I0628000

Women

WOL-VRIEY

Other Books By Wol-vriey:

The Bizarro Story of I
Meat Suitcase
Chainsaw Cop Corpse
Vegan Zombie Apocalypse
Boston Posh (Bud Malone #1)
Vegan Vampire Vaginas
Vagina Mundi
Melanie Nemesis Catchpole
Bizarro 101: A Basic Primer
Boston Corpse (Bud Malone #2)
Dr. Orgasm
Boston Lust (Bud Malone #3)
Pussy Transmission
Hell Dancer
Girls Are Not Smiling
Brainchew
Brainchew 2: Out of Their Heads
Blue Nightmares
Daria (An Erotic Nightmare)
Wet Bones
Mr. Ugly
Brutal
Evil
666
The Cleaverman
Perverse
The Virgin
The Book of Atrocities
The Final Girl

Novellas and Short Stories By Wol-vriey

Big Trouble in Little Ass
Forever Ago Sunshine

Women

WOL-VRIEY

Burning Bulb

PUBLISHING

Women
By **Wol-vriey**

Burning Bulb Publishing
P.O. Box 4721
Bridgeport, WV 26330-4721
United States of America
www.BurningBulbPublishing.com

PUBLISHER'S NOTE: This book is a work of fiction. Names, characters, places, and incidents are either the product of the author's imagination or are used fictitiously, and any resemblance to actual persons, living or dead, events, or locales is purely coincidental.

Copyright © 2021 Burning Bulb Publishing. All rights reserved.

Cover designed by Gary Lee Vincent and Wol-vriey using images from SKG Photography, EVG Culture, Pavel Danilyuk, Ali Pazani, and Two Dreamers from Pexels.

First Edition.

Paperback Edition ISBN: 978-1-948278-43-0

Printed in the United States of America

1

Women are the true spice of life.

CHAPTER 1

Megan

Megan Kemp parked her black Harley Davidson in front of the white Toyota SUV at the top of Dave Lowry's driveway and then took off her pink crash helmet and hung it over the bike's handlebars.

Megan was a tall young woman, and, sitting framed in the moonlight like this on this late spring night, in her jeans, gray tee shirt and black jacket, while clearing her long brown hair out of her eyes, she could easily have been a model posing for a photo shoot.

What destroyed this impression was the totally pissed-off look on her face.

Megan was here for business. Dave Lowry owed her money—two thousand dollars to be exact. He'd owed her the money for six months and had promised to repay her this Wednesday. Today—tonight, actually—was Friday, and Dave seemed to be maintaining radio silence. Megan had neither heard from him nor had she been able to contact him this week. His phone was going straight to voicemail and he wasn't noticing her WhatsApp messages either.

Which clearly meant he was avoiding her. He either didn't have the money or simply didn't want to pay up. As Dave was a great friend of hers, Megan suspected the first option to be the case; meaning Dave was still broke. But if that was so, why avoid her then? Why not simply come out and admit it?

Anyhow, combined with the other current issues in her life—her being between jobs and trying to stretch her dwindling financial resources until she got reemployed—Dave's evasion had sufficiently angered Megan to make her get on her Harley and ride over here to his house to come find him.

Well at least he's home, she thought with a mixture of relief and anger as she scanned the lit windows; though the white SUV parked in front of her was already proof enough of his presence in the house. The living room drapes were drawn but Megan clearly saw the silhouette of someone moving about behind them. She also heard music playing inside the house; the noise sounded like Slain Jane.

After the week I've just had it would be a total bummer riding over here to find no one home.

She actually lived close by, on Ruth Ellen Road, but had been up north in Boston all week—staying at her brother Brian's house and attending job interviews. None of the interviews had gone well. Boston was seemingly full of waitresses. The town seemed to need strippers though, but Megan wasn't interested.

For a moment Megan sat there contemplating the house; a medium-sized bungalow on Raynham's Macy Street. The place didn't really belong to Dave; it was his older sister's. But Lucy Lowry was constantly out of town, flying cross-country on business, and so Dave had the run of the place. Just like he had the use of her Toyota SUV too.

Though a very nice guy, Dave Lowry was generally broke. And when he wasn't broke he was very free with spending his money, which was why he was generally broke. Which was why Megan had had to lend him money in the first place—because free-spending Dave had maxed out his credit cards.

She smirked. *You'd think a lowly truck stop cook would know better than to splash his cash about like he was a movie star.*

Dave's spendthrift financial philosophy was another reason why Megan had decided to come over now on Friday night instead of waiting till tomorrow morning. Assuming he did have her money ready, she didn't want him going off to some gay nightclub and spending it all in trying to impress a prospective new boyfriend. And this wasn't an idle worry; she'd seen it happen before: Dave buying everything in the bar to impress some pretty boy and that person later leaving with another man.

But still, she'd left it rather late tonight; by her phone the time was 9:30 p.m.

Hey, I'm lucky he's still home.

She figured she'd sat on her bike long enough.

He's definitely heard me pull up and knows that I know that he's home and so . . .

She got down from the motorbike and stretched. *Dave, you better have my money in there with you or I'm gonna give you a course in drama you'll never forget.*

Though normally quite a calm and well-balanced young woman, at the moment Megan Kemp felt pissed off enough to give her friend several good pieces of her mind.

She paused by the bike and looked at her pink helmet. She considered taking it along with her, so some passerby didn't filch it while she was in the house, but then decided she couldn't be bothered if someone did. Either she had too much hair now or her head had gotten bigger or the helmet had gotten smaller, but each time she wore it recently it felt uncomfortable. If someone stole the helmet, she'd be forced to buy a new one.

Megan walked over to the front porch and climbed the steps. As she reached the front door, she heard the music turn off in the living room. Suspecting foul play—that Dave might have just noticed her arrival and was preparing to bolt through the back door—Megan hurriedly rang the doorbell.

There was no initial response from within the house, so she rang the buzzer again, keeping her finger on it till she heard someone approaching the door.

The door opened, but it wasn't Dave standing there. It was his sister Lucy.

"Yes, yes, I heard you the first time. What is the matter, girl? What do you want?"

"Oh, I'm sorry," Megan apologized. "Hi, I'm Megan—I used to work with Dave at Rudy's Truck Stop."

Lucy Lowry was thirty-five years old, was as tall as Megan and had piercing blue eyes and long black hair cut in razor-sharp bangs. She had a boyish, almost breastless body. According to Dave, she'd been married once, but was now divorced and had since reverted back to her maiden name.

Lucy was a cosmetics company executive, and just like on the few previous times that Megan had seen her, she was dolled up now too—a walking advertisement for lipstick, eyeshadow, blusher, sensual perfume and nail paint. At the moment though, she was casually dressed in faded denim and flip-flops and had a small overnight bag slung over her right shoulder.

"Yes, yes, I remember you," Lucy said, sounding distracted, her gaze darting behind Megan as if she was in a hurry. "You were waitressing at Rudy's right?"

"Yeah, that's right," Megan agreed, "though I quit working there two months ago. . . . But hey, I need to see Dave urgently about something. Is he home?"

At the mention of Dave's name, a furtive look entered his sister's eyes. "No, no, no, he isn't," she quickly replied, and then, before Megan could respond to that, added, "Why don't you just phone him anyway? I'd have thought you'd do that before coming over here."

Megan nodded. "But that's the trouble, see? I *have* been calling him. I've been calling him for three days now but he's totally incommunicado." Though she knew it was a rather rude thing to do, she made an attempt at peering around Lucy, trying to see into the house. "Are you *sure* he isn't home? This is real important."

Lucy shook her head with finality and stepped out through the door, afterwards reaching back inside and flicking a switch which put the house interior in darkness. "No, he isn't home." She laughed as she said this, but it came out sounding forced. "And no, girl, I'm not hiding him from you. My brother is a grown man and can handle his own affairs, so there's no reason why I'd need to do that."

But there was something false in both her voice and her eyes that told Megan something odd was going on here.

"Listen, I'm late for a dinner date," Lucy told Megan, stepping past her and hurrying down the porch steps. "I don't know what you mean about not being able to reach Dave on the phone—I spoke to him just this morning."

"Oh?" Megan said, descending the steps after her. "So, where is he now? Maybe I can ride over there and see him."

Lucy walked over to the white SUV, opened the driver's door and then turned to face Megan. "Oh, he didn't say where he was. I didn't ask him. All I know is, he has a private cooking job somewhere—big money and you know how broke Dave always is so he couldn't turn the offer down—and he won't be back for about a week." She shrugged apologetically. "I was in a hurry then just like I am now." She flung her brown overnight bag into the car and then got in and shut the door. "Hey, I'm sorry, girl, but I really gotta run, okay? Like I said, I'm meeting this guy for dinner and it's a hot date and . . ."

"Yeah sure," Megan nodded and walked over to her motorbike. Her mind was elsewhere though. She was thinking: *Hey, lady, you're wearing flip-flops.*

Okay, now Megan would actually have believed Lucy *was* off on a hot date, but for that one detail—those flip-flops she had on. Yes, Lucy was as perfectly made up as always and her hair was equally flawless . . . she was even wearing fake eyelashes . . . but that footwear . . . Her feet soft and pampered and sleek, her toenails perfectly pedicured pink, but . . . flip-flops? Flip-flops on a hot date?

From the little that Megan knew of Lucy Lowry's fashion sense, that single detail was so out of place as to be a wardrobe malfunction of 'Janet Jackson–Justin Timberlake at the Super Bowl' proportions. A completely unacceptable fashion disaster, and it instantly confirmed to Megan that Lucy was lying to her.

She glanced first at the house, then back at the white SUV, which Lucy was already reversing onto her lawn so she could head down the driveway. *The thing is, what the hell are you lying to me about, Lucy? Alright, I can bet my last dollar that Dave isn't in the house—it isn't like I'm the mafia, I ain't gonna break his legs if he hasn't got my money, so there's no reason for him to hide from me. So what's going on here?*

Megan no longer felt angry. Rather she felt mystified. *Lucy is behaving as strangely as if she's killed her brother and hidden his corpse in the house.* Her gaze roved over the white SUV, which was now flashing its headlights as Lucy got it properly aimed at her driveway. *Or perhaps she's stashed him in the trunk of her SUV and is off to bury him in the woods. Which would explain her haste.*

Megan shook her head and cautioned herself. *No, even suspecting that is crazy. Whatever would they fight about? Well, there's money, I guess, but . . .*

But no, they couldn't have had a fight, because Dave was an easygoing chap, without a violent bone in his body. No way was he going to get into a squabble with his sister.

Megan watched Lucy put the SUV in forward motion. *That overnight bag she has with her is a clue to her actual destination. That bag is stuffed with stuff, so she's clearly not returning home tonight. But where's she headed then?*

She stood there looking confused.

"Okay, see you around!" Lucy called out, waving as she drove past Megan. "If Dave calls me again I'll tell him you're looking for him!"

"Thanks!" Megan waved back and then she watched the SUV leave the yard, make a right turn and then speed off.

After a few seconds of reflection Megan climbed on her motorbike, rode out of the yard, and made a similar right turn to Lucy's.

She followed Lucy.

Normally Lucy Lowry's destination would be no concern of Megan's. But the older woman's secretive behavior, which had begun immediately Megan mentioned her brother's name, now had Megan curious as to her destination.

Megan smirked as she turned the Macy Street curve, with the white SUV a hundred yards ahead of her and just making a left turn onto Judson Street. *She's dressed, not like she's off to romance some guy, but instead like she's off to a slumber party somewhere. And she did mention dinner—twice. And yeah, she also said that Dave has a private cooking job. So there's a very good chance that he's cooking dinner for she and her friends.*

The tall young brunette sighed grimly. *And oh, what the hell—I've nothing better to do tonight anyway. Better keep searching for my money.*

So, taking care to ensure that Lucy never suspected she was being followed, Megan tailed the departing SUV.

CHAPTER 2

John

"Sex and Death,
Yeah, sex and death.
That's all we get,
Here on Earth.
So use that damn bed,
And get enough sex,
Before Death collects . . . you!"

The Slain Jane lyrics swam in John Miller's head as he stared around his prison cell.

Sex and death . . . sex and death. That had mostly been his life for the past week. Here in this large room with nothing in it except a bed, a table, a digital clock on the wall, and a giant television. The cell's steel door was situated at the room's opposite end, beside the TV.

John smirked, turned his head right, and stared at the recessed space in the wall about four feet from the bed, its border lined with bright blue ceramic tiles. Oh yes, there was also the toilet and shower in that adjoining cubicle.

And of course, himself, chained here like someone's dog.

John was naked but the room was warm. He had been lying down, but now, galvanized by fear and worry, he shifted his thickset middle-aged body to the edge of the large bed and sat there, scratching his thinning brown hair, scuffing the thick blue rug with his toes, and once more trying to make sense of his current situation.

Why the hell was I kidnapped? And by who?

No, no, no, that latter half was a silly question. John knew who had had him kidnapped. He saw the deranged woman every day, several times a day in fact and each time she came here, they . . . they . . .

He was grateful that, at least where he was concerned, she wasn't making a point of living up to her horrible name.

No, the real question here, the overwhelming puzzle, was: *WHY? WHAT THE HELL DOES THAT CRAZY BITCH WANT WITH ME?*

With no immediate answer to this, John once more ran his mind over the events that had led to his arrival down here:

I was out partying with Barbara . . .

Barbara Barbanell was John's fiancée. Last Friday night they'd gone out for dinner and afterwards gone clubbing. John Miller was fifty-three years old, and considered himself too old for all-night dancing, but even though Barbara was herself fifty-two, she acted like she was twenty-eight and still liked to shake her ass to music; so he'd obliged her. At about 3 a.m. they'd driven home, with Barbara insisting on handling the silver Bentley, and John, who'd given his chauffeur the night off, hoping they didn't get stopped for a breathalyzer test as she'd had even more to drink that he had and was clearly only keeping the car in their lane with difficulty while giggling all the while and chain-smoking into the bargain.

But all had gone well . . . until they'd gotten home, that was. 'Home' was a palatial two story residence in the southern Boston suburb of West Roxbury. John Miller was a very wealthy man, but didn't like to flaunt his wealth.

Barbara had managed to park John's Bentley without crashing it into the house, but then, once she'd gotten the driver's door open, she spilled out of the car and lay flat on her back in the driveway giggling at the moon.

Not doing much better himself, but nonetheless concerned about his girlfriend's wellbeing, not least because she'd promised him some hot butt sex that night and wouldn't be able to make good on her promise if she was sick, John had drunkenly opened his own door and gotten out of the car, intending to go help her. But then . . .

"Hello, Mr. Miller," a male voice had called out. "Excuse me a moment, sir."

Swaying on his feet, John had still been trying to make out exactly where the voice was coming from when a sweaty hand had clamped a napkin over his nose and mouth.

The napkin hadn't been drugged; it had merely been used as a gag to prevent him calling for help. John knew this to be true, because the next moment he'd felt a sharp prick sting the right side of his neck and for a few seconds he'd seemed to grow even drunker till . . .

Blackout . . .

And then I woke up down here. And I've been trapped here for the past week, with that crazy woman. . . . And I still don't know what she wants with me!

'Down' was John's subjective location for his prison. His cell had no windows and so he naturally assumed it was a basement room, an assumption buttressed by the complete absence of sound 'down here' other than from footsteps out in the hallway when his jailor visited him, and from the television positioned opposite the foot of the bed.

Oh, how John wished he could turn that damn TV off. He cringed now as he stared at the giant 120-inch unit as it idled on standby, with its blank screen promising to show him fresh horrors soon.

John dreaded the TV coming alive, dreaded what it would show him next. Up until his incarceration here he'd never believed such horrors really existed. And that evil woman . . .

But there was no way for John to reach the TV. The chains attached to the steel cuffs around his wrists and ankles didn't even extend as far as the foot of the bed. The chains were long enough to permit John to comfortably use the toilet and shower in the cubicle near the bed, and to lie down on the bed, but that was all.

There was also nothing near him that he could throw at the TV, not that doing so made any difference. He'd tried that approach on his second night here, after being woken by the noise of a looped video of a man's head being chainsawed off his neck. Horrified by the sight, John had hurled a coke bottle at the TV. Sure, the TV had exploded, but his relief had been brief; barely five minutes later the cell door had opened and his captor's two male assistants had carried in a brand new television, set it up and taken the destroyed one away.

Neither of the men had said a word to John. But when next his female captor had visited him, she'd warned him that if he destroyed another television she'd cut off his hands.

John had by then watched enough videos of her brutality to believe she'd carry out her threat. So since then he'd behaved himself.

Sitting on the edge of the bed now, he once more tugged on his chains in frustration. The chains were thin and silvery in color. Those restraining his wrists were about eight feet long, while the pair attached to his ankles were about two feet longer than those. The steel hoop to which the chains were attached was situated up on the wall to the right of John's bed (presumably so he could sleep in comfort) and was locked with a keypad. But even if John knew the combination that unlocked the hoop, freeing himself was out of the question; four CCTV cameras situated up in the angles of the cell's corners ceaselessly monitored his every motion from the moment he got up, swiveling to follow him as he crossed the room to use the toilet for instance, or took a shower.

And why wasn't he allowed some underpants? It was completely demeaning to be kept here as naked as an animal.

At first this nakedness and total lack of privacy had worried John, but he'd quickly realized he had other things to worry about.

On first waking up down here, John had been very concerned about his fiancée Barbara.

"Did you kidnap her too?" he'd asked the woman.

She'd laughed. "No, I didn't."

"I don't believe you," John had said. "Don't you dare hurt her, you hear me?"

She'd laughed even louder. "Tough words for a helpless captive. No, I didn't capture her; it was just you I wanted."

"You're lying."

"No, I'm not." And on her next visit she'd brought him a tablet device and opened the website for the Boston Globe.

He was news:

'WEALTHY BOSTON SOCIALITE ABDUCTED!'
John Henry Miller, heir to the Miller fabrics business, was last night kidnapped outside of his home in the Boston suburb of West Roxbury. The kidnapped man's fiancée Barbara Barbanell is pleading with the abductors to return her boyfriend. There has so far been no demand for a ransom and the police are baffled as to the motive for the kidnapping. Boston law enforcement officials say . . .

There was some more, but John stopped reading at that point. His real question had been answered—the article showed a picture of Barbara leaning on her older sister Grace and weeping. There was no way that could have been faked.

Since then John had forgotten about Barbara. She was safe and as such unimportant in his current crisis.

This woman who'd captured him, this crazy person who'd ripped him from the comfortable womb of his rich and cozy middle-aged life to cage him naked in her basement, what did she want? This was his biggest question.

Sure, John had known many women in his life, had even married several of them . . . but he'd never seen this particular woman before—meaning she couldn't have any kind of personal grudge against him.

Or is she angry on someone else's behalf?

This thought once more plagued John Miller's mind. Okay, that was a possibility, that she wanted revenge for someone else. But he doubted it.

Yes, just like every other guy I know, I have angered a few women too, but . . .

But his captor never seemed angry at all when she visited him. Rather, she only ever seemed amused. Even when she had threatened to cut off his hands if he damaged another of her televisions, she hadn't acted like she was angry with him.

John stopped reflecting when he heard his cell door opening. He realized he'd been so caught up in his thoughts that he'd not heard the sound of footsteps approaching along the corridor outside his cell.

He looked at the clock suspended on the wall above the TV. It was now 9:30 p.m. Apparently his jailer wanted a sexual nightcap.

John groaned. Despite his absolute dread of her, his penis was already stiffening in anticipation of her visit.

***

Mrs. Pain had very pale skin. To John's expert eye, she seemed to be in her mid-thirties. Mrs. Pain looked like a Real Doll come to life—like a porno actress—all breasts and legs and ass. The porno impression was enhanced by her face—she had large black-painted lips, a perfectly sculptured nose and a flawless complexion.

She was completely bald, both upstairs and downstairs, with not a single hair on either her scalp or pubis. The few stray hairs that John had noticed on her body spoke of her being a blonde in a past life.

Despite calling herself 'Mrs.' she wore no wedding ring.

"Mrs. Pain? Does that mean you're married to Mr. Pain?" had been his sarcastic question on first meeting her. "Or is it spelt 'P . . . A . . . Y . . . N . . . E,' or even 'Pane' like in 'windowpane?'"

"I'm married to pain," she'd replied him in her soft voice. "I simply *love* inflicting it on others. But not on you, honey. Never on you; you're simply too precious to me." While explaining this she'd gently raked his cheek with her black fingernails.

He'd thought she was merely being cute, but the first video she made him watch quickly disabused him of that vanilla notion. Watching that video had also cured him of any future attempts to sass her.

***

She walked into the room now in her usual casual state of undress—she always came to him naked, not even wearing sandals—and carrying her empty silver goblet in her hand. She never came to him without the goblet.

John wouldn't have found her perpetual nakedness unusual—this was after all her home—but for the fact that she never visited him alone.

Accompanying Mrs. Pain into the room now were her two assistants. Two muscular goons wearing just sweatpants and sneakers and as bare-chested as boxers, both of them about six feet tall, and both as ripped as fitness trainers. The pair fit any stereotypes that one might have about evil henchmen, down to ugly moronic faces, total subservience and suggestions of subnormal intelligence. Neither man ever spoke to John even when he addressed them directly. They just loomed around him.

Yes, 'loomed' was the right word. These two guys were menacing presences providing the muscle to Mrs. Pain's deranged brain.

John avoided his captor's eyes. He hated looking directly into them.

Mrs. Pain nodded at John's stiff penis and laughed her flat, emotionless laugh. "Honey, I'm so glad to see you're glad to see me." Then she waved her hand at the two bodyguards. "Wait for me outside."

The two men stepped outside the cell and shut the door. Once more John felt the immense relief that he always did when they departed. He couldn't control his dread of them. He knew those hulking men were the ones who had kidnapped him and brought him to this place.

Once the men had left, John was forced to look at Mrs. Pain, who had now walked over to the bed and sat down on it and was stroking his thighs with her right hand; not going near his penis yet, but just tracing circles in the borders of his pubic hair with her fingers. Her flesh felt very cool against his. Her fingernails and toenails were painted the same glossy black as her lips—'bright black' was how John thought of it, black that shone with darkness. The black nail paint and lipstick had the unsettling effect of setting off the paleness of her skin, making her look ghoulish to John.

He already knew she was a ghoul of sorts, but she really looked it too.

Her loveliness ended at her eyes. Her beauty and the Junoesque perfection of her body ended there. Her eyes, which existed in a thick circle of red eyeshadow that totally eclipsed her eyebrows, were gunmetal gray and seemed lifeless. They looked as dead as her voice sounded. Whenever John stared into his captor's eyes, he had an instant and deep understanding of how she could be so cruel, how she could do all the horrible things she made him watch her do on the TV in his cell.

'Enter*pain*ment' was how she described her videos.

Mrs. Pain terrified John. She really did. In all of John's years of life, he'd never met a woman as inexplicable as this one. Sure, he'd read of them in fiction and watched them in the movies, but that was merely imagination. To actually meet such a person in the flesh was beyond imagining.

It bothered John even more that his body responded to her very presence with sexual arousal. Yes, they were both naked and she was a sexy woman, her figure easily comparable to that of any A-list porno actress, physically entrancing even if her soul's corruption beamed from her eyes—but . . . but . . .

She grabbed hold of his penis and pumped it as if milking it. "You're wondering why I turn you on so much when you're terrified of me, aren't you?" she asked with a sinister smile.

John just managed not to gasp at the pleasure of her fist on his manhood. Oh yes, he was wondering why his penis kept getting hard once Mrs. Pain was in the room with him. Was it really because she turned him on? Or was it because he was subconsciously scared of what she might do to him if she felt she didn't turn him on?

He replied, "No, I'm merely wondering what you want with me, holding me captive like this. You've kept me down here for a week now, and yet I'm none the wiser as to why. Lady, for God's sake, gimme a break. I've got a life to return to, people who care about me and are looking for me, and all you do is feed and fuck me."

She laughed. "So be grateful for small mercies, Johnny boy. There are lots of people begging for someone to feed and fuck them and not getting either. They're dying of hunger and not getting laid either."

He scowled. "Lady, you know what I mean."

She laughed again, let go of his penis and instead raked him with her eyes, which had the effect of making him want to shrivel into himself, although his manhood adamantly refused to shrivel and stayed hard as wood. "But it's much better that I feed and fuck you than torture you, don't you think?" She gestured over at the still idling television, which, as if reading her thoughts, now came on to show a half-naked man bound to an upright X-shaped whipping frame while she mercilessly lashed him. "Or would you prefer this latter alternative? Would you like to be one of *them?* Would you like to be one of those I hurt for my pleasure?"

John watched the video (its picture in 4K clarity) and cringed. The man on the TV was almost dead on his feet in the literal sense. His head hung back in the top angle of the whipping frame and his eyes were shut, with blood dribbling from his gaping mouth. The man's entire chest and belly were shredded in pieces by the bloodied whip that Mrs. Pain wielded against him. Her whip had four tails and bright strips of razored metal glinted through the blood that coated those tails. The video's only sound was that of the whip whistling through the air and striking mangled flesh; though occasionally John heard Mrs. Pain grunting in pleasure too. Flaps of skin hung down like red tassels from the victim's torso and the muscle beneath that shredded skin was ripped up like meat hacked with a cleaver. His genitals were as shredded as the rest of his body and there was a widening pile of blood and detached flesh between his spread legs.

Despite which Mrs. Pain, who was as naked as the day on which she was born and who was covered both bald head and body with the dying man's blood, continued whipping him. And whipping him. And whipping him; the muscles of her buttocks and thighs visibly tensing as she lashed him. At one point her ass remained tightened as if she was coming.

"No, no, no, please turn it off!" John pleaded, looking from the TV to her with desperate eyes. "Turn it off."

He was speaking to the back of her head since she'd been watching the video also. And now she turned to smile at him. Her smile chilled him to the bone.

"Surely you wouldn't like that to be you?" she asked gently. "If you desire to experience the terrors of the flesh too, I can easily make it happen."

John glanced once at the shredded man on the television, his ribs now visible through the flesh of his destroyed chest, and violently shook his head. "No no no no no!"

Mrs. Pain's smile hardened. "Then don't fucking complain to me anymore." She moved her hand to his penis again and squeezed it hard. "And don't ask me any more silly questions. I've already told you—you're here because I need you to be here. And when I no longer need you, I'll let you go. Understand?"

John nodded. "Yes, yes, yes. She was squeezing him painfully now, despite which his erection felt harder than ever.

She let go of his manhood and waved the silver cup in her other hand at him. "And now let's have our little nightcap, shall we? And afterwards you can get some sleep."

"Please turn off the TV," John pleaded. "I can't stand seeing all this stuff. It's driving me nuts."

She laughed at him. "Honey, pain makes me horny. Just be glad that it's not your pain. I need you for another purpose." She pushed him down on the bed. "Lie on your back. Tonight we'll do it reverse cowgirl so I can watch torture porn at the same time."

He lay back and she got up on top of him and slid him into her body. He sighed with relief as her toned back blocked off the sight of the TV, and then sighed again when she began moving up and down on him. He reached his shackled hands around her sides and gripped her breasts.

She rode him like she was riding a motorcycle along a bumpy road. Bang, bang, bang, bang, bang! There was no tenderness in it, just raw sex, her love tunnel seeking friction against his manhood. Still, her body was velvet on his and he didn't last long. He never did last long when she fucked him like this. He was soon ready to come.

As she always did, Mrs. Pain timed his climax perfectly, leaping up off of his crotch at the critical moment and instead catching all his come in her mouth. She jerked him off so she got every drop of his semen. Then, while John lay gasping in appreciation of the great orgasm, Mrs. Pain picked up her silver cup from the bed and dribbled all his semen from her mouth into it, spitting out the last bits.

She measured the amount of semen with her eyes, nodded in satisfaction, and placed the goblet on the table by the foot of the bed. Then she stood smirking down at John, who just gazed up at her in amazement.

"Okay, baby, that's it for now," she told him. "Try to get some sleep, you've got a heavy night ahead of you."

"What d'you mean—'a heavy night?' " John managed to ask her. He always felt completely winded after sex with Mrs. Pain, even when, like now, she'd been the one doing all the hard work.

She laughed and playfully smacked his cheek. "Oh, you'll find out later tonight, baby. I've got a huge surprise for you."

John was about insisting that she answer him, but then his eyes flickered again to the TV, which was frozen at the end of the video, where the whipped man's abdomen now gaped open with his guts visible through his shredded abdominal musculature. John gulped and shivered. He remembered that Mrs. Pain had cautioned him about questioning her.

Instead he pleaded, "Turn the TV off, please. I can't sleep while it's on."

She shook her head. "No. Okay, baby, I'll play you a nicer video. How's that?"

John made no comment; he already knew what her definition of 'nicer' was.

Someone must have been listening to her because the image on the screen instantly switched to red words on a white background: WHAT HAPPENED TO THE TEENAGED BRAT WHO SMARTMOUTHED ME LAST WEEK AT THE SHOPPING MALL.

"Sweet dreams of blood, baby," Mrs. Pain said as the video began, this time showing a room, maybe even the same room that the previous video had been shot in, but with no whipping frame in it, just a naked blonde teenager strapped to a bed. The girl looked to be maybe fifteen or sixteen years old.

"Oh, my dear God, no!" John gasped to himself as the video camera swept around the bound and terrified girl, who was pulling against her bonds and howling to be released. The camera focused on a tray of morbid tools on a table beside the bed: gleaming scalpels and knives and bone saws and circular saws and a hammer and chisel.

Mrs. Pain stepped into view. She was naked as usual, but maybe as a joke, was wearing a surgical mask.

"Let me go, you nasty witch!" the teen yelled at Mrs. Pain. "You'll never get away with this! My dad's a cop. He's gonna hunt you down and kill you if you dare hurt me!"

"Oh, but *I will* get away with it, brat," Mrs. Pain said in a teasing voice, the outline of her lips visible as a smile against the fabric of her surgical mask. "I already killed your father."

The girl gasped. "No you didn't. Please, tell me you didn't kill my dad!"

"I whipped him to death. I'd show you the video, but I don't think you'll survive long enough to watch it."

The girl fell silent and tears filled her eyes. Winking, Mrs. Pain gestured to the camera and then picked up a scalpel.

"Please . . . no!" John gasped, feeling really nauseated now. "I don't want to watch this!" He turned to plead again with Mrs. Pain to turn it off, but found that he was now alone in the room; she'd left while he'd been entranced by the video.

"Now this is a lesson to little brats to be nicer to their elders," the onscreen Mrs. Pain said, stepping up close to the bound girl and running her fingers up and down her torso.

"NO, PLEASE DON'T! I BEG YOU, PLEASE DON'T HURT ME!"

But as if the girl wasn't speaking to her, Mrs. Pain dug the scalpel into the flesh between her breasts and began slicing down towards her belly. The pink skin parted and blood spurted out of the wound, spattering Mrs. Pain's face and turning her surgical mask a bright red.

"NOOOOOOOOOO!" the teen screamed.

John leapt out of bed. Navigating his way through his steel chains so that in his haste he didn't trip himself up and go flying headlong, he fled into the bathroom to escape the horrible sight.

In there, he sat on the toilet seat and shut his eyes and plugged his ears to drown out the young girl's screams.

This is insane, he told himself. *Completely insane. Oh, God, what am I doing here? What am I doing here?*

CHAPTER 3

Megan

With the night as her accomplice in her pursuit of Lucy Lowry, Megan followed the white SUV out of Raynham and eastward along State Route 44.

Her suspicions that Lucy was headed for the coast were soon proven to be wrong however, when the other woman turned left off of Route 44 onto a side road.

Megan reached the turnoff and stopped for a few moments. This side road was bordered by woods and she watched Lucy's taillights grow smaller in the distance for a while. Then, shrugging, she once more reminded herself that she had nothing better doing this Friday night.

Megan had bought her Harley Davidson secondhand, from a biker who'd originally used it for running cocaine between Boston and Dresden, Ohio. In addition to several concealment spaces he'd had built into the motorbike, Bill 'Ferret' Morris had also modified the Harley's lighting, building in a switch that completely turned off the bike's lights, both headlights and taillights.

"Stealth mode," he'd called it with a laugh, while demonstrating the function to Megan. "I can't begin to recall how many times this switch has saved my ass from the DEA." Then he'd laughed some more, while Megan surreptitiously examined his nose for stitches. Ferret's nose looked odd. It wasn't broken like a boxer's, but it wasn't properly set on his face either. Megan had heard a rumor that Ferret had had to have his nose stitched back on again after an irate gang boss had sliced it off.

Before tonight, Megan had never had any use for Ferret's 'stealth mode.' The mod had seemed pointless. The whole idea of headlights staying on all the time was so that drunken motorists didn't think you were some species of metal creature they could ram into extinction, right?

But what about this kind of situation, when you didn't wish the driver you were tailing to realize you were following her? This side road was deserted; it looked like it would be just their two vehicles motoring along it. If she left the Harley's lights on, it wouldn't be long before Lucy realized someone was tailing her.

Megan grinned as she flicked the 'stealth mode' switch and the bike's lights died. *Alright, from here on I'm gonna have to navigate by moonlight and hope someone hasn't splattered a huge chunk of roadkill in the road ahead.*

She put the black Harley Davidson in motion again and sped after Lucy.

To further conceal herself, Megan also rode as close to the road's border of trees as she could. She was soon glad that she had done this, because shortly after she'd set off after Lucy again the wall of trees on her left abruptly became an actual wall, one that extended ahead for two or three hundred yards.

Then, barely two minutes further into her pursuit, Megan stomped her brake again. Two hundred feet ahead of her, Lucy was slowing down and parking in front of a large dark gate.

Well, here we are, Megan told herself. She cut the motorbike's engine and freewheeled as far forward as she dared, skidding sideways off the road and under the trees only when Lucy got out of the white SUV.

Watching Lucy walk towards the gate, Megan felt defeated. *Well, I guess the pursuit is over now, time to just return home again. This is some kind of private estate. I was expecting a party at a house, not a huge place like this, with a wall like a jail and a gate and guards who'll be monitoring who comes and goes.*

But even though there was a guardhouse by the gate, no guard attended to Lucy. Sure, the gate was shut, but Lucy simply walked up to it and slid it aside. The gate made no noise either as it slid open.

Then Lucy Lowry walked back to her Toyota SUV, got in and drove it inside the enclosure, out of Megan's range of vision. Then after a short period of time, Lucy reappeared at the gate on foot again, this time to slide the gate back into place.

Oh, now this is weird, Megan thought as Lucy vanished from view for the second time. *Why aren't there any guards here?* A breeze ruffled her hair and she absently swatted at a bug that bit her neck, but she really hardly noticed either.

Beyond the gate she could hear Lucy's vehicle start up again and pull away. After a few seconds consideration (meaning without giving it much thought) Megan rolled her motorbike out of sight behind a large maple, hung her pink helmet on its handlebars and then hurried over to the gate for a look.

The gate was night black in color and, while mostly solid, had several cutout circles in its upper half that were protected by grilles. Megan peered through one of these. She saw that the driveway which led from the gate stopped at a huge house three hundred feet away. The building was really a mansion, which she figured was to be expected considering the size of the grounds it stood on.

More interestingly though, Lucy's SUV was parked at the head of the driveway. Squinting, and with the help of the house's exterior lights, Megan could make out that Lucy was still seated in her car.

Looks like she's looking for something in her bag. Or is she waiting for a servant to come open the front door for her?

Whatever the reason, Lucy hadn't gotten out of her SUV yet. Megan now walked across to the guardhouse side of the gate for a quick check. She tugged carefully on the side of the closed gate. Once more it slid silently sideways at the slightest pull of her fingers, meaning its rollers were very well oiled.

Yes, the gate is still unlocked . . . and . . . I mean, but . . . where the heck are the guards?

This simple question had begun worrying Megan. She'd once worked as a pizza delivery girl and if there was one thing that experience had taught her, it was how security-conscious rich people were. The rich were paranoid about the poor taking away their riches.

"So where are the guards?" Megan asked herself aloud, mental alarm bells starting to clang in her mind. "How come there aren't any? And at night for that matter?"

It made no sense. *Something really odd is going on here and I'm not sure I want any part of it. Okay, girl, it's time to leave and go home.*

But Megan didn't leave her vantage point at the gate. Peeking in through the space she'd created by pulling the gate aside, she saw that Lucy was finally getting out of her white SUV. She had her overnight bag slung over her shoulder and was holding another bag that Megan hadn't earlier noticed.

Maybe a servant was finally at the door.

Reaching a decision, Megan shrugged and slid the gate open enough to squeeze through. *Hey, hey, wait a minute? What on earth am I doing this for? This is how people wind up getting shot for trespassing.*

But despite realizing the trouble she'd be in if she was caught, Megan still slid the gate shut behind her and then hurried up the driveway towards the mansion. After about twenty yards, she stepped off of the concrete and walked on the lawn instead. In her opinion this was a safer way to approach the building; the grounds had many trees she could duck behind.

Megan was still bemused as to the reasons for her actions.

But Lucy wasn't paying any attention to her surroundings anyway. She was stepping up onto the front porch and striding for the house's front entrance. And judging from Lucy's lackadaisical demeanor there didn't seem to be any dogs around to worry about either; which was a huge relief to Megan, who'd just remembered that a private estate this large might reasonably be expected to have several unfriendly canines in its security employ.

Megan paused behind an oak tree to see who would answer the mansion's front door. If there were people home, that would be her cue to leave. Around her the night seemed brooding and moody. An owl cooed up in a nearby tree, startling her. Then, almost like it was speaking to her, it cooed again. The bird's voice had an eerie note to it, something mournful like the sound of an approaching or departing ambulance siren announcing a tragedy; or the other kind of siren, the seductive female who in olden times was believed to lure unwary seamen to their dooms.

But then, Megan felt, being outside in the dark beneath the trees like this was bound to give one the creeps.

Still, she shivered.

Megan now discovered that she'd been mistaken about Lucy's waiting for a servant to let her into the building. Lucy didn't even press the buzzer. Just as she'd done with the front gate, she simply turned the doorknob and opened the door.

Megan was about thirty yards from the house when Lucy did this, and so, looking through the glass window that formed the door's upper half, she clearly saw that there was no one on the other side of the door. Megan also saw that Lucy simply clicked the door shut and walked off. She hadn't locked it behind her either.

Which means (Megan thought) *that the front door is still open.*

Which means (here she glanced back down the driveway at the gate) *that other people are very likely expected to arrive tonight.*

Which means (she bit her lip and furrowed her brow) *I should leave this place right now before someone comes and finds me here.*

She looked back towards the gate again. *But . . . where are the guards and servants?*

She found it impossible to overcome her curiosity over this last detail. She now took a proper look around the mansion grounds.

The mansion itself was just that—a huge moonlit construction of masonry that loomed ahead of her with concrete wings spread left and right like a bird of prey about to feast on the night; an object too large for her to get any true idea of specifics so close to it, and yet something that filled her brain with impressions of its vastness. It had two floors and, viewed from where she was standing, most of the ground floor lights seemed to be turned off.

Almost as if the building was trying to hide itself tonight, most of its exterior lights were also switched off.

Megan's view of the surrounding acreage was very restricted by the trees and by this scanty exterior lighting, but she made out several cars parked in a garage over on the mansion's far side. She saw a navy blue Escalade and a cream-colored Rolls Royce, and the shadowy outline of two more cars, both of which looked very expensive. Then, closer to her side of the building and not counting Lucy's white SUV, stood three more cars; less expensive models: a blue Ford pickup truck, a battered black Honda sedan, and a red Camaro.

*So there's guests staying the night, and possibly more are expected to arrive soon. But there's four cars parked in the garage and this is a rich person's residence, and I've been out here for five minutes now and still not seen any signs of anyone else other than Lucy being here. At the very least there should be several servants about—a house of this size would have at least three or four—and at least one chauffeur . . . a gardener and—*she made another furtive look back at the gate—*several guards.*

Megan did her best to leave. She really did. She understood that simply turning around and walking back out to where her motorbike was parked was the sensible and law-abiding thing to do, but she felt unable to walk away.

The obvious absence of any form of security presence on these premises tonight was too much of a lure to ignore. She was an intrepid enough young woman at the worst of times, and not the sort to turn down this God-sent opportunity to simply walk into a building where her money was at stake.

She was now certain that Dave Lowry was somewhere in this mansion; clearly to cook for Lucy and her friends, and so . . .

Seeing as no one seems to be around anyway, who's to stop me from seeing him? I'll just look for the kitchen, remind Dave to repay his debt and leave again. And if I get caught snooping, I'll tell them I followed Lucy over here to ask her about something.

While thinking this last Megan had already set off for the front porch. Once there, ten steps took her to the front entrance.

She squinted once through the glass window in the door—*Yes, just like I thought, no one's home*—and then quickly tried the doorknob.

The door clicked quietly open and Megan slipped into the mansion.

***

Once she'd shut the door behind her again, Megan took a moment to compose herself. The front door opened into a large anteroom. The anteroom lights were turned off but the light from the adjoining living room on her right was bright enough to see by.

Megan hid behind a marble bust and listened for footsteps and sounds from the living room; it wouldn't do to walk right into a meeting. Then she remembered her cellphone and switched it off; it wouldn't do either to have it ring when she was hiding.

She didn't hear anyone in the living room and a quick peek through the connecting archway confirmed her impression that the living room was empty. Lucy was nowhere in sight.

Megan now began feeling a deep sense of unease and eeriness.

I still don't know what has gotten into me tonight to make me do this, but since I'm already in here I'd better just get it over with. I'll hurry through this deserted place, find Dave and then leave.

However, just as she stepped out of hiding and started 'following her nose,' to locate the mansion kitchen (which was where Dave was certain to be), she heard footsteps coming her way.

Megan was already through the connecting archway then and so couldn't duck back into hiding quick enough. All she could do was freeze in place, hold her breath and hope she wouldn't be seen.

But it didn't matter. Lucy was the one returning down the hallway on Megan's left, and she had a totally preoccupied look on her perfectly painted face, with her exquisitely shaped eyebrows knit together, as if at the moment the rest of the world didn't exist. Seemingly lost in thought, she was twirling the ends of her black hair around her fingers and humming to herself.

In a way, Lucy reminded Megan of her brother Brian's wife Valentina, but Valentina was older and didn't seem as plastic, though she and Lucy both looked like they'd stepped out of the same reality TV show for makeup-obsessed wives.

Lucy was still dressed the same as earlier, and as she stepped past Megan without noticing her and began ascending the stairwell on their right, her flip-flops made soft slaps on the polished wood floor.

Megan heaved a sigh of relief when Lucy vanished around the turn in the stairwell. Then, after taking a few seconds to compose herself again, she headed down the darkened hallway.

This shouldn't take too long, she thought, *I smell food ahead. Ugh, smells like some really stinky cheese!*

***

As Megan proceeded down the hallway, the smell of cheese grew stronger and stronger until she reached a large dining room. The size of this hall and its distance from the living room made her think the mansion must have more than one living room. God knew the building was large enough to contain three or four parlors.

Megan was now feeling quite spooked by the combination of darkness and silence in the mansion. As was seemingly the case for most of the building, the dining room's lights were turned off too, its present illumination coming from the hallway she stood in and on the dining room's far side, another hallway into which light spilled from an open door.

That'll be the kitchen over there, Megan thought, setting off across the dining room.

She felt relieved when the smell of food intensified once she reached the opposite hallway. *This won't take long. I'll just read Dave the riot act and be gone from here before any more guests arrive.*

But as she stepped into the hallway that approached the kitchen, Megan heard gasping noises coming from the open door ahead of her.

What the hell is going on in there? she asked herself, though she thought she already knew the answer to that. Still, she hurried forward and peeked through the door.

As was to be expected from the size of the house, the kitchen was a giant space, with several cooking ranges along its walls and at least three islands that Megan could see from where she stood.

There were two men in the kitchen: Dave and another guy whom she remembered from somewhere, a tall muscular fellow. Both men had their pants down and Dave was down on his knees and was sucking on the other guy's manhood like a baby at its mother's nipple, a baby desperate to feed when the mother's breast seemed to have run out of milk.

Then Dave deep-throated the other cook. At that point crotch and face were so mashed together that Megan could not tell what was pubic hair and which was moustache.

"Yeah, baby, suck it like that," the other guy (she remembered now that his name was Ron) told Dave, holding him by his ears and ramming his head back and forth over his penis, while spit dribbled from Dave's lips.

Megan blushed. Like many women, she was as fascinated by gay sex as men were with lesbian intercourse. She choked back a giggle and wondered what to do now.

Yes, I'm in a hurry here, but it seems wrong to disturb them.

Especially as at that moment, Ron pulled his erection out of Dave's mouth, pulled him up from the floor and bent him over the nearest kitchen island. Then he bent down and began licking Dave's ass.

"Okay, baby, now I'm gonna fuck you so hard, my come's gonna squirt out of your mouth."

"Yeah, baby, gimme that big dick!" Dave gasped back, reaching a hand behind him and pulling Ron closer.

Megan just kept staring. Ron had a really big penis, but Dave's anus swallowed it up like it had had lots of practice in stretching to accommodate it.

"Yeah, give it to me deep, baby," Dave gasped as Ron began thrusting into him; at which point Megan decided she'd seen enough and walked away from the door.

She sat in the dining room, with the noise of the two lovers reaching her. The sound of them having sex helped her relax:

Hey, they don't seem concerned about anyone discovering them screwing, so maybe no one's home. But no, someone is definitely home—Lucy is here and so are the owners of those other cars parked out front.

Then she winced and got to her feet again. *Ouch, I gotta go pee . . . somewhere away from the smell of that cheese. That cheese they've got in there smells utterly atrocious—it ain't parmesan, that's for sure. And is that fried shrimp I can smell along with it?*

She had noticed a tray of uncooked orange crustaceans on the island that Ron had bent Dave over. Shrugging, she crossed the dining room back to the hallway.

Now, where do I find a toilet? Yeah, I know—a house of this size is certain to have one attached to the living room.

So Megan set off back the way she'd come.

She was in the living room when she heard footsteps again. She glanced around but didn't see anyone; but she was on the opposite side of the living room from the anteroom now, which meant she could no longer see all the way down the hallway. The footsteps sounded like they were coming from that direction and were quite nearby. They also seemed to belong to more than one person.

Megan considered waiting and giving whoever was coming her prepared explanation of being here to see Dave and letting herself into the house when she found the front door open. But then she decided against letting anyone see her.

They might call the cops on me anyway.

So, instead of waiting, she ducked left into the stairwell and climbed it instead.

She heard a woman's voice downstairs just as she made the turn in the stairwell that took her out of the newcomers' range of vision. But the footsteps didn't continue away from the living room as she had expected them to. Rather, Megan got the impression of several people walking into the living room and sitting down.

Dismayed, she risked a peek around the turn in the stairwell. Yes, she'd been correct. She made out a pair of bare female legs crossed at the knee, with the crossed foot swinging back and forth while its owner laughed at something. The unseen woman had a throaty voice.

Oh, dammit, what do I do now? Megan worried. *I can't go back downstairs until they leave and*—she winced—*I really, really, really do need to pee now.*

Hoping that the people downstairs would remain there and not suddenly decide to ascend the stairs too, and silently cursing Dave for choosing right now to have sex with his new boyfriend, Megan quietly made her way upstairs.

***

The second floor was as dimly lit as the ground floor and seemed just as deserted. The stairs had brought Megan up to another hallway. This hallway split off into several alcoves and passages, one of which seemed to end in a distant living room with a huge television hung on its wall. The TV was off though.

How big is this place anyway? Megan pondered. *All I want is a bedroom with an en suite bathroom that I can quickly use. I just hope I don't get lost up here.*

She set off looking for a guest toilet. The most obvious place to search for one would be in the living room at the far end of the corridor, but that living room seemed to be almost on the other side of the building and if she met someone over there, her story that she was looking for Dave wasn't likely to hold much water.

Thankfully, she quickly found a bathroom. The bathroom was opulent and lavish, with taps that seemed made of real gold, and while using it Megan fantasized about how great it would be to own a bathroom exactly like it, and a mansion like this one.

She flushed and then winced. *Oops, what if someone heard me flushing the toilet?* Then she shrugged. *It's too late to worry about that now.*

Then she froze because she thought she'd heard voices. Cracking the bathroom door open, Megan peeked out. She hoped the mysterious woman downstairs hadn't now decided to come upstairs.

But, what am I worried about? If she has come upstairs, it means I can now get the hell out of here. . . . I really shouldn't have entered this building in the first place . . . I really could get shot in here and it'd be written off by the cops, because yes, I know I'm trespassing. My entering this house was explainable while I was downstairs, but now that I'm upstairs, I'll just be accused of burglary or home invasion.

But there still seemed no way for her to leave yet; the woman in the living room was apparently still down there. The hallway was empty. So where were the voices coming from?

Megan didn't want to investigate the voices, but she decided to do so anyway. She was stuck up here until the woman downstairs and her companion (she'd just heard a male voice laughing) decided to take themselves off elsewhere.

Oh dammit, lady, get off your fat ass and just leave so I can leave too . . . I mean, Dave and Ron must've both have come twice by now.

So rather than remain in the lush bathroom until it would be safe for her to return downstairs, Megan left it and began tracing the female voices that she'd heard. One of them had been Lucy's—that was certain of.

Strangely, the closer she got to the voices, the more the smell of cheese and fried shrimp increased.

Megan's search for the voices ended at the right rear corner of the mansion. At least she judged that was where she now was.

And now that she'd arrived here, Megan suspected she'd made a huge mistake by entering this mansion at all.

The chamber she was peering into was large and seemingly windowless. It was painted red and black in color. Its walls and ceiling were red; the black color component came entirely from the large pentagrams drawn all over them, including down on the red rug.

Oops. Megan repressed a shudder. She knew as well as anyone else what pentagrams signified. Witchcraft . . . black magic.

There were five women in the chamber (Lucy and four others whom Megan didn't know) and they were all seated on high-backed chairs arranged around a circular table of white marble. As though she'd just entered the chamber herself, one of the women was taking her seat at the table when Megan arrived to spy on them.

Just like the red chamber's walls, the top of this white central table was designed with a black pentagram. This pentagram, however, was cut into the table top and covered its entire extent. The five women were each seated at one of the points of the pentagram's engraved star. The other thing that immediately stood out about the room was the large stone oval that was propped up like a mirror in its far corner. The oval was gray stone, was about seven feet high and just like the table, had its center decorated with a giant and deeply-carved pentagram.

Megan just stared. Nothing wicked or evil was happening, but she sensed an air of almost palpable malice hovering over these five women.

She looked from face to face, noticing their looks of grim expectancy. *Wow, what in the world have I just stumbled on?*

One of her questions had already been answered. The source of the seafood smell up here was the piled plate of fried shrimp coated with melted cheese that was set before a heavily pregnant brunette who was hungrily stuffing the cheese-drenched shellfish into her mouth.

The brunette's food was the only refreshment on the stone table—this clearly wasn't a recreational meeting, but a business one.

"Okay, ladies," the blonde woman who'd been sitting down when Megan arrived said. "Now that Lucy has finally joined us, we can get down to business."

"Yes, and it's about time too," the other blonde in the room agreed. "I was beginning to think you'd changed your mind about doing this."

"Change my mind? Josie, are you out of yours?" the previous speaker retorted.

The women all laughed. Megan laughed quietly too, and then after glancing back down the corridor to ensure no one was coming, and also peeking again around the door jamb to ensure the five women in the room couldn't see her, she settled down to hear exactly what was going on.

CHAPTER 4

John

Since fleeing into the bathroom of his cell, John Miller hadn't reemerged from there. He'd remained seated on the toilet with his hands clamped over his ears and with his eyes tightly shut.

But whoever was transmitting the enter*pain*ment videos into his cell had simply turned up the volume of the recording, so that the tortured kid's screams penetrated his attempt to mask them.

And oh, how the girl had screamed and screamed.

The bathroom cubicle had no door. All John had to do to see the TV from in there was open his eyes and turn to the right. He had been sorely tempted to look; at several points during the sonic barrage of the teenager's agony, John had wanted to know exactly what Mrs. Pain was doing to her to make her howl so loudly.

But . . . *Hell no, I don't wanna watch that!* he'd told himself repeatedly and kept his eyes closed.

The video of Mrs. Pain operating on the once-rude teenager finally ended. The tormented girl's screams ceased as abruptly as if her head had been chopped off. John felt intense relief when she stopped moaning; for the past few minutes he had been wondering where she'd found the strength to remain alive for so long. By his estimation, Mrs. Pain had been mutilating her for at least twenty minutes.

Heaving a huge sigh, John opened his eyes and nervously glanced out at the TV. Then he instantly threw up.

On the giant television screen, Mrs. Pain stood beside the teenager's brutally eviscerated corpse, holding her removed heart overhead like an Aztec sacrifice.

The camera zoomed in on her, its lens tracking up her blood-spattered Junoesque body, her muscles taut and quivering from her murderous exertions. The camera's focus lingered on her breasts, so that John clearly saw the drops of blood that hung from her stiff nipples. Then the POV moved up to Mrs. Pain's face. She was laughing behind her blood-soaked surgical mask.

Sighing in horror, John got up and took a shower to wash the vomit off of himself.

***

Five minutes later John was seated on his bed again watching another of Mrs. Pain's abominable murder videos. This one was titled 'STUPID MARRIED DEBTORS.' In this video, Mrs. Pain was hard at work skinning a man and woman who were bound to twin tables on either side of her. She was scraping their skins off with a large woodwork plane. Both the carpentry tool and Mrs. Pain's hands and arms were covered with blood, and the pink strips of skin that emerged from the plane looked as absurd as flattened worms.

Thankfully, the couple being tortured were gagged. As Mrs. Pain ran the hand plane up and down over their bodies, they jerked like they were being electrocuted, but John was spared the noise of their screams.

This is insane, was all he could think. He didn't run to the bathroom again. He'd lost the willpower to flee from Mrs. Pain's enter*pain*ment.

What's the point of even trying? John thought miserably, with his gaze moving from his shackled wrists to his similarly clamped ankles and then tracing the chains that led from all four of them up to the hoop on the wall where their ends were fixed. *Why try to escape from her? I can't get away from her.*

Watching Mrs. Pain slide the huge plane over the bound man's face from chin to forehead, completely peeling his lips and nose off, to the accompaniment of massive squirts of blood, John just felt relieved that he wasn't the one being tortured like this.

But there was major craziness to come. Mrs. Pain suddenly stopped torturing the man and woman. What she did next was to dip her hands into a bucket of water in which several strips of their skin were submerged and pull one long strip out of it. The extracted strip of skin was hairy and had a nipple attached, so it must have come from the husband.

Then, with a pair of scissors, she cut up the strip of skin into roughly dollar-sized lengths, got out a green Sharpie and drew '$100' in two corners of each piece of skin, along with a central smiley face that John assumed was supposed to represent Benjamin Franklin's head.

Then, grinning, she flung this make-believe 'skin money' at the camera, which then froze the image with the 'money' in midair and placed a bright yellow banner over the image. The banner read:

'BEST Y'ALL PAY YOUR DEBTS ON TIME, ASSHOLES. OR ELSE MRS. PAIN IS GODDAMNED COMIN' FOR YA! YOU BETTER BELIEVE IT!'

Unable to make any logical sense of what he was seeing, tears filled John Miller's eyes. He sat there weeping, occasionally lifting his hands and tugging at the shackles on his wrists.

What on earth am I doing here? he kept wondering.

***

John had a brief respite after this, with the TV screen beaming, of all things, images of Mrs. Pain masturbating with a wand vibrator. This innocuous sex video played in a continuous loop for thirty minutes, until John had begun forgetting the horrors that had preceded it and was thinking he'd actually manage to get some sleep tonight after all. The video's soft sounds, the vibrator's hum and its user's moans, had a hypnotic rhythm to them, one that was fast lulling him into slumber.

It was now 10:45 p.m. Sleep would be a welcome release. If he slept for a few hours, in the morning he'd feel refreshed enough to resume wondering what was in store for him.

But just as his eyes were closing, he heard the cell door opening.

Oh, heck! he thought, opening his eyes wide again.

Mrs. Pain stood there with her silver goblet. He looked from her to her onscreen image, and back at her again.

"Milking time, cow!" she announced, then waved to her two hulking assistants to leave them alone.

He understood then why she'd played him her masturbation video—she'd been subconsciously conditioning him with desire for her. Because now, seeing her standing there, his body was already responding to hers. It was as though none of her enter*pain*ment craziness had occurred in the interim since she'd last visited him.

"Now there's a good cow," Mrs. Pain said mockingly as John's penis came erect. "My John has such a lovely john. Alright, now let's milk that sweet love milk out of you."

Still smirking mockingly at him, she sat beside him on the bed and took his erection in her hands and began expertly stroking him, till he gasped in ecstasy and gave her what she wanted.

CHAPTER 5

Megan

Megan was still at her eavesdropping post by the door of the chamber in which the five women sat around the white pentagram-inscribed table. With the corridor as dark as most of the rest of the house, there was no way those Megan was spying on would notice her except if perhaps she coughed or was loud in some other way, or if she actually stepped right into the doorway and showed herself to them.

The last woman to seat herself at the table, a fiftyish blonde who was clearly the mistress of this mansion, was speaking: "Lucy, you're late again. Josie was the one expected to arrive last, because she didn't know exactly when her babysitter would show up; but even she got here before you."

The middle-aged speaker was the oldest woman present, the other women's ages all falling somewhere between thirty and forty-five years of age. Her voice was soft but lacked warmth. When she turned towards the doorway and Megan got a proper look at her face, at the icy blue eyes, plump lips and cheeks and large nose, she also saw ruthlessness in the woman's features, like she was not the sort of person who would forgive even the slightest slight.

"I'm sorry, but it was unavoidable; I got delayed at home," Lucy replied her. Then she seemed to remember something and added: "Hey, Candice, I should mention that I left both your gate and your front door open." She shrugged apologetically. "Yes, I know that our agreement was to leave them both open so Josie could get in on her arrival, but I had no idea that Josie had gotten here ahead of me. Remember, you said to all turn our cellphones off at six p.m. and not to turn them on again no matter what happened, so I couldn't call ahead."

"It doesn't matter," the older woman, Candice, said in her soft but cold voice. "What matters is that you're here and didn't chicken out on us. I can easily have someone lock both the gate and the door." She frowned at Lucy. "Why are you so late anyway?"

Lucy shrugged again. "Some girlfriend of Dave's came looking for him, and I—"

The pregnant brunette, who also had the hairiest legs that Megan had ever seen on a woman (hadn't this lady ever heard of razors? her bare legs honestly looked like bear legs), paused a moment from crunching on her meal of fried shrimp and cheese to interrupt: "Girlfriend? Lucy, I thought your brother was gay?"

Lucy scowled. "Yes, he *is* gay, Maryanne. I meant 'girlfriend' as in a girl who is also a friend of his? 'Girlfriend' doesn't have to mean they're sleeping together."

"Oh, sorry, didn't know that's what you meant," Maryanne quickly apologized, then she dipped her hand back down into the plate of cheese-coated shrimp and shoved more of them into her mouth.

"Can't you stop eating those damned things for even a moment?" the statuesque brunette seated on Lucy's left growled at Maryanne. This woman's dark skin immediately marked her as being of mixed race.

"Oh, leave her alone, Donna," Candice said with a chuckle. "We've both been pregnant before and gotten cravings too. When I was pregnant with Jenny, I got cravings for ice cream, and it was in the dead of winter then."

"Yeah, but ice cream doesn't stink up everywhere like that mess she's stuffing down her throat does." The speaker was the fifth woman in the room, the skinny blonde seated on Candice's immediate left, a woman with a pinched face whom by process of elimination Megan assumed had to be 'Josie.' "All four times when I was pregnant, I only had a craving for sausages, not for . . . Look, that stuff she's eating smells like baby poop, okay?"

Josie left off speaking and looked disgusted.

From her vantage point, Megan sympathized with Josie. She'd worked as a waitress long enough to know what parmesan-garlic shrimp smelt like and that wasn't it by any stretch of the imagination. Whatever cheese Maryanne's shrimp were coated with had to be the smelliest cheese available on the planet. She made a mental note to ask

Dave what it was once she got downstairs again and then to avoid it forever afterwards.

"Hey, don't knock it till you've tried it," Maryanne said disinterestedly, and then fed another cheese-coated shrimp into her mouth. She was quite plump and very pretty with it too. "It's not my fault that these are the only things I feel like eating at the moment." She grinned at Candice. "Thanks for having Dave make these for me."

Candice smiled coolly back at her. "No problem, girl. And don't forget there's more where those came from." Then her expression turned serious again. "Okay, now back to business. Lucy, you were explaining about your delay. This girl who was looking for Dave, I hope it wasn't anything serious that might jeopardize our purpose here tonight."

Lucy quickly shook her head. "No, the girl just wanted something from him. I didn't ask what it was, but I think he owed her some money that she'd come to collect. Anyway, I gave her a story about not knowing where Dave was and left her there."

"She bought your story?" Candice asked.

Lucy looked surprised at the question. "Yes, sure. Why wouldn't she? Listen, she's just some kid who used to waitress at Rudy's Truck Stop. I don't see why she should concern us tonight."

"Just being careful," Candice said. "Alright, let's get on with things, shall we?"

***

But no, Lucy, I didn't buy your damn story, Megan thought sourly. *No I didn't. I followed you over here and now, I'm not even sure why I did so. And now that you've mentioned Dave, hey, I really should head downstairs again. That woman in the living room surely must have left there by now.*

But Megan didn't leave the door yet.

Something about this gathering of five women around this stone table intrigued Megan immensely. And then it struck her what it was:

On the surface, the five of them seemed to have nothing in common:

They weren't the same age, which would speak of them being friends or possibly old schoolmates having a reunion. Candice was the oldest and Donna clearly the youngest, in her mid-to-late twenties at most. Lucy and Maryanne seemed to be the same age—mid-thirties—with Josie filling in the age range between them and Candice.

Nor did the five of them share the same social status—which might have been another reason for their association. Candice was obviously rich, while pregnant Maryanne just as obviously wasn't (Maryanne's clothes were old and faded). The other three women fit somewhere in-between, with Lucy's and Donna's designer clothes indicating that they had some money, and Josie somberly dressed like a hassled suburban housewife who was stretching her husband's salary as far as it would go.

Nor were they related as sisters—sharing eye and hair color was as far as any facial similarities extended. To drive home the point of this, Donna was clearly half Negro and half Caucasian.

Nor did their personalities mesh. Candice seemed cold and regal, while Lucy was laid back; Josie looked nervous and was clearly high-strung; Maryanne just seemed bored; while Donna . . . Donna gave off a clear vibe of A-grade sultriness—she clearly wouldn't be good friends with Candice or the others; they would all want to keep their boyfriends or husbands well away from her.

But something in the air connected these five women and Megan was curious as to what it was.

But hey, curiosity killed the cat, she thought, glancing back down the corridor to see if anyone was coming.

But the coast was still clear and she kept eavesdropping.

***

"First off, all of you must remember the 'no cellphones' rule," Candice said. "You keep your cellphone or tablet turned off at all times while you're here. That way, so long as you each kept mum about your destination tonight, there'll be no way to actually place you in this mansion at this point in time."

"But . . . but, do we really have to do this?" Josie asked nervously. "I mean . . . the cops . . ."

"Forget the cops!" Candice barked at her in a steely voice. "And yes, Josie, we do have to do this. We're going through with it here tonight."

"Yeah, sure," Josie said quickly, looking like a soccer mom whose son has just conceded a penalty to the opposing team. "I was just . . ."

Candice smiled at Josie. "Don't worry about the police getting involved. Just don't turn your cellphone on." Then she glared at Donna, who was seated on her immediate right. "That particularly applies to you, young lady. Yes, I know you're an escort, but . . ."

"Yeah, yeah, I'm cool," Donna said, pulling out a cigarette from her large handbag and then searching through it for her lighter. "You've already told me how my clients can wait. Sure they can. My pussy will appreciate the break. My ass needs a rest from time to time."

Lucy smiled at that, but Josie rolled her eyes.

"Hey, I'm bored," Maryanne said with a yawn, shoving away her empty plate and then patting her protruding belly. "Except you guys want me to fall asleep on you here, you'd better let me go on social media." Then, noticing that Donna was staring at her with something like awe on her face, she added: "What's the matter?"

Donna pointed to the empty plate. "I can't believe you actually finished eating all of that."

Maryanne burped and patted her baby bulge. "Oh, you know what they say—I'm eatin' for two." Giggling, she stared in turn at Candice. "Social media, pleeeease. I promise not to call Tony."

"No, Maryanne, and that's final," Candice said. "You wanna keep up with the Kardashians, do it on the smart TV in your bedroom."

"Tony's very jealous and possessive," Maryanne protested. "Yeah, yeah, he thinks I'm over in Richmond now, but he's gonna be worried as hell if he can't get a hold of me. I don't want him running off to the cops and starting a search."

"Okay, you can call Tony if you want to," Candice grudgingly conceded to her. "Just do it from one of the house phones, and tell him you're still down in Richmond, Rhode Island. If he asks you why you're not using your cell to call him, tell him you dropped it into something and it conked out."

"Yeah, tell him it fell into the oil used to fry your damn stinky shrimp," Josie said.

Maryanne pouted and kept quiet.

"But listen, I'm still worried about the police," Josie said. "What if we don't succeed in getting rid of all the evidence? I've seen this happen way too many times on cop shows: someone commits a so-called 'perfect crime,' but they leave one tiny shred of evidence behind and then the police . . ."

"Yeah, she's right," Donna agreed, leaning forward over the stone table after first stubbing out her cigarette in one of the carved furrows of its black pentagram. "My clientele includes several cops, and one thing they've told me is that there's no such thing as a perfect crime. We could get busted for this."

They're here to commit a crime? Megan asked herself. *These five women who seemingly have nothing in common? What could these five possibly plan to do together? Is this 'Ocean's Five' or what?*

Candice, however, had begun laughing. Megan shifted her attention back to her.

"Stop worrying about the police," Candice told her four guests. "You can rest assured that when we're done here there'll be not a single trace of evidence left for anyone to find."

"But your husband?" Maryanne asked, with another yawn. "You sure he won't suddenly surprise us while we're at it?"

"Yes, I'm really worried about that too," Lucy seconded.

Candice snorted. "You girls worry too much. I've already told you—my husband Richard is handling some shipping company's lawsuits down in Panama at the moment, and is stuck in some nasty little town where the internet is still in the stone age and it literally takes forever to ram a phone call through to anyone. He won't be home for a fortnight. And you've noticed yourselves how I've sent all of the servants home for the weekend—which is why you all had to let yourselves into the house." She laughed. "Girls, even our dogs have the weekend off—they're over at our vet's for spurious medical reasons. The servants and security guards won't be back till Monday evening earliest, by which time you ladies will all have returned to your everyday lives."

So who is the woman downstairs, then? Megan asked herself. *Another person who'll soon join this meeting?*

Candice got to her feet and pushed her chair back. Looking immensely powerful, she leaned forward over the table, the gaze in her blue eyes like steely knives stabbing at the other women. "Now listen, girls, no more excuses, okay? John Miller has had it coming to him for the longest time, and the five of us—his ex-wives—are going to do to him exactly what he deserves to have done to him." She stared coldly from face to face. "Agreed?"

"Agreed," Lucy instantly replied.

"Yes, agreed," Donna and Josie said at the same time, with Josie adding, "We'll pay him back big-time."

Candice peered at Maryanne. "Agreed?"

Maryanne seemed to jerk awake. "What? Oh, sure. Agreed. Yeah, it's time we paid old Johnny back." She moved her heavy body on the leather chair and frowned. "You know I'm beginning to feel hungry again? Hey, can I have some more shrimp now?"

"Oh no!" Donna and Josie both immediately said. Along with Lucy, the pair of them flung imploring glances at Candice.

Candice nodded back at them and next wagged a finger at Maryanne. "Uh uh, preggers, not yet. Once we're through here, you'll have all the cheese-coated shrimp you and your little fetus can eat. But first let's get matters sorted out."

Plump Maryanne pouted prettily. The other three women heaved sighs of relief.

Megan also heaved a sigh of relief. True, Maryanne's plate was now empty, but the smell of her meal still hung in the air like a vengeful ghost summoned during a séance.

CHAPTER 6

The Ex Club

Exes? Ex-wives? So the five of you women were actually married to the same guy?

Megan thought this odd because . . . because there was simply no uniformity to the five women seated around the white marble table, nothing that would suggest their errant ex-husband had a particular type of female he was attracted to:

Candice and Josie were blondes, while Donna and Maryanne were brunettes, and Lucy had black hair.

The graying Candice was a matronly woman, one well-filled-out with middle-age, and she seemed to have always been a bit on the heavy side. From Megan's vantage point, Donna seemed to be of average height and was quite statuesque. Lucy and Josie were both slim, but Josie had very large breasts and Lucy had almost none at all. Maryanne was short (seated there on her chair, her feet barely touched the floor), and pregnant as she was, looked even shorter. Yes, she was also very plump now; but seeing as most women tended to put on weight while pregnant, Megan had no idea what Maryanne had looked like before getting knocked up. (Megan also couldn't understand how any sane man wouldn't consider the amount of hair Maryanne had on her legs a turnoff in bed—*Wow, it's like a brown-carpet factory down there. And she doesn't shave her armpits either?*)

Candice, Lucy and Maryanne had blue eyes, while Josie and Donna both had brown eyes.

Finally, there were also Donna's mulatto milk-chocolaty skin and partly negroid facial features to consider.

So, absolutely no uniformity to the women at all.

This is sort of like being in a lover's supermarket, Megan decided. *Like this John dude just walked in there and selected whoever was nearest to him on the*

'Girlfriend' shelves. Then her eyes widened. *Hey!—now I remember! Dave once told me his sister was married to a rich guy named Johnny . . . Johnny something or other.*

Candice was speaking again. She'd actually been speaking for a while, but Megan had zoned out and hadn't heard what she'd been saying. Candice was holding up a thick sheaf of papers.

" . . . Just don't ask me how Richard got a copy of this."

"What's that?" Josie asked, her eyes gleaming with curiosity.

Candice handed the sheaf of papers to her. "The copy of John's will that I promised you girls." She waited until Josie had made an attempt to read it and given up in defeat at its legalese, before adding: "You can all look through it later; but I'll summarize the relevant part of its contents for you now."

"We're listening," Donna said, tapping the table with her long fingernails.

"Alright," Candice said, holding out her hand and taking the will from Josie again. "It's simple. John may have been a scoundrel of a husband, but at least the son-of-a-bitch is a conscientious father. John Henry Miller has four children—my daughter Jennifer, Josie's two kids Simon and Lisa, and Donna's son Toby—and at the moment his estate is set to be partitioned equally between the four of them in the event of his death."

Candice suddenly seemed caught in the grip of an emotional storm. She looked like she was blinking back tears from her eyes and at the same time looked madder as hell. When she finally got control of herself again, she shook her head in obvious disgust. "Oh, you girls have no idea how much I want to kill John Miller."

"Well, you're about to do exactly that," Lucy laughed, while scratching at her left breast with a long pink fingernail. "And so are the rest of us."

"Oh, I'm not really *that* interested in killing him," Maryanne said. "Sure, he's the world's greatest douchebag for what he did to us . . ." She shrugged. "But hey, I never had a kid for him and I'm real glad now that I didn't." She leaned towards Lucy. "Neither did you, hon. Yeah, I understand about your other issues with him, but see, I really think you should just move on with your life."

"No, John Miller must die," Lucy said. She looked enraged that Maryanne would suggest otherwise, and her demeanor made Megan wonder what in the world the absent John Miller could possibly have done to hurt her so much.

What could he have done to piss them all off so badly that they've gathered here to murder him? Megan was still dealing in abstract concepts; the concrete horror of what she was listening to hadn't yet stuck her.

"Hey, preggers, I *have* moved on with my life," Lucy finally retorted. "And I don't see why you're judging me anyway—you're here too, aren't you?"

"I'm both dirt poor and dead broke," Maryanne replied easily. "Candice promised me a hundred grand if I took part in this. Tony and I wanna buy a house to raise our son in. A hundred grand sets us up nicely."

"You're very pretty," Donna told Maryanne. "I don't see why you couldn't just have dated someone richer."

Maryanne shrugged and looked regretful. "That's what I had in mind too. But"—she lifted her bare left leg above the table and wiggled her toes at the others, with her green toenails catching the light—"most rich guys seem turned off by how hairy I am. They all conclude I'm too redneck for upper-crust society. And besides, Tony was the only other guy I ever met who really looked at me as more than a large set of tits and a hole to satisfy himself in." Her gaze turned dreamy and she giggled. "I mean, he satisfied me too." She tapped her pregnancy. "You know, the joys of motherhood?"

"Whatever," Lucy said coldly. "My point is that despite your feigning boredom with all this, Maryanne, you've got to be as pissed off with John as the rest of us here, to be willing to exchange his life for a measly hundred thousand dollar payout."

"Alright, yeah, I am," Maryanne grudgingly admitted. "I can't stand men who're cheapskates."

Josie stared at her in disbelief. "That's all you're angry about? Girl, I was in therapy for two full years afterwards."

"And I'm *still* in therapy," Lucy said, leaning back in her chair with a bitter smile on her perfectly made-up face. "I loved that human turd with all of my heart—"

"But not with all of your pussy," Donna laughed. Then her expression turned sad and cold, but not unkind. Her sad smile was bittersweet, holding much understanding in it. "Hey, sistas, calm down, wilya? Let's not made an issue of this. We've all got the same reason for wanting our ex-husband dead and"—here Donna gestured across the table at Candice, who had remained silent through the impassioned vocal exchange—"we've been offered a platinum-plated opportunity to exact our revenge. What more can you possibly want?"

"Yes," agreed Josie, who'd also been silent for a while. "The three of us who've got kids will be securing their inheritance, because, once dead, John Miller can't father any more sons and daughters and rewrite his will. And Maryanne and Lucy both get a hundred thousand bucks out of—"

"Lucy turned down the money," Candice said. "She asked me to give her hundred grand to Maryanne instead, to finish paying for her house." Candice laughed at Maryanne's surprise. "I just haven't told her yet."

Maryanne looked at Lucy in shock. "Hey, you did that for me? I'm real sorry about being nasty to you just now."

Lucy waved it off, her long pink fingernails fluttering like butterflies in front of her face. "It's okay. I know you need the money and I really don't—I've already spent more than that in therapy to clear my brain of what our ex did to me. I'm just in this for revenge."

"So that's nicely settled then," Candice said. "We're all good friends again. Okay, girls, the sacrifice will be at midnight and . . ."

Sacrifice? Megan kept listening; she didn't want to miss a thing.

Candice went on: ". . . After that, everything will proceed as I've already outlined to you all: John Miller's body will never be found, but his heart will be. His heart will be delivered to the police station near his home, with a note explaining who it belongs to and also giving some bogus reason as to why he was killed . . . something plausible like an unpaid mob gambling debt. That'll confirm him as dead. The cops just need to run a DNA test on the heart to confirm his identity."

"Ugh, sending them his heart seems so gross," Donna said, her lips twisting up in disgust. "Why not send them a hand or a foot instead?"

"Yeah, or even just an ear?" Maryanne suggested.

"Girls, girls, use your brains," Candice chided gently. "A severed hand or foot or ear is no proof that John is dead—you don't need any of those body parts to stay alive. Even if we sent the cops his penis, it still wouldn't prove he was dead, just that he'd been badly tortured and mutilated. On the other hand, his heart . . ."

"Yeah, I guess you're right about that," Donna conceded. "Yeah, you're most definitely right about that. His heart it is then."

***

Megan was still finding it hard to process what she was hearing.

Those five women in there are going to murder their ex-husband tonight. They aren't kidding. This isn't some joke. Sacrifice. They said they're gonna sacrifice him at midnight.

She peeked into the pentagram-decorated chamber again, once more noting the grim expressions on the five women's faces. The coldness of their eyes, speaking as it did of a uniformity of purpose, frightened Megan.

Dammit. Whatever this John Miller ex of theirs did to them must've been really bad. Lucy looks incensed, while Maryanne doesn't seem to care about the guy's dying anymore than if someone told her they were gonna stomp on a bug at twelve p.m. Donna doesn't look like she cares either—to her, the guy's death is nothing more than good riddance to bad rubbish. And Josie—Megan scanned the thin woman's long-nosed face for a hint of compassion—Nah, all she's interested in is her two kids inheriting their father's wealth and herself not being caught by the police.

And the overseer, Candice? Well, she assembled this gathering, didn't she? Candice sounds pleased: both pleased that she's convinced the others to do her bidding and be participants in this, and also pleased that her ex-husband will soon get what's coming to him.

Megan kept wondering what John Miller had done to the five women. *Hey, did he marry them all at once in different parts of the country? Yeah, that has to be it.* She felt angry on the ex-wives behalf. *No man has the right to treat a woman like that. And five women at once too. But no . . . that's not right, is it? 'Cos while . . . Okay, I don't know where Donna and Maryanne drove over from, but Lucy lives in Raynham, just a short distance from the old girl, Candice, and . . . and Josie spoke of needing to get a babysitter set up before driving over, which means she lives close by too, and even Maryanne was talking about telling her guy that she's down in Rhode Island for the weekend, which means she likely lives here in Massachusetts as well. Oh shoot—don't tell me he married all five women in the same state at the same time! That'd be more than sufficient reason for them to want to off him! If he did that to me I'd wanna kill him too.*

But even this theory didn't seem right to Megan. *No, there's something even worse than polygamy going on here—it's the way the five of them keep referring to John Miller as having specifically hurt them in some way. Wow, the scumbag did something so bad that Lucy and Josie both needed years of therapy.*

The gathered women were for the moment silent, with Maryanne spitting into a paper napkin. When Candice started turning in Megan's direction, she ducked back behind the door jamb again.

Okay, now what do I do? Megan wondered. *I can't just sit here and let the guy die, can I? Yeah, sure he's got to be a scumbag of the lowest sort for them to all be so set on murdering him, but . . . what kind of a person does it make me if I just let them go ahead and do it? I need to call the cops. There's still time—they're planning to sacrifice him at midnight.*

Then it hit her; suddenly she understood what the word 'sacrifice' implied and the color drained from her face. *Oh no! They're sitting around a table which has a pentagram carved into its top and they're in a room which is painted with pentagrams . . . and over in that far corner is that giant stone egg-thing with another huge pentagram carved into it! Why haven't I worked out before now what all of this means? At midnight tonight, these five ladies are going to perform some kind of magical satanic ritual here!*

Megan considered what she should do. In a situation like this, calling the police really was the most sensible step to take. Once the cops got here, they would . . .

Her fingers had found her phone inside her jacket and she was pulling it out when she remembered that she was actually an intruder here. *Oh, shoot! If I call the cops from inside here, I'm going to wind up in a world of trouble. Sure I may save John Miller's life* (she envisioned the women's hated ex as a repulsive old lecher with an overflowing potbelly and sagging jowls), *but what if he's not being held here and they simply deny everything? Best that I get out of here, talk to Dave about my money—nah, forget Dave—I'll just scram and once I'm back home I can call the police anonymously and tell them I heard a rumor that some guy named John Miller is going to be murdered at midnight in this old mansion. No, I won't call from home, I'll make the call from a bar along the highway where no one knows me; definitely not from Rudy's Truck Stop. That way even if the cops do later track me down, I can claim I just heard two lowlifes talking and figured it might be true and I'd better report it to save the guy's life.*

Megan turned to sneak away, but then inside the room, Lucy said: "Okay, Candice, so I'm cool with us offering up Johnny to this demon of yours or whatever it is . . ."

A demon? Megan delayed leaving again. She just had to hear this bit too.

" . . . But I'm worried about my brother Davey. Look, he's innocent of any wrongdoing here and I don't want a situation arising where after John is dead and the police start asking who delivered his heart to the police station, you're gonna suggest that we off Davey and Ronald too to really dispose of the evidence."

"Yes," Josie agreed. "Because after that, how long is it going to be before you think that we too will be unable to keep our mouths shut, and you start disposing of us as well?"

"Oh, don't you girls worry your pretty heads about that," Candice reassured the worried pair. "Dave and Ron are in no danger whatsoever. Neither of them will have any memory of being here tonight." She laughed and added. "It is magic after all. The spell I've placed on our two cooks means that everything that we—and they— see or do or hear tonight will be forgotten once they leave this house."

"Hey, speakin' of cooks, can I have my damn shrimps now?" Maryanne moaned.

Candice nodded. "Yes, you can, honey. You've certainly earned them."

Ignoring the other women's scowls of disgust, Maryanne began pulling herself to her feet, saying, "And the kid's kickin' my bladder again. I gotta go pee."

Megan took that as her cue to get out of there. As Maryanne began lumbering her way towards the door, she turned and headed at speed for the other end of the corridor. It wasn't just the fear of being discovered that spurred her on now. There was maybe about an hour and a half left till midnight, and she needed to get a move on if she wanted to call the police from a bar on the highway.

Why do I even care what happens to the guy? Maybe I should just let them kill him.

But Megan knew she wouldn't do that. No, she'd do what she could to save this John Miller douchebag whom she'd never met and whom she prayed she never would meet.

She turned off the corridor into the main hallway and half-ran for the stairs. She was about stepping down into the stairwell when she heard voices below her. A peek down revealed a bare female foot just appearing around the turn in the stairwell.

God, no. She's coming up the stairs!

Megan raced for the nearest open door. This was the door to the bathroom that she'd earlier used. She was about ducking inside it, but then remembered that Maryanne had just said that she needed to pee; and what if the pregnant woman decided to pee in here?

So instead, Megan dashed past the bathroom and turned into the next shadowy corridor.

Once safely concealed, she glanced back down the hallway. A bald and naked woman with a fantastic figure was just stepping up onto the stairwell landing, flanked by two very muscular and bare-chested men with ugly, forbidding faces.

Brave as she usually was, Megan found herself shivering at the aura of intense menace that she felt coming from those three at the stairwell entrance. There was no doubting or debating what she sensed—that the trio standing over there were three very nasty people; and not individuals she should tangle with or even introduce herself to.

The naked and bald woman headed down the corridor that led to the women's satanic meeting room. Her two muscular companions remained where they were beside the stairwell, as silent and motionless as statues.

Aw shucks, I'm trapped up here, Megan realized. *I'd better find somewhere I can hide for a while, until the coast is clear again.*

She set off silently down the corridor, checking each door she came to.

2

Women are like bombs; ensure you don't drop 'em.

*

Sometimes a cat needs ten or more lives.

CHAPTER 7

The Six Wives of John Miller

John Henry Miller had always been wealthy. Rich grandparents, rich parents, etc., down to himself, the present head of the Massachusetts line. The family's fortune had originally come from mining, and then from buying large amounts of both Microsoft and Coca-Cola shares, and finally from the fabrics industry.

By a conservative estimate, John Miller was worth forty million dollars.

John was a relatively frugal man, meaning that while he liked spending and enjoying his money, he also restrained himself from going overboard with his spending and hated wasting his wealth on frivolities. His late parents had schooled him very well in the principle of 'waste not, want not.'

And so for most of his time on Earth, John Miller had lived a luxurious if simple life.

The only problem John ever had concerned women.

No, this is an incorrect statement. It would be more correct to say that women weren't John's problem—marriage was. Or, even more correctly stated, *divorce* was John's problem with women.

Rich men never have a problem attracting women. The fair sex swarm around rich men like ants around sugar, bees around blossoming flowers . . . or (if one was of a cynical mind) flies around both corpses and excrement.

And in this regard John was of a very cynical mind. Once he'd begun seriously dating his biggest dread had been of marrying some pretty girl and then one day waking up to hear her tell him that she no longer loved him and wanted a divorce . . . and then off she'd walk into the sunset . . . along with half of his inheritance.

To John, it seemed a very unfair trade to give a woman half of everything his grandfather and father had labored to amass just because he'd slept with her a few hundred times. Now if that wasn't the living definition of prostitution, what was?

And so, despite the pretty girls fluttering around him like butterflies, John didn't get married until he was into his thirties. By then his friends were all settling down and having kids and he had begun feeling left out.

But not so left out that he didn't first fully research prenuptial contracts and get a lawyer to draw him up an ironclad one.

If he got divorced, his wife would get the sum of five million dollars; and that only if they had remained married for seven full years. If she divorced him before then, she only got a half-million.

John figured this was a fair enough trade. Five million dollars wouldn't make too big of a dent in his wealth.

As he had told lots of women through the years, "honey, it's my money. I can't afford to trust anyone."

With this settled, John then settled on the pretty and plump Miss Candice Bowler to be his wife. Candice was a nightclub receptionist. The blonde Candice was practical to the point of ruthlessness, but much less of a gold digger than the other girls who hung around John and his rich friends. Candice was very loving and very agreeable to the idea of being a millionaire's wife. And the 'if-they-split' payoff of five million dollars seemed even more reasonable to her than it did to John. After all, she came from a poor family.

So they got married.

At first things went very well between them, Candice soon got pregnant and John enjoyed parading his rapidly fattening wife before his friends. The good times continued even after their daughter's birth, with John being the loving and attentive husband and Candice the equally loving wife.

But then things turned sour. John was never afterwards certain what had gone wrong. He had no idea if Candice had actually gotten postpartum depression like she'd claimed and so really hadn't felt like having sex with him, or if she'd been angry that he'd not bought her the yacht that she'd wanted for her birthday and that was why she'd given him the big freeze. Or maybe he was the one who'd done something to offend her.

Sometimes hindsight really isn't 20/20 vision.

Anyway, they'd begun arguing a lot. These sort of things happen in every marriage of course and after a while of being jackasses, sensible couples kiss and make up. But both Candice and John stubbornly persisted along the warpath.

Now, John wasn't the kind of man to ever force a woman to have sex with him. While he didn't believe it was technically possible to rape one's spouse, he'd always felt sexual abuse of any sort was wrong. Even as a single man, John had believed it was dumb to commit a rape, because, even aside from the ethics of it, you were putting yourself in danger of going to jail for something which the woman in question was giving to other men for free.

So while it would have been easy enough for him to simply push Candice down on the bed and have his way with her whenever he felt like it, he decided not to.

And so their situation just kept on degenerating.

The problem now, from both of their perspectives, was that they had only been married for four and a half years. And both spouses were very aware of the wording in John's prenup contract which gave a seven-year minimum time limit for Candice to get her five million dollars divorce settlement.

So Candice wasn't going anywhere; she intended staying married to John for the remaining two and a half years that would make her eligible to collect her money. And at the same time she wasn't sleeping with John either, thinking she had him by the blue balls. She did; John was forced to masturbate. He was going nuts and thinking about hiring hookers; which seemed crazy to him, when he had a pretty and perfectly healthy woman of his own at home.

But both spouses had sexual needs and needed them taken care of.

Enter Mark Fisherman. Mark was the young man John employed as his chauffeur after the previous and much older chauffeur resigned over his refusal to give him a raise. Mark Fisherman was Canadian and dashingly handsome. He was a rich kid fallen on hard times. Mark was understandably vague about the circumstances of his fall from grace, but it later emerged that he'd seduced his young stepmother and his enraged father had then disowned him.

Looking at 'poor Mark' (as she shortly came to think of him) Candice could understand why his stepmother (whom she was certain would be about her own age) would find him irresistible. Mark was impossibly cute, with blonde surfer-boy looks and physique and . . .

Long story short, it wasn't long before Candice had enticed Mark into her own bed. By this time John was taking long trips down to Texas and Florida where Candice was certain he was screwing lots of prostitutes; so screw him too.

Things continued like this for three months, with the two lovers growing ever more reckless. Mark confessed to Candice that no woman had ever made him feel like she did when they were making love and that were she not married and himself broke, he'd sweep her off to the altar, toddler included.

For her own part, Candice assured him not to worry, that she'd soon have money and they could get married then. She told Mark about the prenup money she stood to gain in two years.

All this while, Candice noticed her estranged husband staring suspiciously and angrily at herself and her lover. *But,* she decided, *screw him; this Canadian kid is twice the stud John ever was in bed and then some.* She meant this literally, not figuratively, as Mark had an exceptionally large penis.

And besides, there was nothing John could do to her anyway. She realized this when he angrily moved out of the house.

And then, imagine Candice's surprise, when, after making love to her all night, one morning Mark received a phone call from home in Calgary, Canada.

"My father's dead," he informed Candice in a shocked voice. "And that's not all—the old boy left me all of his money."

Candice, naked and covered with summer sweat from the night of passion they'd just spent, could only gape at him.

"For real?" she'd finally asked.

It turned out that Mark the humble chauffeur was now worth about two hundred million dollars. That same morning he quit his job with John Miller.

Then Mark turned to Candice, got down on one knee and proposed: "Honey, will you marry me?"

Candice considered Mark's request for thirty seconds. She spent that short period balancing off Mark's two hundred million dollar inheritance against her paltry (as it now seemed) divorce payoff of five million.

"Yes, darling, of course!" she finally gushed. After which, to celebrate their engagement they spent the entire morning making love, with Mark's very impressive manhood making her come over and over again.

The next day, after giving detailed instructions to her daughter's nanny in case she couldn't make it back home that night, Candice called John and pestered him until he grudgingly got on a plane with her, flew down to Reno, Nevada, and divorced her.

"Screw you and your money," she told her perplexed husband.

Then he flew off to Florida again and she flew back to Boston.

But once back home in Massachusetts, Candice now discovered she couldn't reach her new fiancé. Mark had flown up to Calgary to handle some family business (she'd seen him off to the airport and watched him board the plane), and now . . . nothing.

Had he been killed in an accident?

Her answer came two days later, when Mark sent her an email, with several photos attached. In the photos he was seated in a restaurant and was kissing a ravishingly beautiful redhead.

'Sorry, babe, but I can't go through with it,' Mark apologized in his email. 'Yeah, I did love you, but once I got back home and met Marie again (Marie was his stepmother and the redhead in the photos), I realized where my heart and true loyalties lay. So it's over between us. I'm sorry if I've hurt you, but goodbye, babe.'

What? Candice almost had a nervous breakdown right there and then. She'd been shot both in the heart and in the bank account, and at first didn't know which one hurt her more. Mark had dumped her after she'd just thrown away both her marriage and her prenup payment for him?

Once she'd gotten over her initial shock, Candice instantly ran to a lawyer with the desperate question: Was it possible to have a divorce annulled?

The answer was of course 'No.' Candice didn't qualify for the big payout anymore; she'd been married to John for just five years and three weeks.

She did have the option of the half-million dollars she'd get if she left him prematurely, but even there she discovered she'd been foiled.

***

John Miller had of course arranged everything. Mark Fisherman wasn't a rich man's son. The kid was a Canadian porno actor whom

John had hired to play the part of a chauffer and seduce his wife into the bargain.

John had taken his time with selecting Mark. Once the young man had passed the 'looks test,' John had then watched a couple of his porno films to discover how big his penis was. He'd come away from the viewing more than a little envious, but completely satisfied that Candice would find the kid irresistible, both in bed and out of it.

He'd paid Mark a hundred grand to play the part.

See, pretty and plump Candice's mistake was to not read her prenup closely—i.e. all that small print stuff everyone dreaded missing.

If she had, she'd have realized that it really hadn't mattered if she'd divorced John or not; their prenuptial agreement clearly stated that if she cheated on him with anyone before the seven year time period was up, she'd get nothing. Not a red cent.

And so Candice was left with nothing except she and John's daughter Jennifer, while John smiled all the way to the bank.

By being sneaky, John Henry Miller had just saved himself five million dollars. He didn't mind in the least having to pay child support, after all the kid was his.

Poor Candice had no idea that she'd been set up. She just moved out of John's palatial house and spent the next few years regretting how dumb she'd been.

***

After Candice came Josie.

And it was now that the perverse side of John Miller's nature came into play. While his underhand treatment of Candice could possibly be excused, as it could reasonably be argued that Candice Bowler brought her fate on herself, by the time John tied the knot with Josie Milewski, he'd realized he had something good here.

All he had to do was repeat the same process when he got tired of his new wife.

Josie Milewski was an airline stewardess when John met her. In fact, he took attention of her because their jet encountered a random pocket of turbulence while she was handing him his coffee somewhere in the sky over Colorado and she ended up spilling it all over herself (not him, thank God), which completely splattered her chest wetly brown and made her breasts stand out as prominently as the presidents sculptured on Mount Rushmore.

John had always been a 'breast man.' Matters were further helped along when the turbulence resulted in Josie falling on top of him, so that he got a good 'up close and personal' view of her exceptional mammary endowments.

Courtship rapidly followed, and marriage came hot on courtship's heels.

This time John lowered the payout clause in the prenuptial agreement to five years. He just suspected that he'd tire of Josie rather quickly.

The problem was that Josie was very clingy, extremely possessive. Yes, she loved him, but it was the kind of love that flared up in rage the moment a pretty girl glanced John's way or smiled at him suggestively. Josie wasn't really pretty herself—she had an elegant face at best, but she did have her exceptional points—those wonderful points being the tips of the two large mounds of womanhood on her chest.

Ironically, Josie should have spared herself the bother of being jealous—John Miller never cheated on his women. He might not have wanted to share his wealth with them, but he wasn't a philandering rat.

Anyway, John was happily married to Josie Milewski for two years and eight months, during which time they had a son and a daughter. After which Josie's clinginess and jealousy became so irritating to John that he simply stopped sleeping with her, and then, when he knew she was desperate for physical intimacy, he fired his new chauffer on some bullshit charge, rehired Mark from Canada again, and watched the same adulterous drama unfold as it had the first time.

This time John also relocated the family to an isolated villa outside of Denver, Colorado that he had rented for the summer.

Josie had protested against moving to the villa. "Why don't we just go to California instead?" she had asked. "There's nothing to do at that darn villa except get bored."

But that was the whole point of the move: in addition to preventing his friends and associates from noticing any similarities between this divorce and his first one, John was also counting on this boredom at the Denver villa to help drive Josie into Mark's arms.

This time Mark got a payment of two hundred grand. Women apparently couldn't resist getting pregnant for him and the child support payments were crippling. John, who now had three children himself, of course sympathized with Mark's plight.

The difference in Josie's case was that she wasn't hung up on Mark enough to divorce John—she'd merely wanted some sexual intimacy until her husband stopped ignoring her.

She'd refused to divorce John, so he'd divorced her instead, invoking the 'infidelity' clause in the prenup. But in Josie's case John had felt sad because she cried so much, so he'd paid her the half-million dollars compensation anyway.

Josie also went her unhappy way without suspecting either that she'd been set up to take a fall.

As a wife she'd lasted three years and five days.

***

Wife number three was Maryanne. She'd been the waitress in a greasy spoon in Trussville, Alabama, where John had stopped for lunch on his way to Birmingham.

Maryanne Hawkins perfectly fit the popular politically-incorrect definition of 'southern white trash.' When she'd plopped the fateful plate of cheeseburger and fries in front of John Miller, she'd been thirty pounds overweight, had a garish pink hair weave tangled up with her natural auburn locks, had several ugly tattoos on her bare arms and neck, and was chewing green gum to boot.

But she'd been irresistibly pretty too; nice and fresh-faced, a seeming calm in the storm of smells and loud redneck voices all around him.

He'd asked her what time her shift ended and if she'd like to have dinner with him . . . somewhere else of course.

Maryanne was the first woman John had ever dated who never shaved her legs or her armpits. Maryanne would have loved to be as smooth-legged as her friends, but razors, depilatory creams and even waxing all gave her the most horrible rashes. The single time she had given her lady parts a Brazilian treat she'd developed bumps down there that were almost the size of grapes. It also didn't help that she was a brunette, which meant the dark hair color showed up against her pale skin; if she'd been a blonde her natural furring wouldn't have been as obvious. (And unfortunately for Maryanne, she was allergic to hair dye too.)

John had initially found Maryanne's hairy legs off-putting, but once she'd wrapped them around him in bed a few times, that reservation went flying right out of the window. She was one passionate southern belle, that was for sure.

Their trip to the altar came shortly afterward.

John had tired of Maryanne because she wanted children. Already having three of them, John was tired of kids.

"I don't see what your problem is, hon," Maryanne had protested against his own protests. "You're rich, so what's it matter how many kids you have?"

John wasn't actually thinking of the cost of the children themselves, but the problems involved in coordinating another one once he divorced Maryanne. Because now he seemed unable to conceive of being with any woman for too long.

Maryanne might have remained wed to John for longer, but for a particular idiosyncrasy that she had: she liked smelly food. John had never worked out if his third wife had a defective nose or not, but whenever they went out for dinner, Maryanne always seemed to choose the stinkiest item on the menu.

There was one particular French cheese that Maryanne loved—Époisses de Bourgogne—which John absolutely hated the smell of. But Maryanne loved that stuff. She called it her ambrosia—her food of the gods—and stocked their giant fridges with it.

Anyway, three years of Maryanne was all John could manage. She'd gone the way of her two previous comrades in his bed. But not without a change of seducer.

John had just been about to summon the super-effective Mark Fisherman back from Calgary, Canada, when Maryanne summoned his attention to a newspaper article about a Canadian porn actor who'd died in a car crash along with his girlfriend.

Mark Fisherman was the dead man. The dead woman was the hot porno redhead John had hired to play Mark's stepmother.

John had shrugged and instead found Leroy Brown—a handsome sometime rapper from Queens, NYC with a body that seemed carved from rock and a penis like a mule's. (John knew Maryanne was partial to black guys.) Except for the fact that Leroy had a shaved head, the kid looked like a young 'Arnold with Denzel's face,' as the Salt-N-Pepa song went.

Long story short, Maryanne was shortly on her adulterous way out of their marriage too, Leroy having lied to her that he was a disowned African prince who wanted lots of kids . . .

***

In the meantime Candice had remarried to a super-wealthy lawyer named Richard Penderson III, a guy whom John knew by reputation as being both ruthless and apparently heartless as well. The sort of guy that had no problem with robbing orphans to feed the rich. The kind of man that you asked for a break and he broke your arm.

***

Lucy Lowry was wife number four. A sales executive for a cosmetics company, she'd sat next to John on a flight home from Los Angeles and they'd gotten to talking and had talked non-stop throughout the flight. They'd seemed to have everything in common.

Marriage had followed two months later.

Lucy had really loved John. John had had no doubts on that score, although over the years he'd often wondered if it was really himself or his money that his wives desired so passionately.

Anyway, after about a year or so of wedlock, John decided that he and Lucy weren't as much soul mates as he'd initially thought. In particular, he hadn't understood how anyone could be so obsessed with their appearance.

It was time to get rid of Lucy too.

He'd called Leroy Brown again, but the negro politely declined the offer.

See, Leroy had wisely invested the hundred grand he'd gotten from John into the music industry and had just launched his own record label—Alimony Records—a joke only he and John understood.

"Motherfucker, why the hell don't you just look for one bitch you *can* love?" Leroy asked John when they met in his Alimony Records office. "I mean, dude, big tits, big ass, White, Black, Mexican, Japanese, whatever; you name it, bro—I can find the woman for you."

"Nah, man, I got it like pussy wanderlust now," John explained. "You know, how some guys just have to keep traveling and can't stop no matter how good it'd do them to settle down in one place and put down roots? I got it like that, you know, pussy to pussy to pussy. I can't help it; can't stop myself."

Leroy had scowled and rubbed an itch on his bald pate. "So just don't marry 'em then, Johnny boy. I don't mind tellin' ya: this shit of yours is gonna backfire on you sooner or later, and you'll be real sorry then."

"Nah, they'll never figure it out."

Leroy looked thoughtful for a moment, then said: "Hey, listen to me, man. I happen to know this stripper chick named Cancer that you might like."

"Why would I wanna date a woman named Cancer?"

Leroy sighed. "To do me the great favor of taking her off my hands. Cancer's got her talons into this Chill Bill kid that we had the album drop party for the other night. She's eight years older than him but don't seem to care, and the kid don't care either. And worst yet, he listens to whatever the bitch says. So, say you were to show interest in her and flash some cash at her—I mean, Cancer likes millionaires as much as the next girl, see?"

Leroy gazed hopefully and pleadingly at John.

But John shook his head. "No, and that's final. I'm here trying to fix my current problem, not to find another one." He stared at the muscular negro in mock disbelief. "Cancer? Leroy, you gotta be kidding me."

Leroy accepted defeat with good humor. "Aw, man, I figured it was worth a try."

"Well, forget it. Hey, man, alright, now I know you can't do the job anymore. That's cool. But do you know anyone who'll fit the bill?"

"White, Black, or Latino?"

"White. Lucy shows no interest in colored guys. And one more thing: I don't want a porno guy—with the internet there's too much chance of her having seen the porno guy's face somewhere before; they're all on talk shows now. So find me someone unknown. Yeah, and he's gotta have a huge cock too."

The bald negro scowled. "Motherfucker, what the hell is you obsessed with huge dongs for? You on the down-low or sumthin?"

John shook his head. "Nah, it ain't that. Yeah, yeah, I know the size of a guy's package doesn't matter to a woman if she loves him. It's just that . . . I just want the psychological impact of it, you know— so that Lucy thinks she's getting more with the guy than she's getting with me. She's very petty like that."

Leroy at first hemmed and hawed. "Well, Johnny, you know I'd love to help you solve your li'l problem, but at the moment I don't think . . ."

John had already realized that Leroy was merely stalling and he knew why. He got to his feet, walked over to the window of the sky-high office, stared down at the mob of the Big Apple going about their daily business, and said over his shoulder in an exasperated voice: "You bald negro motherfucker, find me someone, someone young and reusable, and I'll make a quarter-million bucks investment in Alimony Records."

At that statement, a greedy glint entered Leroy's eyes. He'd crossed his legs, scratched his chin and grinned. "Well, there is this one dude I know . . ."

***

The 'one dude' Leroy knew was Maxwell Hutchins, or just 'Hutch,' as everyone called him. Handsome. Nineteen years old, six foot two inches tall and rippling with muscles; and once John had him drop his pants, all he could do was gape and wonder how God could be so unfair when sharing out penises.

Anyhow, long story short again, Lucy Lowry was soon on her unhappy way out of John's life as well. And just like Candice and Maryanne before her, Lucy left her marriage to John Miller without a cent.

And then six months later, she discovered that she'd contracted the HIV virus from Hutch. Lucy's discovery that she was now HIV-positive sent her crashing, turned her almost suicidal, and put in therapy for years.

John, however, was already settling down with wife number five.

***

John was never sure afterwards exactly where he'd first met Donna Goines. He knew he'd met her in New York City, but where? Was it in Leroy Brown's office, or was it during another album release party that Leroy held for 'Chill Bill' Wachowski, a teenaged white rapper who was literally the most untalented human being John had ever heard on a microphone, but whom everyone (Leroy Brown included), acclaimed as the best thing since Eminem?

Or was it during the drunken ride home in the back of someone's car that John had met Donna? Or had he drunkenly offered her a lift home? Or maybe they'd ridden up together in the hotel elevator, or did they met outside in the hotel corridors or bump into one another in the parking lot?

By next morning, however, none of that mattered. He'd woken up with a beautiful mulatto woman sucking his penis.

By John's own admission, despite his raging hangover, that morning's blowjob counted as the best one he'd ever had in his life, and having been married four times that was really saying something.

There and then he'd proposed to Donna.

She'd taken her mouth off his erection long enough to say, "Sure, honey, it'll make a positive change for me," and then resumed sucking on him.

"You crazy, man?" Leroy Brown had asked over the phone when he'd heard about John's proposed new marriage. "That girl's a hooker; all the rappers and players here have had a taste of her honey pot."

But John didn't think he was being silly by marrying a prostitute.

"Don't worry," he'd calmly replied. "So long as she ain't carrying any diseases, I can cope." Then he'd laughed. "Remember, I've got my 'wife-disposal' system properly figured out now."

"Man, you're one sick puppy," Leroy had told him. "I done already told you to stop that shit before it backfires on yo' white ass."

That said, Leroy hung up.

John shrugged at the silent cellphone, then dialed Donna instead and booked their flight down to Reno.

Five months later Donna happily announced that she was pregnant.

Marriage to Donna was strange to say the least.

She was loving enough and the sex was increasingly fantastic, but the new Mrs. Miller simply had no concept of fidelity.

Maybe it was to be expected considering her previous employment, but one evening, a year and six months into their marriage, and when their son Toby was five months old, John came home unannounced from a trip and found Donna giving a blowjob to their cook. And from what she was saying before he interrupted them, she'd also earlier sucked off both the gardener and the old chauffeur as well and had also had sex with both of them.

"I was bored 'cos you weren't home, honey," Donna apologized. "But I assure you it won't ever happen again."

Oh, it most certainly won't, baby, John thought in disgust and then pretended to forgive her.

However, all the male house staff got sacked the next day, with the errant old chauffer replaced by the ever-randy Hutch.

In Donna's case, John had rented an isolated and 'boring' villa in Salt Lake City to relocate them to so as to ensure that the seduction went faultlessly ahead.

John's previous wives had needed a little prompting to descend into infidelity, but in Donna's case, hiring Hutch was like setting cheese in front of a mouse. Immediately the former prostitute set her eyes on Hutch and sized up the massive bulge between his legs, she was caught up in a spiral of lust and simply had to have him.

Donna also didn't bat an eyelid when she was served with the divorce papers and then dumped by Hutch. She made few phone calls, left her son Toby with her parents, and then departed on a three-week cruise with a rich lawyer.

Little Toby caused John some trouble. Donna herself didn't believe the child was his. She'd begun sleeping with their staff just two months into their marriage and so the boy could have been fathered by any one of six people. But John had the boy DNA-tested and the tests were conclusive—the kid was beyond a shadow of a doubt his.

Donna, who'd been married to John Miller for two years, a week and two days, also didn't contact HIV from Hutch.

But, if considered objectively, the reason she'd not gotten HIV like Lucy had before her was a simple one: Donna had been a prostitute. For her, putting condoms on men's erections was a conditioned response, practically a reflex action. Housewives like Lucy only thought of unwanted pregnancies and abortions when they screwed the hired help, not about diseases.

And, to Donna's jaded mind, even in that case condoms tended to work better than morning-after pills.

Once she'd met Hutch, Donna had quickly realized that, unlike the hired help she'd previously fooled around with, this new lover of hers was likely to have a long and very checkered bedroom history. And so, claiming she wasn't on the pill and that she was scared of falling pregnant again so soon after her last baby, she had insisted on them always having safe sex.

Call it hooker intuition if you liked, but in her case it had worked.

***

Samantha Lincourt (or Wife No. 6) was just eighteen years old when John met her. She was a mathematics major at Boston University.

They were married four months later, and while John, who was now fifty-one years old, was still questioning the wisdom of hitching himself to her at all. Was this his mid-life crisis, when he needed the firm young flesh of a barely-legal teenager to combat the depressing feelings brought on by his own sagging body and declining virility? Was this his attempt to convince himself of his desirability to women half his age in comparison with younger men, studs where weren't thickening around the middle and who also didn't need hair transplants?

Whatever the case, whatever the answers, John married Samantha Lincourt.

With young Samantha, the problem was sex. Not that she didn't want it, but that she wanted it all the time.

John still remembered being a teenager, when it seemed impossible to get his penis to soften and he was happy to service a girlfriend four consecutive times at a single sitting, but those days were long behind him, and if now he had sex three times a week, he felt he was doing okay.

But meanwhile, his young bride wanted sex at least three times a day, and if she didn't get it, she began weeping loudly that he didn't love her.

(And unlike Donna, she seemingly had no intention of sleeping with anyone except himself.)

John never saw this side of Samantha's personality until after they'd gotten married. Okay, yes, he'd known from the start that she was highly-strung, but that hadn't worried him. After a while he figured she had some deep-rooted trauma she was compensating for.

To meet her incessant sexual demands he used Viagra, but even if his penis stayed hard, his body began feeling the strain; he got serious back and arm aches and stitches in his side at the most inopportune moments.

So after about a year and a half of bedroom athletics that occasionally made him glad he'd recently rewritten his will to include Donna's son Toby, John Miller placed another phone call to Hutch.

After which he abruptly stopped sleeping with Samantha. When she began getting violent about it, John moved out of their house.

It took four whole months after Samantha stopped getting any sex from her husband before she capitulated to Hutch's charms. She really did love John, it was just sex that was the problem.

(Just like Mark Fisherman and Leroy had done before him, Hutch spun the wives the same tale of being a rich kid disowned for sleeping with his stepmom. After all, like they say: 'If it ain't broke, why fix it?' The ruse worked a treat each time.)

When Samantha did however fall for Hutch, she did so with complete and reckless abandon.

"Fuck you, you pencil-dicked asshole," was all she told John when he served her with the divorce papers. "I'm glad to see the last of your impotent old ass."

John was relieved to see the last of her too. But of course, neither of them knew about the HIV that she too had now contracted from Hutch, who had known all along that he had the HIV virus, but simply valued money over other people's lives and happiness and so hadn't bothered to tell anyone about his infection or to use condoms either.

This time Hutch had charged John two hundred grand for his seduction services.

Samantha Lincourt had been John's wife for two years and two days, exactly a week shorter than Donna, the wife before her.

***

John Henry Miller had successfully gotten away with doing this to his wives for twenty years. The actual time that he'd been married through all this had been seventeen years, then there had been three years of 'rest-periods' between marriages.

John himself never had figured out why every single woman he'd set his adulterous honey trap for had fallen into it. It was almost as if all six ladies he'd married had been born brainless. Or maybe their brains were between their legs? But wasn't that saying supposed to only apply to men?

Even after the amount of planning he'd done, it still struck him as odd that not one of the six successive Mrs. Millers had ever questioned the possibility that the studs he fed to them might be lying about being disowned heirs. And also, that not one of them suspected that she wasn't alone in the fate she'd suffered. John credited his low-profile lifestyle for this. He'd never courted either publicity or the press, and so his marriages and divorces didn't interest anyone.

But still, John sometimes wondered at night, when the wind blew outside his bedroom window and his conscience wouldn't let him fall asleep: *Six beautiful women, six similar divorces, twenty years, and none of them has yet worked out what's going on? Maybe I'm a genius then.*

But it wasn't really that. The successive wives' lack of suspicion was easy enough to explain. It was mainly due to the fact that most of them had never even met one another.

In the early years, Candice and Josie had met each other thrice, but of course neither of them cared to advance the information that she'd been played for a fool by her husband's driver. And then Candice had married the attorney Richard Penderson anyway and had instantly become rich again, and as such had easily forgotten her sordid past; while Josie, who with two young children to care for could no longer work as an airline stewardess, had moved on into a series of bad marriages, each of which had her viewing her time with John Miller as a season spent in Paradise.

Of the last four women, Maryanne simply wasn't smart enough to figure out that she'd been fooled out of a fortune and try to do something about it, Lucy was too distracted and distraught by the knowledge that she'd gotten HIV to dwell on the past . . . and Donna, who *was* streetwise enough to later suspect that something dirty had gone on, had just shrugged it off and gotten on with her escort's lifestyle and looking after John's son Toby.

Which of course left John's last wife Samantha . . .

***

Now, any unbiased observer would reasonably have expected John's close friends (or at least their gossipy society wives) to wonder too about his string of similar divorces. And at first a few people did, but then everyone just assumed that John sucked in bed and the hunky chauffeurs didn't.

No one really bought John's explanation as to why he'd rehired both Mark and Hutch after they'd stolen women from him, which was that he didn't blame them, but rather blamed the erring wives.

Those two temporary shifts of 'divorce home,' to Denver (while divorcing Josie) and to Salt Lake City (while disentangling himself from Donna) had served to quell gossipy tongues a little, but even despite these precautionary shifts of location, the rumor spread in some circles that John was in fact impotent, and that he kept hiring handsome chauffeurs to keep his wives happy in bed and get them pregnant.

More malicious rumors (usually begun by those girlfriends he didn't marry) even claimed that John was himself sleeping with the chauffeurs.

In the end though, for whatever reasons or by whatever combination of implausible occurrences and coincidences, or maybe even because he had a guardian demon watching over him and keeping count of his sins against a day of reckoning, John Miller got away with it all.

The John Miller 'Wife-Exchange Express' rolled on for two full decades, with no one the wiser as to what was really going on.

Or was I simply an unsatisfying husband to those women? John also wondered sometimes. But then, instead of feeling repentant and vowing to change his ways, he'd always laugh and say out loud: "But if that's the case, then I'm a *rich* unsatisfying husband. And I'm about to move on to wife number seven—oh yeah!"

***

But then had come the twist in the tail that even John hadn't anticipated. And ironically, like divine retribution, this twist came right at the point when he had finally fallen hopelessly head over heels in love with Barbara Barbanell, and was hoping she'd be the woman he'd spend the rest of his life with.

Because then, John's last wife, the borderline nympho nymphet Samantha Lincourt found out that Hutch had given her HIV.

And that was when the wheels came off of John's romantic wagon.

CHAPTER 8

Candice Inc.

On that fateful evening Candice Penderson had been channel-surfing on her giant television when she'd stumbled on a gruesome news item—a murder-suicide down in New York City.

For want of anything better to do at the time, she had paused there before switching channels:

". . . Shot Mr. Hutchins at his apartment before driving home and committing suicide by shooting herself in the head also. . . ."

A picture of a young woman—a redhead barely out of her teens came onto the screen, while the bored-sounding anchorman gave further details about the case:

". . . In the suicide note she left behind, Ms. Lincourt accused Mr. Hutchins, a Bronx playboy popularly known as 'Hutch,' both of breaking her heart and giving her AIDS into the bargain; she also accused him of making her cheat on her ex-husband, Mr. John Miller . . ."

Candice had been about changing channels—the news was full of crazy young people nowadays—but the newscaster's mention of her former husband's name froze her finger on the remote control.

John? What does John have to do with this?

Nowadays Candice hardly ever thought of John at all. Now that she was living in opulence again, she'd long ago put the circumstances of her divorce behind her. Her only contacts with her first husband concerned their daughter, Jennifer, a brilliant young woman now studying Computer Science at Harvard.

So John married this red-haired kid and . . .

". . . Early investigative reports reveal that Mr. Hutchins had previously been Mr. Miller's chauffeur and that it was Ms. Lincourt's affair with him that led to the breakup of their marriage. In her lengthy and rambling suicide note, Ms. Lincourt wrote that Mr. Hutchins had lied to her that he was a disowned heir and . . ."

Candice stared at the TV in horror. Listening to the circumstances that had led to Samantha Lincourt's divorce and her shooting her lover sounded like someone had leaked her own personal history to the press.

Oh no, it can't be true, she'd gasped with her lips trembling in shock. *It simply can't be true.*

But a few phone calls later, Candice had confirmed that it was indeed true.

And then Candice had gone on Facebook and begun searching out John's other exes, first Josie and then the others. And she'd invited them to a meeting at her home on a weekend when her husband Richard was out of town.

***

"So what exactly are we all doin' here?" Donna Goines asked once they were all seated in one of the giant upstairs living rooms with drinks set before them, her creamed-coffee face crinkling up with curiosity. "What's this 'big deal' you were talking 'bout on the phone? 'Cos I know you didn't fly me up from the Big Apple just to share parenting tips."

"No, she didn't," Lucy told Donna with a grim smile. "I've an idea why we're here, but I'll let Candice tell us herself."

"I'm here 'cos she said there's money in it for us," pregnant Maryanne said, taking something yellow-and-orange and stinky from a large paper bag and popping it into her mouth. "Money's a magic word where I'm concerned," she added between chews.

"I could do with some more money too," Josie had agreed. "I've got four children and no husband and my two teens are running me towards a nervous breakdown." Then she'd frowned and wrinkled up her nose. "Girl, what on earth is that nasty stuff you're eating? Smells like a seafood restaurant's dumpster."

"Oh, it's just fried shrimp with Époisses cheese smeared on top." Maryanne patted her immense belly and shrugged apologetically. "You know, for the cravings?"

Josie nodded, though her eyes showed her revulsion. Then she returned her attention to Candice. "Hey, this isn't just about us setting up an ex-wives club, is it?"

"Okay now, ladies, calm down," Candice told them in a cold voice that permitted no argument. "Now, I'm going to tell the four of you a story I've never told anyone else, the true story of how I got divorced from our ex-husband John Miller. I want you all to listen to me without asking any questions. And then we'll discuss your own divorces, which I suspect will turn out to be very similar to mine."

"Alright, we're listening," Josie said.

***

The results of Candice's tale were even more dramatic than she had expected.

"Hell no!" Donna screeched, looking mad. "He did that to you too?"

"That's exactly what happened to me as well," Josie said. "It was also Mark Fisherman. So I was set up? But I thought John . . ." She shut up and looked confused.

"Oh, that Johnny's a total rat," Maryanne said. "I can't believe I ever loved him. She-it, I can't believe either that I fell for that honey trap, like I got me no brains at all." Then she giggled. "The sex was hot though, even if it did loose me five mil."

"I'm going to kill him," Lucy said, her teeth clenched in rage. "Read my lips—I'll kill him for this!" She was so angry that her porcelain-flawless complexion seemed about to shatter in pieces and shed her exquisitely painted cherry-red lips onto the table like overripe fruit.

"No point in going to jail on John's behalf," Candice chided her. "He's not worth it. And besides, us wives have already had one casualty."

"Casualty?" All four women stared at Candice. Candice nodded back at them, then she picked up a printed copy of the full text of Samantha Lincourt's suicide note from the end table next to her chair and read it out to them.

". . . And so I just can't go on," Candice read. "Maybe it would be different if I was thirty or forty years old when I caught this disease, but I'm just twenty-one now and instead of me looking forward with hope and happiness to the rest of my life, now I can't even look at myself in the mirror; when I do all is see is death. . . . Even though I know there's lots of drugs to control HIV so I don't get full-blown AIDS . . . well, I still feel like a living dead person. And I don't know if this is just me having an adverse reaction, but my ARVs make me feel like I'm losing my mind. So I'm going to end it all and . . ."

Candice stopped reading because Lucy had suddenly burst into tears.

"What's the matter?" Josie asked her, with the other women nodding.

"I know exactly how Samantha felt," Lucy said, with tears flooding down her cheeks and smearing them with lines of mascara. "I feel exactly the same way she did."

It took a few seconds for the rest of the women to understand what she meant, and then Donna tentatively asked: "Hey, you've got HIV too?"

Lucy nodded. "Yes, it was the same guy, Hutch."

Donna, who was wearing her hair in a large Afro, dug her fingers through its kinky fibers and scratched her scalp with her long nails. "Aw, shit, honey. I'm so sorry; I didn't know." And then, in a show of solidarity, she got up and went over to Lucy and hugged her tightly.

The other three women got up too and did the same. It was a long group hug, with Lucy weeping all through it.

After that revelation, as if their shared emotional outburst was a sort of glue that now bound them together, the five women sat close together on two adjacent couches while talking.

"Hey, Donna," Maryanne asked, "if you married John between Lucy and Samantha, how come you didn't get AIDS from Hutch?"

Donna shrugged; she looked confused herself. "I dunno. I'm just lucky, I guess. Or maybe it's 'cos as an escort I always use rubbers with guys?"

Her words caused Lucy to start crying afresh, so Donna hugged her again.

"Okay, ladies, let's not get distracted here," Candice said. "I think it's now obvious to us all that John set us all up so he could divorce us. Well, yes, we were all idiots to fall for it, but the point is he's not going to get away with it."

"I want revenge," Lucy said. "I want revenge on John. That miserly jerk traded away my happiness for five million bucks." Her perfect makeup was now a perfect mess, with, in addition to the mascara lines, her lipstick having gotten widely smeared across her left cheek; something that she thankfully wasn't aware of, as it would have made her even more distraught.

Candice laughed. "Revenge is easy enough to have, but first I think we need confirmation from at least one of the studs he hired to seduce us."

Josie winced at the word 'seduce.' "Oh, please no, Candice. "Even after all this while I don't think I could bear seeing that bastard Mark Fisherman again."

"Mark's dead," Candice calmly informed her.

"Did you kill him?" Maryanne asked hopefully before popping another smelly shrimp into her mouth.

Candice shook her head. "No, girl, he died in a car crash ten years ago—I like to view it as bad karma biting him in the ass. And now Hutch is dead too, which leaves just Maryanne's seducer Leroy Brown alive. So we'll—"

"Hey, did you just say *Leroy Brown?*" Donna asked. "Tall and bald black guy?"

Candice nodded. "Yes, the same one, if he lives in New York."

Donna instantly dropped all her culture and sophistication and reverted back to 'ghetto bitch' mode. "Shit, I should've known that bald nigga was up to no good." She glared at Candice. "I got news for y'all—Leroy and John are real good friends." Donna looked completely irate now. "So Leroy was in on this too? Oh, I'm gonna fucking kill that skinhead nigga!"

"Calm down," Candice told her. "If anyone should be angry with Leroy, it should be Maryanne."

Donna glared at Maryanne. "I don't think pregs there is capable of being pissed off at anyone or anything."

Maryanne giggled and ate another smelly shrimp. "It was ages ago and like I said, the lovin' was great. Yeah, I got screwed, but wow, I *really* got screwed."

"Then your brains really are in your pussy, girl," Josie said angrily. "We're talking serious stuff here—those assholes even gave Lucy AIDS and all you remember is how great the sex was." Her expression turned even more annoyed. "And do you really have to keep plopping those horrible smelly things into your mouth? Can't you put them away till this meeting is over?"

"Don't pick on her," Candice told Josie firmly.

Josie frowned but kept quiet after that.

"So what we gonna do now?" Donna asked, with hatred blazing from her eyes. "I wanna off that asshole Leroy Brown so bad I can taste it."

"Not him," Candice said. "He was merely a tool John used. John Miller is our target."

"But . . ." Donna protested.

"No," Candice retorted. "No . . . and that is final. We are not going to kill Leroy Brown." She fixed Donna with a cold stare. "What you're going to do for us, Donna, is to fly back down to New York and have a talk with Mr. Brown, and get him to confess to you everything that happened between himself, John Miller, and Maryanne here."

Donna snorted. "Get that nigga to talk? How? Old woman, looks like you don't know how tough those gangsta rap guys are. Leroy would rather go to the penitentiary before confessin' to doin' somethin' like that. Imagine word getting out that his hip-hop empire rests on him performing gigolo services for white bitches." She sighed. "Sorry, I don't mean to call Maryanne a 'white bitch,' but I guess y'all know what I meant by what I said."

Maryanne waved a hand. "No offense, girl. Trust me, I'se been called a whole lot worse at the diner where I work now. You'd think political correctness don't apply to us whites."

"Don't worry about getting Leroy to talk, Donna," Candice said confidently. "Just offer him a hundred grand in cash to tell us what really happened. I'll give you a package of money when you leave here." She frowned. "What's important though is that you record Leroy's confession on your cellphone so we can all listen to it."

Donna nodded and smirked. "Yeah, I think I can handle that."

"Good," Candice said. Then she looked around at the other three women. "I suggest we wait until Donna has brought us Mr. Brown's confession before I tell you exactly what I have in mind to do to Johnny Boy."

The meeting broke up after that, with another one scheduled for the next weekend, when Donna assured everyone that she would have the required recording.

***

Donna never gave Leroy even a dollar of the hundred grand that Candice handed to her after the meeting at the mansion.

What she did instead was to stash the cash in the wall safe she had in her penthouse apartment and then call up Leroy on the pretense that she wanted to talk business; not sex business, but about her little sister Tasha, an aspiring rapper who needed a mentor. She made it very clear on the phone to Leroy that she was willing to do 'whatever it took' to get Tasha a record deal.

Leroy bit the bait. Donna still had the reputation for giving the best blowjobs in New York City, so he invited her over to his penthouse for dinner.

They talked business and Donna played him some of Tasha's demos.

"The kid's good," Leroy lied over drinks. "Yeah, yeah, maybe we can do something with her."

Donna knew Leroy was lying; even she hated Tasha's rapping. But what was important was the way Leroy couldn't take his eyes off her breasts, which were practically popping out of the low-cut dinner gown she'd worn to his place. And each time she licked her lips, she imagined she could see his penis thumping against his pants as he imagined her sucking on it.

Anyhow, one thing led to another and Donna and Leroy went to bed, where Donna gave Leroy some of the best sex of his life. When they were done, Leroy fell asleep and Donna quickly went to work on him.

Leroy Brown woke up about an hour later to find himself tied hand-and-foot to the corners of his bed with silk scarves that Donna had brought along in her purse.

Two things however assured the bald negro record company CEO that this wasn't just some S&M scene Donna had set up to pleasure them both further:

1. The Sony camcorder that Donna had set up beside him on the nightstand. And . . .

2. The fact that while grinning at him like a wolf, she was holding a huge meat cleaver against the base of his penis.

"Shit, bitch, what the hell's the matter with you?" Leroy protested with his eyes bugging out. "You high on crack or what?"

Donna tapped his penis with the flat of the cleaver blade. "Listen, nigga, don't you dare waste my time now. I wanna know everything that you and my ex-husband John did about setting us wives up with his chauffeurs so he could divorce us without paying alimony." She scowled at Leroy. "Either that or, motherfucker, you'll soon be known as 'No-Dick Leroy Brown.' "

Leroy saw she was dead serious. But even if she wasn't, no man ever jokes with a woman holding a meat cleaver to his penis and threatening to cut it off.

"Oh shit, girl. Not that damn matter. Listen, yeah, Johnny's a good friend of mine—but I done already warned that crazy white motherfucker to stop doing that shit to all of you girls. I warned him it was gonna backfire on his ass. But the dude just won't listen to me."

Donna couldn't help but laugh. "Well, guess what, nigga—it just did backfire on yo' black ass. Now, which is it gonna be? Are you gonna tell me how you guys went about workin' it, or do you wanna make a trip to the ER? But if you choose that latter option, I'm first gonna chop your dick up like salami so it can't ever be reattached to you."

"NO, I'LL TALK, I'LL GODDAMN TALK!" Leroy was almost weeping now. "Don't you dare chop up my package, woman."

Donna patted him condescending on the cheek. "Good boy, I knew you'd see reason. And hey, Leroy, I also wanna know everything 'bout that bastard Hutch as well."

Leroy talked and talked and talked and talked and talked. He told Donna everything he and John had done, including how he'd hooked him up with his boy Hutch.

Leroy confessed: "I mean, girl, Johnny was so desperate to be rid of Lucy that he even bought shares in Alimony Records . . ."

Donna almost castrated him when she heard that. But she managed to control herself.

She filmed everything with her camcorder and left Leroy unharmed but still tied up; though she also gagged him with duct tape now so he couldn't yell for help. She figured someone would find and untie him in the morning. And Leroy Brown was certain as hell not going to tell anyone what had gone down between them.

Donna got back home, transferred the video recording to her laptop, and then uploaded it for Candice to view.

***

At the next meeting, Candice was so impressed with Donna's handling of the situation that she didn't even demand her money back, not that Donna would have returned it anyway.

"Sista, you got what you paid for," was all she told Candice, when the latter enquired what she'd done with the hundred grand.

Anyway, now that they had Leroy's confirmation of what John Miller had done to them, all five exes were irate—including the usually phlegmatic Maryanne.

"Yeah, I agree the jerk deserves to die," Maryanne said even before Candice proposed that they sacrifice John to some demon she called Boku Java.

"Me too," Donna agreed. "No one who treats his wives like that deserves to live. But how're we gonna get him here? If you invite him over for dinner and he vanishes . . . you know . . . the fuzz?"

"Yes, she's right," Josie agreed, her worried expression making her thin face seem haggard and lined. "The police will be onto us in minutes, like glue on envelopes. Then we'll all go to prison for kidnapping John."

"Please permit me to just drive over to his house and stick a shotgun in his face and pull the trigger," Lucy pleaded through a fresh outburst of tears that had Donna hugging her to comfort her again.

Candice laughed. "Oh, don't you worry your heads about kidnapping John," she told her guests. "I'll take care of bringing John to us. All I wanted was your agreement that he needs to be dealt with. The ritual to dispose of his remains requires the participation of five people."

The five women turned then as someone entered the living room where they were seated. This person was a completely naked bald-headed woman.

But despite her nudity and baldness, what was most surprising about the newcomer were her eyes—cold grey eyes that instantly filled Josie, Maryanne, Lucy and Donna with dread. The fact that those merciless eyes were completely circled by red eyeshadow (as if she was wearing giant red sunglasses) didn't help matters either.

Candice, however, smiled warmly at the naked woman and gestured her to sit in the chair beside hers.

"Ladies, I'd like you all to meet my good friend Mrs. Pain," she introduced the woman to them.

CHAPTER 9

Meet The Ex: Candice

Candice Bowler had always been the kind of person who saw a thing and went for it, but after her divorce from John Miller she'd drifted aimlessly for a while and just narrowly avoided having a nervous breakdown. Having a child had stabilized her; she'd realized that for Jennifer's sake, she couldn't crack up.

Though originally from Bedford, Indiana, she'd remained in Massachusetts after the divorce and had worked a series of low-income jobs to get by.

A far fall from grace indeed for a millionaire's wife.

She had met Richard Penderson at a cocktail party she attended with her younger sister. The young lawyer had been handsome and very sexy, but most importantly, from Candice's point of view, just like herself he was recently divorced.

They had been married for fifteen years now, most of it blissful, though recently there had been a slightly rocky patch.

Candice had been unable to have any more children after Jennifer, but Richard (who also had a daughter from his previous marriage) was too much of a workaholic to make a good father anyway, so that too had worked out for the best.

What Candice hadn't told John's other exes—because she still found it embarrassing to recount after all these years—was that her own cravings during pregnancy hadn't been for ice cream like she'd claimed, but that she'd had serious pica—she'd begun eating dirt and had wound up with lead poisoning, with the doctors just managing to save both she and her unborn daughter from serious harm.

So she totally sympathized with Maryanne, whom she thought was actually getting off quite lightly as far as pregnancy cravings were concerned.

3

A woman's heart is more fragile than
glass,
And yet will survive a nuclear blast.

*

*Life's a dream, and then you wake up in
Heaven or Hell
- Kimchi Chocolate Stereo (Propaganda to
Calm the Tortured Soul)*

CHAPTER 10

Megan

The third door that Megan tried opened into a study. The room, which contained several chairs, a wide reading desk and several large bookcases, was large and was also airy because the drapes were open.

Leaving the study door slightly ajar so she would hear any footsteps approaching, Megan sat in an armchair and pondered her increasingly precarious situation.

This stuff is beginning to snowball. The longer I remain in this house, the harder it's going to be for me to explain my presence here.

She considered returning outside to the corridor and trying to find another stairwell that led downstairs; a mansion of this size had to had several more. But she cautioned herself against doing so: *I can't return to the main hallway while those two muscular goons are standing by the stairwell . . . and who the hell was that girl with them? Why is she walking around butt-naked like that, with that creepy makeup on her face—black lips and her eyes looking like giant sores? Oh, dammit. If I start prowling these corridors looking for an exit, I'll be just a step away from encountering someone who'll raise an alarm at my presence in the house.*

She got up from the chair and crossed to the left of the two study windows, pushed apart its billowing green-striped drapes and peered down at the acreage of lawns that bordered the building and at its dotting of fruit trees; and then she looked up at the night sky. The oval moon was lovely; it made her wish she still had a boyfriend. But the US Marines had recently sent Tommy off to Japan and since tearfully breaking up with him, Megan hadn't dated anyone else. Still, looking up at the moon put her in both a radiant and a depressed state of mind.

She sighed. *Except I want to climb out of the window, I'm stuck in here. I just hope this isn't an often-used room. Well, at least I hope no one needs to use it tonight.*

She did consider jumping down from the window and walking away. She'd not leapt down from a second-floor window before (the drop seemed to be about twelve feet), but it didn't seem too far of a fall and she should survive it without breaking her ankles.

But if I'm noticed doing so, then I'll really be considered a burglar. Although with what those women plan to do . . .

What the ex-wives planned to do. What the ex-wives planned to do. That, of course was the real problem here—the elephant in the room, so to speak, that Megan had been avoiding really thinking about. She was in a house where a murder would be committed in . . . she got out her cellphone, turned it on and checked the time on its screen . . .

An hour and twenty-five minutes. That's how long I've got to leave this house and call the police. She scowled and then, after making sure her phone was muted, put it back inside her jacket. *But for the moment, I'm stuck here. Not yet trapped, thankfully, but with the Fates seemingly conspiring against me leaving.*

And then a chilling wind of realization seemed to blow in through the open windows and swirl around her. *Oh shoot, if those angry ex-wives catch me and realize . . . if they even suspect that I've overheard them, I'm done for. But no no no, it hasn't yet gotten to that. If I do get caught by them before I can leave, then I'll throw caution to the wind and call the police anyway. Going on trial for breaking and entering or trespassing on private property is way better than becoming a sacrifice myself.*

She crossed from the window to the study door and peeked out through the slight gap she'd left.

She heard female voices conversing a short distance away, but they didn't seem headed her way. Then the voices faded; but whether this was because the speakers were thinking or looking at something or because they'd left the corridor, Megan couldn't tell.

She decided to wait here a short while longer: if she tried to leave now there was a good chance that she'd find those she was trying to avoid sitting and drinking coffee in the living room downstairs.

Frustrated, she turned and studied her temporary cell.

A picture of a man whom she assumed was Candice's husband— Richard, she'd called him—scowled down at her from the wall above the reading desk. Megan walked closer to study his face. Richard . . . (she had no idea of his and Candice's surname) was a very handsome middle-aged man with graying black hair, but there was also something unpleasant about him.

This guy doesn't look like your average old lecher, Megan thought. *No, what's off about him is much worse than that. Oh yes, I get it now—he looks like he doesn't have a conscience; the sort of person who enjoys doing bad things to other people just because he can.* Then she shook her head. *But no, I'm just being silly; it's just a photo. He's really dashing though. I'd love to have a husband who'll look this good at his age, not some overweight beer-guzzling slob who does nothing but burp and fart and watch baseball while yelling at our teenage kids. Yes, despite his mean eyes, this guy Richard is cute*—she giggled—*not to mention VERY rich, another very important consideration for us ladies.*

She grinned at the picture for a while, imagining what her life would be like if she was this wealthy man's wife instead of Candice.

Maybe I should have a baby now, she thought. Then she froze, upset that she'd once again been drawn into a lulled state, one in which the specter of maternal life haunted her.

She was twenty seven, almost thirty, and sometimes, seemingly out of nowhere, the desire to have a child hit her like this, like a sucker punch to the gut, and then all her other plans and ambitions seemed as fragile as a castle built from playing cards or dominos, and then she would sit in one spot for hours convincing herself that the free and roaming life she had now was the life she really wanted, and that she wasn't yet ready for nature to attach a baby anchor to her body.

Then she considered her present straits:

Okay, yes, so I wanted excitement. This—tonight—would never had happened if I'd had the baby in question, or even remained at my cushy Boston job.

***

After leaving university Megan Kemp had worked with Ellis Drake Biotech for four years, but had then grown tired of her job.

The problem hadn't been either her workload or her salary. Rather, as if a switch had been thrown in her mind, she'd felt a sudden desire to travel for a bit; an inexplicable yearning for the freedom that the highways offered instead of the structured and predictable life of a white-collar professional. So she'd quit her job, sold her Honda SUV, bought Ferret Morris's Harley Davidson instead and had hit the road, riding up and down the eastern seaboard with friends.

And this was how she'd gotten into waitressing too. Serving tables paid a whole lot less and the hours sucked, but unlike in her biochemistry lab, she actually got to meet interesting people during the course of her day. That's the way she viewed the customers anyway.

But the temptation to return to her previous well-paid employment in a laboratory was always there, and nowadays it was a nagging one each time she viewed her dwindling bank account, which had dwindled a lot more since she'd lent Dave that two thousand bucks.

Her older brother Brian had never understood how anyone could ditch an assured future for something as unreliable and low-income as serving tables. What motivation could anyone have for such behavior? He and his wife Valentina (who was a bank executive) kept pressurizing Megan to 'wake up and smell the coffee before it got cold.'

Megan had been living this way—biking and waitressing—for three years now. She figured she'd spend maybe another six months following her present course, make a couple more bike trips north and south, and then reach a final decision.

At least she'd had her fun. But what the future held, she wasn't sure. Occasionally, at stops during her travels, she'd felt she wanted kids; then the next moment, she wanted to be the top woman in her biochemistry field; and the moment after that she just wanted lots and lots of money; and then suddenly she'd want everything—husband, family, professional success, and piles of cash—which she knew could be attainable if she was willing to give up her passion for riding and concentrate her energy towards attaining those goals.

***

Megan soon got over her funk. Several leather-bound volumes were open on the reading desk below the photograph that had set her thinking, and she walked and sat down beside one of them and turned its pages, which were also made of the same old leather as its cover. The script on the pages was in red and brown ink.

'. . . To raise Boku Java the mage or sorceress requires a human sacrifice. This sacrifice should preferably be a man in the prime of life and in good health and unharmed—not wounded or mutilated in any way . . .'

What's this? Megan made a face and kept reading.

'. . . When the clock strikes midnight or a little bit afterwards (but not prior to the Witching Hour), the victim, who has previously been bound on the marble altar, must be killed. The victim's blood will then flow along the Grid of Agony . . .'

In addition to these morbid instructions, the strange book also had diagrams. The full-page diagram opposite these last lines that Megan had read was labelled 'A Summoning Room' and showed five people sitting around a table with a pentagram drawn on it, and a naked man tied on top of the table/pentagram with his four limbs and his head each pointing to one of the pentagram's angles. A person in a hooded robe was holding a knife with a wavy blade to the naked man's throat.

This table is exactly like the one in the room where the exes are talking now. So, according to this book, that room is a 'summoning room' and they really do mean to sacrifice John Miller.

In the background of the diagram stood a stone oval exactly like the one Megan had noticed in Candice's summoning room, with a pentagram etched into its center.

Entranced by what she was reading but at the same time revolted by it, Megan turned the book over to see what its title was:

'LOTUS: Volume 3317.'

When Megan read this her fingers seemed to quiver with a weird sort of electricity. She had turned the cover and was staring at the book's first page before she realized that she was frightened. Very frightened.

But what on earth is scaring me? This is just a book for chrissakes! Everyone knows magic is just smoke and mirrors . . . but . . . but . . . Oh, my God, no!

She had just understood what had scared her. The book she was holding was bound in human skin, and had pages also made from human skin. What she'd assumed was normal leather wasn't—this was proven by the unmistakable human navel positioned above the additional title on the book's first page: 'LOTUS Volume 3317: The Purposed Incarnation of Demons.'

With a shriek Megan dropped the ghastly book on the reading desk. Then, realizing that the noise she had just made might have given her presence in here away, she clamped her palm over her mouth and began shivering.

Occasionally her eyes lifted to stare worriedly at the man in the picture over the desk.

What would a handsome and well-off man like this Richard guy be doing with a book bound in human skin in his lavish home?

CHAPTER 11

Josie

Josie Milewski walked carefully and quickly down the corridor. And then, after checking and making sure that there was no one around who could report her actions to Candice, she quickly slipped through the doorway that led to the basement stairs.

This has gone too far already, and it has also gone on for way too long, she thought. *I need to put an end to it while I still can. Now, while everyone is resting before Candice's so-called 'big event,' which is really just a cold-blooded murder, I'd better break Johnny out of here!*

Josie had never really bought into what Candice was selling them. As far as she was concerned, Candice's version of sanity had long ago overstepped the boundaries of insanity. In short, the woman was cuckoo.

Whatever she spiked our Kool-Aid with, I'm not drinking that stuff. Yes, John did treat us like dirt, but if we kill him, we're no better than he is. And besides . . .

And besides, Josie was still in love with John Miller. Yes, she sometimes hated to admit it to herself, but eleven years and two failed marriages later, she still couldn't get John out of her mind.

And, truth be told, she really did still blame herself for their divorce and losing her prenup payout. *Yes, John did set us up. But why didn't we all just keep out thighs closed? Cheating is cheating, no matter how you color it. I don't mind admitting that I really did think the grass would be greener on the other side when Mark Fisherman was romancing me! So I partly share the blame for what happened to me; we're all culpable.*

Josie's plan was simple: to rescue John and remarry him. She had no doubts in her mind that once John Miller realized what she'd saved him from, he would also realize that he'd been very wrong to divorce her. Saving his life would more than make up for cheating on him back then.

And once that was understood and her adulterous past forgiven, the children she'd borne him would once more be home with their father. Now that they were teenagers Simon and Lisa were both totally unmanageable. Josie hadn't been exaggerating when she'd told the other women that her older two kids were driving her towards a mental breakdown with their rebellious behavior.

John had requested twice that the children come live with him, but on both occasions Josie had turned him down. She'd been happy in her second marriage then—the one that had produced her younger daughter Erica, and had wanted to show John that he'd really lost out when he'd lost her.

But not now. Now Josie had seen the light and was ready to risk her life to free the man she loved and reunite her family.

Of course, if Candice found out what she was up to . . . the consequences didn't bear thinking about.

Her and that crazy bitch named Mrs. Pain . . . strutting about like . . . We're not lesbians, why can't she put some clothes on? And Candice sees nothing wrong with her nakedness. Has to be because her husband Richard isn't around. Now, there's a truly handsome man for you. I wonder what he even sees in fat Candice?

Not that Josie would dare say this to Candice's face of course. Mrs. Pain was clearly a brutally effective woman; Josie had watched a video of her whipping a man's body to shreds and she had no desire to be on the receiving end of Mrs. Pain's brutality.

As she stepped down off the stairs into the mansion's basement, Josie tightly gripped the knife she'd sneaked into the house. She would have preferred a gun, but doing this quietly was essential. Once she shot anyone, the noise would alert the others. And Candice was certain to have some guns of her own in the house.

***

In keeping with the mansion's sprawling size, this basement was a large place, running about half the length of the building overhead. Josie knew this because once all the exes had agreed to go along with Candice's plan to sacrifice John, Candice had given them the grand tour of the basement so they could see that she meant business.

Along with the usual rooms full of unneeded things, the store for the kitchen was also down here. This pantry was a giant room that contained several walk-in freezers. The kitchen had a separate stairway to access this underground room.

(Aside from the stairs that Josie and the others had descended to the basement that day, they'd also seen two side alcoves that contained stairways, but Candice hadn't explained where in the mansion either of those connected to.)

As Josie remembered it, there were four corridors down here, two that ran lengthwise along the axis of the mansion and two that crossed those at right angles to the building's length, all four of them with doors to storage rooms. The cell in which Candice was holding John was near the end of the second of these turnoff corridors.

Josie gave a slight start when she heard a noise. But it was nothing serious, just a scared rat hurrying away from her. Seeing the rat calmed her somewhat.

She returned her attention to her task. After peeking into the first intersecting corridor and seeing no one, she stepped quickly past it and headed for the second one, which was about forty yards ahead.

Her heart was pounding with anticipation now. Just a few seconds more and she would be with the love of her life again.

Oh, Johnny, don't worry, honey. Your pussycat Josie is here to save you.

And then, just as Josie was about turning right into the second corridor, someone stepped out of it and bumped into her.

Josie yelped in fright, almost scared out of her wits. Though she initially thought that it was either Candice or Mrs. Pain that she'd run into down here, she somehow managed to control herself, to not panic and turn and flee.

She was surprised to see it was Maryanne who'd bumped into her.

Maryanne had of course hit Josie pregnancy-first and had now reeled back gasping against the blue corridor walls. She looked every bit as scared as Josie.

"What are you doing down here?" each women asked the other at the same time once they'd gotten over their fright.

Then Josie nodded to Maryanne. "Sorry, you go first." She was relieved to see that her pregnant companion wasn't carrying any of that stinky shrimp and cheese mess she was so partial to at the moment.

Now, Josie disliked Maryanne. Yes, Lucy for instance, also disliked Maryanne, but that was a totally different situation. Lucy's dislike of Maryanne stemmed from petty causes: she disliked the pregnant brunette's hairy legs, her cheap tattoos, her even cheaper perfume and her atrocious fashion sense. Lucy Lowry was a fashion Nazi and she considered it a 'final-solution-level' crime that frumps like Maryanne even existed on the planet.

But Josie *totally detested* Maryanne Hawkins. And the reason for this was simple to understand: Maryanne was Ex-Wife No. 3—that is, she had become John's wife after he'd divorced Josie. Josie disliked the other exes too, but this single fact—that Maryanne was the woman who had replaced her in John's affections—gave Maryanne a special place in any hell that the Devil asked her to stock with people she wanted tormented for all eternity.

***

Never believe a woman who says she doesn't want to have kids; particularly a wealthy man's wife.

(Wanting a fruitful and fulfilling career is for poor or middle-class girls, who need something to boost their self-esteem because they don't have sufficient money to burn.)

Because to be honest, once your husband had lots of money, what else was there to do to alleviate your boredom, except create society-approved biological work for yourself? Because like it or not, once a woman had a baby, she'd be busy—and very gainfully employed indeed—for the next two decades.

Sure the government said your responsibilities to the kid ended when the child turned sixteen, but every mother knew that was nonsense. Sons, for instance, sometimes needed maternal overseeing well into their thirties, until they could be handed over to suitable young wives who would take over the pampering from where mom left off. And even then Mother had to check in every now and then to ensure that the wives in question were doing a good job.

Daughters, on the other hand, were a different kettle of fish entirely. In most cases, one had to watch over one's daughters for life, part of which included terrorizing one's sons-in-law so they could be expected to take good care of your girls. And then you had to be there for them when they gave birth to your grandchildren. And of course there was all the advice on child-rearing which you then gave to your daughters and which they never appreciated at all.

Oh, being a mother never ended; once kick-started into motion, it was a lifelong profession.

***

"I was on my way to the kitchen to pick up some fried shrimp and got turned around and confused," Maryanne explained a little drowsily to Josie. "I got the cravings again and . . ."

Oh, shit, Josie thought, gaping at the other woman in disbelief. Yes, Maryanne was dumb—that much had been obvious from the first time she'd met her—but how much of an airhead did you have to be to not count flights of stairs correctly? *We're rooming up on the second floor, for chrissakes, and the kitchen is one floor down! Even as sleepy as she is she should be able to realize she'd passed the ground floor landing. Or is that shrimp and cheese nonsense she keeps eating burning out her brains?*

"So what're *you* doin' down here? And with a knife too?" Maryanne asked. "Hey, d'you know where the kitchen is?"

Josie groaned in rage. *I really ought to murder this stupid preggered bitch right now. She's just completely messed up my rescuing John.*

And Josie really was angry enough to do so, to just slit Maryanne's throat and leave her to bleed out onto the basement floor.

But then, with Maryanne staring at her expectantly and awaiting a reply to her questions, particularly the second one, Josie caught the sound of footsteps approaching. The footsteps were coming from the interconnecting corridor behind them.

And then she heard Mrs. Pain laughing.

Panic filled Josie. *I'm dead. Oh, Jesus, I'm done for. At least this cow Maryanne has a plausible excuse for why she's down here. But me . . .*

Then a mad thought occurred to Josie. Quickly, before she had the chance to reconsider her intention and chicken out of acting, she slashed herself across her left forearm with the knife.

Maryanne watched in horror as she gasped in pain and blood spurted from her self-inflicted wound.

Then, realizing she hadn't a moment to waste if she intended to save herself from disaster, Josie handed the bloody knife to Maryanne and then slumped to the floor.

And that was how Candice and Mrs. Pain met the two of them, with Josie lying on the floor bleeding and Maryanne holding the bloody knife.

"What's going on here?" Candice immediately asked, hurrying to Josie's side and kneeling beside her while Mrs. Pain quickly disarmed Maryanne.

"I-I-I . . ." Josie muttered.

"Take it easy," Candice calmly instructed her. "We're here now. Everything is alright."

Faking shock and weakness, Josie pointed a shaky finger at Maryanne. "She . . . she stabbed me! She . . . stabbed me. I was looking for the kitchen and got lost and I found her down here . . . she told me that we're all crazy and that she was going to free John and . . . I tried to stop her and she stabbed me . . . ouch!"

Candice rose swiftly to her feet and glared at Maryanne, who was still staring in shock at Josie and hadn't yet realized the gravity of what she was being accused of.

"How dare you betray us?" Candice asked Maryanne.

"But I didn't," Maryanne tried to explain. "She's lying. I didn't—" While protesting she pointed her fingers at Josie. But, with her hand bloody from the knife she'd been holding, the gesture merely served to confirm her guilt to the two newcomers.

"She told me she's still in love with John and that she's going to sell us all out to the police," Josie groaned from the floor.

Candice nodded to Mrs. Pain. "She's all yours now."

"But . . . but . . . I didn't say that!" Maryanne gasped in shock. "I was just looking for—"

Before Maryanne could explain herself, Mrs. Pain chopped the edge of her hand hard against the side of her neck and she slumped down unconscious.

"Stupid fool," Candice growled as she bent to help Josie up. "It really is impossible to trust anyone these days." She gently pulled Josie to her feet. "Damn, that's a nasty cut—let's see what we can do to stop the bleeding."

"It's not too bad," Josie said when she'd straightened up. "My teenagers have had worse. Once it's bandaged up, I'll still be able to participate in the sacrifice." Relieved that she'd gotten away with her ruse, she pointed to Maryanne, whom Mrs. Pain was picking up from the floor. "What are we gonna do about her though?"

Candice smirked. "Oh, don't worry about her. Mrs. Pain will send her home."

"She's out of the sacrifice then?" Josie asked with her face twisted up in agony—she figured that she had either sliced her arm more deeply than she'd intended, or had forgotten how badly cuts hurt.

Josie knew she wasn't completely out of the woods yet: there was still the possibility that once Maryanne woke up again, she would tell Mrs. Pain what had really happened down here in the basement and the naked amazon just might believe her, though judging from the immensely cruel smile on Mrs. Pain's black lips, she would clearly prefer not to.

"Sacrifices are only of value to those with faith in them," Candice said. "And that faith is clearly lacking in Maryanne." She tossed Maryanne a dismissive gesture. "Forget about her—like I said, Mrs. Pain will ensure she gets back home okay. Won't you, Mrs. Pain?"

Mrs. Pain smiled coldly back at her. "Of course I will, Candice. You can count on it. She'll have a wonderful trip." Josie wasn't certain, but the naked woman's nipples seemed to have stiffened with excitement.

Blood still dripping from her arm, Josie allowed Candice to help her away from the basement.

Oh wow, I've really screwed this up now, she thought, glancing briefly back from the end of the corridor, and seeing that Mrs. Pain was now holding the unconscious Maryanne upright by gripping her beneath her armpits, so that from a distance the pair seemed to form a four-armed pregnant monster with two heads. *What are they going to do to her now? I'm certain Maryanne isn't about 'going home' like Candice so blithely put it. This is all my fault. But, hey, better her than me . . . it isn't like we're friends or anything.*

And as she and Candice climbed the stairs to the ground floor Josie smiled to herself. *At least with Maryanne gone we no longer have to endure the reek of that awful shrimp-and-cheese mix of hers.*

CHAPTER 12

Meet The Ex: Josie

Though originally from Roseburg, Oregon over on the West Coast, Josie Milewski now lived in Providence, Rhode Island.

John Miller had often joked that God had given such fantastic breasts to the otherwise scrawny Josie simply to compensate her for the drawbacks of her supremely nervous constitution.

Josie was a capable and competent woman and a loving mother also. It was just men and romance that continually drove her crazy.

She also wasn't really as much of a shrew as she seemed to outsiders. As she'd joked to her closest friends, "I'm not the sort of woman given to temper tantrums; but sometimes estrogen gets the better of me."

Josie didn't lack money. In addition to that half-million dollars which John had paid her, her two successive divorce settlements along with all the child support money that came in ensured she had more than enough to look after herself and her four kids.

But for a conscientious woman who was currently going through menopause, a woman who viewed child-rearing as full-time employment in itself, and yet one of a naturally nervous disposition, she lived in a constant zone of stress.

Hers was the sort of stress that having a supportive man by her side would do a whole lot to alleviate. But finding such a man currently seemed beyond her.

As a stay-at-home-mom, Josie had become an expert on other people's lives. She spent long periods of each day watching reality television and socializing on social media; it was her way of reclaiming the glamour she'd lost when she'd quit traveling the world as an airline stewardess.

Now, instead of flying, she ran around after children who seemed intent on driving her mad before they became adults themselves.

Josie really doubted that other mothers had it this hard.

CHAPTER 13

John

The TV screen flickered from blank black to white room.

John was instantly alert. *What is it this time? Why won't she just let me sleep tonight?*

Since his last 'milking' at Mrs. Pain's hands, John had desperately sought slumber but it had eluded him. His worries kept him awake.

"The next time you see me will be the last time you ever see me," Mrs. Pain had told him after his semen had spurted through the velvet grip of her fist into her silver goblet.

What did she mean by that? The last time? Will she free me the next time she visits?

And now, just as his eyes were finally closing, the goddamned TV had come on.

11:15 p.m. But John's mind didn't linger on the time. In her onscreen torture room Mrs. Pain stood beside a pregnant woman who was strapped down on one of her operating tables.

The woman's belly was immense; a shiny white bulge between her swollen breasts and her brown-furred crotch, as though her baby was ready to be born right now. A white hood completely covered her head and prevented John from seeing her face. Still he felt a disturbing hint of familiarity about her. Her legs seemed well acquainted with him in some way; they were very hairy . . .

But John was too worried to notice the glaringly obvious, and before he could make the connection to a similarly hairy ex-wife of his, Mrs. Pain waved at the camera. "Hi, Johnny, see what I found to enter*pain* you with. Really lovely, isn't she?"

John's eyelids felt glued open. "Oh no, she's not going to!" But he already knew that *she was* going to. The only question was *how* she was going to.

Mrs. Pain laid a hand on the pregnant woman's belly, and the woman began squirming.

Something occurred to John then: *Hey, she just addressed me directly. This isn't a recording I'm watching. She's doing this right now!*

Mrs. Pain bent down beside her operating table, so she was out of view for a few seconds. When she straightened up again she was holding a chainsaw. And as John caught his breath in shock and she placed the chainsaw on the pregnant woman's belly and yanked on the starter cord, the screen image froze and dripping yellow words were superimposed over it:

'CAESARIAN SECTION FOR A TRAITOR BITCH,' the words read.

Oh no, I'm not watching this! John thought desperately as the words faded from the screen. He leapt down from the bed to dash into the bath cubicle, but then Mrs. Pain's cold voice came to him from the TV again, somehow louder that the rattle of her chainsaw: "Don't you dare move, Johnny honey, or I'll do you next."

John sat back down on the bed and watched. Clearly waiting for him to do so, Mrs. Pain now lifted the chainsaw up off the pregnant woman's belly and moved its blade down over her legs.

The bound and hooded captive had begun tugging furiously against her bonds immediately the chainsaw started up. But the moment the whirling metal blade touched her thighs, she let out the loudest scream that John had ever heard:

"ARRRRRRRRRRRRGGGGGGGGGHHHHHHHH!!!!!"

The pregnant woman's screaming grew even louder as Mrs. Pain sawed off both of her legs at the crotch.

"No! Stop it!" John screamed at the television as the blood squirted from the victim's stumps. The mutilated woman had now stopped screaming and was merely jerking about in shock, her truncated torso flopping about on the table.

"Fucking stop hurting her! Don't kill her!"

But with a delighted smile on her face, Mrs. Pain merely shifted the focus of her attack. Quickly, before her victim bled out and died, she swung the chainsaw up over her pregnancy and pressed its shrieking blade into the pale flesh just below her swollen breasts. Then she held it there and sawed through the woman, all the way down to the table, twisting the blade about in her body as she did so, as if she wanted to cause her the maximum amount of pain possible while killing her.

John wanted to shut his eyes; but his eyelids still felt glued open.

The unknown woman was now of course dead, sawn in three.

Mrs. Pain switched off her chainsaw and flung it away, out of view of the camera.

For a person who had just butchered another person with a chainsaw, she had surprisingly little blood on her. But that changed an instant later, when she dug both of her hands into the jagged hole between the dead woman's chest and belly and scooped out chunks of shredded flesh. And then, while posing sexily for the camera like a model advertising body lotion, Mrs. Pain began rubbing these handfuls of bloody meat up and down herself, coating herself red from her head to her thighs. Then she reached into the corpse again and repeated the process several more times.

When she was through, she was completely splattered in gore. Her shaved head, face and body were covered with blood and little pieces of skin and meat. Blood ran from her neck down to her breasts and dripped off of them.

Then smiling, she placed her bloody hands on the middle section of the corpse, pressing down on the separated belly.

"Now, Johnny honey, the mother's dead, but"—she tapped the giant belly—"the little child is still alive and well in here. Let's have a look at him or her, shall we?"

Before John could get his mind around what she was suggesting, Mrs. Pain had ducked down and straightened up again. Now she was holding both a large knife and a pair of pruners. Setting the pruners aside for the moment, she stabbed her knife into the sawn-in-three woman's belly, made a long incision, and after a little fiddling about in the hole, pulled out the fetus.

"Wow, it's a boy!"

The child was fully formed, and yes—just like she'd said—it was still alive, eyes shut but squirming and kicking as she dangled it by its left leg. Its umbilical cord protruded thick and fat from its little belly.

Mrs. Pain grinned at the camera. The blood splattered on her head had mingled with her circles of red eyeshadow; she looked truly infernal. "The sad thing here, Johnny, is that bad mommies tend to give birth to bad babies. But let's fix that, shall we?"

"Oh, my dear God, no!" John wailed to himself when Mrs. Pain picked up the pruners and after snipping off the little boy's tiny penis (which made his tiny mouth gape in a silent uncomprehending scream), began snipping off his arms and legs too.

CHAPTER 14

Meet The Ex: Maryanne

Here lies a simple, harmless soul,
Who didn't accomplish her goals.

All Maryanne Hawkins had ever wanted was an uncomplicated life.

From an early age she had understood that she wasn't destined for greatness of any kind. Her bad grades meant she'd never make it to college, and she had no head for figures either, meaning she couldn't start up a business of her own. She couldn't sing or dance either, and although she could be funny when she put her mind to it, she wasn't ambitious (or ruthless) enough to use her looks to her advantage and become a model or actress.

But, oh yes, even though she was a little fat, Maryanne was very, very pretty. Men had remarked on her looks ever since she was a teenager, and she'd also realized she had a weakness for the male sex.

Just like Candice had done, after divorcing John, Maryanne had chosen to remain in Massachusetts instead of returning south to Trussville, Alabama; once she'd run out of money she'd figured the life of a lowly greasy spoon waitress was the same wherever one went. Also, she had lots of family in Massachusetts. Her uncle Ed McKinney owned a pig farm right here in Raynham, her cousin Tina Kravitz (Uncle Ed's daughter) was the town's chief of police and another cousin, Ambrose Duggan, owned the town's most popular and infamous motel, the Sunflower.

Maryanne's greatest ambition was to be a mother. But for her, getting pregnant had proved very difficult. The doctors she'd seen had assured her that her reproductive system was functioning perfectly, and that it was merely a matter of time before she took in and had a baby of her own.

Maryanne had not wanted to go the IVF route; she'd wanted to get pregnant while making love to a man she was in love with. But through the years that just hadn't worked out.

Until now, that is, when she'd gotten pregnant for Tony Cimini.

And now, through no fault of hers, she'd just hit the terminal roadblock known as Mrs. Pain.

And so Maryanne Hawkins would never have that baby she'd so desired to shower her love on.

CHAPTER 15

Megan

For want of anything better to do while waiting for the coast to clear, Megan looked through the bookcases in the study.

Most of the volumes were either about legal practice or magic. But thankfully, the skin-covered magical tome on the table was the only one of its kind in the study.

Even once over her shock at the book of spells' strangeness though, Megan found it impossible to relax. The presence of so many occult volumes in this room had doubly impressed on her the need to make a quick getaway from this house.

Sure, magic might not be real, but Candice and her husband—she sneaked a quick look up at the mansion's handsome but also mean-looking patriarch—*certainly seem to think it is. The sooner I'm away from here the better for my health.*

But despite her concerns, when next Megan checked the time on her cellphone, she discovered that much more time had elapsed in here than she had intended. *11:20 p.m.? It's already 11:20 p.m.?*

She was both surprised and alarmed that time had slipped away from her so easily when she might be in danger.

Alright, now it's definitely time to go. She quickly left the study.

As she padded silently along the corridor toward the main upstairs hallway, she felt a pressing sense of urgency to exit the mansion and dash across the lawn to its front gate and get on her motorbike and zoom off into the night.

She no longer felt the slightest urge to visit Dave in the mansion kitchen and enquire when he intended to make good on his debt to her.

I just hope Candice hasn't yet sent anyone to lock the gate, or else I'll have to find a tree with branches that hang over the wall to climb.

At the end of the corridor, she paused and peeked out into the hallway. *Okay, the coast is clear, the goons are gone.*

She hurried over to the head of the stairwell and listened for sounds from downstairs. Hearing none, she began descending.

And so it was with immense shock that she found herself grabbed by two sets of hands the moment she stepped down off the bottom step.

Oh shoot! Not after all the trouble I went through not to get caught.

She looked left and right and sighed. One of the two muscular goons held her right arm, the other her left. She didn't bother struggling against them when they turned her around and steered her back upstairs.

***

Once Megan was fully inside the summoning room (as the human-skin-bound spellbook in the study had referred to it) and had an unimpeded view of its extent and boundaries, she saw that the red chamber really did seem to be windowless. The four or so floor-to-ceiling curtains in evidence appeared to be decorative rather than functional, as, in addition to the fact that she saw no sign of a breeze moving them, in a reversal of the room's otherwise black-on-red color scheme, these curtains were all black and had red pentagrams drawn on them.

There were also several statues in evidence, blasphemous carvings and sculptures which spoke of a clear and severe departure from the straight-and-narrow where religion was concerned. One of the most prominent of these sculptures was that of a witchy woman wearing a hooded robe and with her hands outstretched as if she was casting a spell on someone. The expression on this sculpture's face was fixed somewhere between rapture and terror, between defiance and compliance, between a desire to stamp her influence on her environment and to behave herself as best she could.

But above all she projected the same aura of dangerousness as the four women seated around the white marble table.

"Maryanne had to leave in a hurry," Candice was telling the women when the two musclemen shepherded Megan into the summoning room.

Once more seated around the white marble table, Candice, Josie, Lucy and Donna now all wore black silk robes instead of their casual clothes. Their robes were similar to that worn by the witch-stature beside Maryanne's empty chair.

"But so abruptly?" Donna asked. "Homegirl was in such a hurry that she couldn't even say 'bye first?"

"I was there when it happened," Josie said. "She got these twinges in her belly and said she felt like the baby was about to come. Her waters hadn't yet broken though—"

"What are you doing here?" Lucy interrupted her on seeing Megan being pushed towards them. "Hey, did you follow me out here?"

Megan shrugged. "I-I-I . . ."

"Who is this?" Candice asked Lucy.

Lucy scowled. "The girl that I said delayed me at home asking about Davey."

Candice looked Megan up and down. "You're really persistent, aren't you? What's your business with Lucy's brother?"

Megan shrugged. "Um . . . he owes me money?" Then she felt bolder and added, "Yes, I followed Lucy. The gate was open and I let myself in. I'm sorry about that."

"There's no harm done then," Lucy said. "She's most likely telling the truth—my brother's always in debt to someone or other. I suggest that we just let her see him and then get lost again."

Candice nodded and waved her fingers dismissively at Megan. "Okay, girl, get going. We're busy here."

"We caught her descending the stairs to the living room," one of the goons said in a rumbling bass voice. "We think she has been upstairs for a while."

On this information Candice's previously benign expression turned frosty. "Oh, so you've been snooping on us, have you?"

Megan tried to talk her way out of trouble: "Oh no, not at all. I couldn't find Dave and so I came upstairs . . . but I didn't want anyone else to see me, so I hid and—"

"She's lying," Josie said flatly.

Candice turned to Josie. "What makes you so sure?"

"Because Lucy arrived here almost an hour and a half ago," Josie replied, with a scowl on her thin face. (Josie seemed to be in some discomfort; Megan wondered how she'd hurt her left forearm, which was now tightly bandaged.)

Josie pointed to Megan. "If this girl tailed Lucy here, they must've gotten here at about the same time. Which means she's been in your house for over an hour now. And besides, your kitchen is downstairs—that's where Dave would be—what the hell would she be doing upstairs, then?"

Lucy looked surprised by this, while Donna seemed undecided.

"And if she's been skulking about upstairs, it's very likely that she overheard our plans and was hurrying off to call the police," Josie went on.

"But I'm not lying!" Megan protested. She could see that Candice was leaning towards believing Josie's interpretation of events. "I don't know what plans you're talking about! Hey, I needed to pee after I arrived here and didn't know where the bathrooms were, so I climbed the stairs to look for one. I really wasn't snooping or anything like that!"

"We don't have time for this now," Candice said, shaking her head. She looked past Megan, at the two goons. "Put her in one of the basement cells. We'll decide what to do with her after the ritual is concluded. And, yes, tell Mrs. Pain that we're ready to start the ceremony."

Before Megan could utter any further protests, she was grabbed again by the two men, spun around and hustled out of the summoning room.

"And so," Candice went on behind her, "We'll have to carry out the ceremony without Maryanne."

"But you said we needed five people for the ritual," Josie said. "Where are we going to find a replacement for Maryanne at this late hour?"

"No problem. Mrs. Pain will take her place."

And then Megan was out of hearing range and being shoved towards the stairs.

***

Down in the basement, Megan and her two burly captors walked down a long corridor, strode past an intersecting one, and then halted before a steel door. The goon on her right held on firmly to her while the other one entered the room.

Megan spent the interval grumbling to herself. The goons had roughly searched her on the way down here and had taken away her cellphone.

The man was inside the room for under a minute and on his return, said, "Mrs. Pain says to put her in Miller's cell, so she can properly enter*pain* her there. Yeah, and we're taking Miller upstairs now so the ladies can properly enter*pain* him too."

Enter*pai*n? Megan instantly disliked the word. What the hell did enter*pain* mean?

"She ain't coming along?" the other man enquired, twisting Megan around and steering her down the corridor.

"We're to meet her back here once we've collected Miller," the other man replied, stepping briskly over to Megan's left.

She winced as the goon's vise-like grip tightened around her left arm. The two men hadn't spoken directly to her since her capture; all their conversation had been between themselves, to Candice, and now to the unseen woman in the room, whom Megan figured had to be the hairless and naked one she'd earlier noticed by the stairwell.

Megan had no idea what to make of the two goons. She was tall, but they both dwarfed her. In addition, each of their biceps seemed the size of her thighs. Their grip around her own biceps felt pulverizing, as if by the time they let go of her arms, each of them would have turned to jelly.

Megan knew she had no chance of fighting the men off. All she could do now was hope for a chance to escape from them.

They walked for another thirty yards or so, made a right turn into a second intersecting corridor, and finally stopped before another metal door.

One of the men unlatched the lock and shoved the door inward.

Megan was pushed inside a large cell. A chained and naked middle-aged man stared apprehensively at them from the bed.

One of Megan's captors immediately let go of her and headed across the room. Without saying a word to the naked man, who cringed back from him, the goon reached up beside the bed and tapped a code into the keypad beside the metal ring that the captive's chains were attached too. The hoop clicked open and the chains dropped in a bunch. The goon picked up their ends and yanked the man off of the bed.

"Where are you taking me?" the man protested as he was shoved towards Megan. "Where are you taking me?"

Neither of the goons replied him. The chained man had a wild and confused look on his face. Finally he seemed to see Megan.

"Do you know what's going on?" he asked Megan as he reached her. "If you do, please tell me. I've been held a captive here for the past week, and no one's told me anything."

Megan's heart went out to him; at the moment he wasn't more than a pathetic wreck. "Are you John Miller?" she asked him, the goon who was pushing him along having relented so they could converse.

"Yes, yes, that's me! I'm John Miller," the man quickly agreed. "What's going on? If you know, miss, please tell me before I go mad here!" His eyes already gleamed with the suggestion of a fast-approaching mental breakdown, as if he'd recently experienced or seen something so crazy it was driving him crazy too.

"Dude, you're screwed," Megan told him softly. "I mean, you're completely fucked. As in, without a safety net of any kind. Your exes have it in for you. I don't know what you did to piss them off that much, but . . ."

He gaped at her in total confusion. "My exes? But . . . but . . . but . . ."

But the goons dragged him outside before he could question Megan further. The removal happened so fast that Megan didn't even realize she'd been locked inside the cell until she heard its lock clicking shut outside.

"Hey, don't leave me in here!" She rushed at the door but stopped just short of banging on it.

Then, defeated for the moment, Megan walked over to the bed and sat on it. She now noticed the giant TV that faced her.

The TV suddenly came alive and flashed the red and dripping banner, 'MRS. PAIN'S GREATEST HITS' at her.

Then the banner changed to a plain background with the black words 'SCENE ONE – MY EX-BOYFRIEND. AND YES, HE WAS VERY GOOD IN BED—HE MADE ME COME MANY TIMES AND HE TREATED ME WITH RESPECT TOO. BUT STILL, A GIRL'S GOTTA DO WHAT A GIRL'S GOTTA DO.'

Then the words faded and the film began.

Confused and having no idea what to expect, Megan settled down to watch it. The camera shooting the video was focused in a room that seemed similar to her cell. In the center of this room, a man—not John Miller—was secured with duct tape to a high-backed and armless chair. His hands were out of sight behind the chair and he was also gagged with several strips of duct tape.

The man was middle-aged and unshaven and wore just boxer shorts. Blood from a forehead cut had streaked all the way down his face to his chin.

Mrs. Pain stood behind him with her bare nipples visible on either side of his bloodied face. She was smiling broadly.

Megan was still pondering how the woman's steely eyes could be so utterly cold and expressionless despite the pleased curl of her lips, when Mrs. Pain grabbed hold of the bound man's left ear and began slicing it off with a knife.

Megan gasped in fright. Bright red blood spurted from the man's head and splattered Mrs. Pain's chest. His eyes bulging out like a frog's, the man thrashed wildly in his chair, but the chair must have been bolted to the floor because it didn't budge an inch.

Once she'd cut her victim's ear off of his face, Mrs. Pain discarded it into a tray set on a metal trolley, grabbed a handful of his hair instead, and now began slicing deeply into his forehead.

Megan gaped in disbelief as the naked torturess first sliced left to right across the man's forehead, and then into the hair above his remaining ear. She did her best to convince herself that what she was seeing wasn't real, but was just great special effects. But the more she watched the man's skin peel away from his skull to reveal the bare bone beneath, the more convinced she became that this was the real deal she was witnessing.

Oh, my dear God, she's really doing this to him! I'm watching a snuff movie!

Megan yelped in terror when Mrs. Pain ripped half of the seated man's scalp off. The man jerked once and went limp.

That scene ended there, with Mrs. Pain leering at the camera; leaving Megan staring bug-eyed at the screen.

*Oh gosh, this is what she meant by 'enter*pain*-ing' me!*

Scene two was: 'WHY ROAD RAGE IS BAD FOR YOUR HEALTH, STARRING THE MERCILESS MRS. PAIN.'

While onscreen an old Mexican couple endured the torments of the damned at Mrs. Pain's bloody hands, beginning with having their eyes plucked out and fed to each other, Megan leapt down off the bed and hastily began searching the cell for something she could use as a weapon.

If I don't find something quickly, before they come for me, I'm not going to leave here alive.

Now that Megan understood just what 'enter*pain*' meant, she had no desire to star in MRS. PAIN'S GREATEST HITS, PART 2.

4

The wrong man can break the heart of
even the strongest woman,
But the wrong woman can drive even the
sanest man completely crazy.

*

*No matter how long you live, life is very
short.*

CHAPTER 16

Tony

Tony Cimini had never considered himself a jealous man. Even now as he dropped over the south wall of the Penderson estate and hurried through the trees towards the sprawling mansion, he saw no reason to revise this opinion of himself.

No, Tony wasn't a possessive or jealous sort of person. But his girlfriend Maryanne's recent behavior had brought him to this point where he was forced to take action.

Now, with the wind blowing around him and a suggestion of late spring rain in the air, Tony paused behind a tree and studied the mansion.

Alright, so I got this far. But what'm I gonna do now? 'Cos I can see she's in the house, that's her Honda parked over there.

Tony was a short, good-looking man, a cab driver in nearby Attleboro. He and Maryanne had been dating for three years now and had been living together for the last two of those. He'd been overjoyed when she'd gotten pregnant—Maryanne had been desperate to have kids and had kept on at him about her 'biological clock running overtime' until the day she'd handed him the positive home pregnancy test.

Which was great. Tony Cimini was thirty-six and felt he was long overdue for a family; his sisters and brothers all had kids and he was the odd one out. His oldest brother Giorgio, who owned an auto repair garage in nearby Dover, already had four children and his wife Chloe was now pregnant with number five.

And yeah, all had been going great—he and Maryanne were saving up to put down a down payment on a small bungalow so they'd have a place of their own when their son was born.

And now this crap has to start, Tony thought gloomily. *Suddenly she's playin' hide and find with me.*

What hurt Tony about Maryanne's behavior was that he'd always been straight up with her. He'd never cheated on her; never treated her any other way but good. Tony's nose didn't work too well either and so he didn't care about that pungent shrimp and cheese mixture she seemed unable to stop eating at the moment.

Why would a pregnant woman start skulking around right when she's about to give birth? was the question Tony had been pondering for two weeks now. The kid was due to be born in three weeks tops and instead of sitting home and watching TV with her legs up on a cushion like a good girlfriend and letting the father-to-be fuss over her, Maryanne had suddenly decided she needed to go visit an old school friend in Rhode Island.

This was the fourth time in the past month that she'd acted like this—given Tony some bullshit story and then headed off 'to meet with some old friend.'

But each time, she'd clearly been lying.

The thing was, Maryanne had never been the smartest bean in the pod. Tony had quickly noticed this about her. No, she wasn't 'airhead dumb,' but she often made the sort of errors of judgment that landed people into trouble, both financial and otherwise.

A good example of this was that tale she'd confessed to him about why her first husband had divorced her. Wow, exactly why would she spread her legs for the dude's chauffer, knowing how much cash it would eventually cost her? Yeah, the black kid had claimed he was rich too, but what was the old saying again, about a bird in hand being worth two in the bush? Damn, if something like that had happened to Tony, he'd have offed himself; stuck a gun in his mouth and pulled the trigger.

But no, Maryanne hardly even remembers that she literally screwed herself out of five million dollars. Five friggin' mil.

And now . . . Tony stared glumly at the mansion again, hating being here, hating having to enter the building and confront Maryanne. *And now she's about to do the same cheatin' thing again—and to me this time. At the moment she's got me so confused with this secretive behavior of hers, I ain't even sure I'm the baby's daddy anymore.*

The mansion ahead of Tony seemed to confirm his suspicions. It was clearly some rich dude's house; Maryanne's boyfriend who was responsible for the pregnancy he'd believed was his for the past eight months.

Oh, damn you, Maryanne.

Tony had never believed that nonsense about her making a trip to Rhode Island anyway. It was clearly a made-up story, the sort of dumb thing she said from time to time.

Who in the hell drives forty-five miles across state lines when they're eight months preggered just to go say hi to someone? Why not just wait till after the baby's born to make the road trip? Or simply have me drop her off there?

Once certain that Maryanne was cheating on him, Tony had installed a GPS tracking device in her car. And then, this afternoon, he'd activated the tracker and found out that just as he'd suspected, she was still in Massachusetts, and close by at that.

And so, here he was now, at close to midnight, coming to confront Maryanne and her lover.

"I'm a dumb fuck myself," Tony muttered miserably as he left his place by the tree and hurried over to the mansion. "I should just go back home, get drunk and understand that it's over between us. Much as I care 'bout Maryanne, she ain't worth getting shot over."

Tony wasn't armed himself and he dreaded the prospect of someone sticking a gun in his face and pulling the trigger once the mansion's front door swung open.

Once up on the front porch, he paused and looked to the right. The moon brightly illuminated the guardhouse down by the gate, but the guardhouse seemed strangely deserted. Tony hadn't noticed anyone over there since arriving. No guards and no dogs either—climbing over the estate wall like he'd done, he'd known he was taking the huge risk of having his ass torn to shreds by Dobermans or German shepherds, but his sense of betrayal had him feeling too desperate to not take that risk.

And was it his imagination or was the gate slightly opened?

Okay, now this is real weird. I'm gettin' a real feelin' that I shouldn't be here.

Still, his heart and his pride hurt too badly to turn back now, so he walked boldly to the front door and rang the buzzer. When no one answered, he rang again. Then he turned and stared worriedly back towards the seemingly deserted guardhouse at the gate.

Then, at a loss for what next to do, Tony gripped the front door's doorknob and twisted it. He was so surprised when the door opened that he almost pitched forward into the house. But he righted himself in time and pulled the door shut behind him.

He stepped out from the entranceway vestibule into a hallway with a large living room on its right. The living room lights were on, but once more there seemed to be no one home. The house had a silence to it that rasped like sandpaper against his nerves.

By now Tony was beginning to get a really creepy vibe about this place. He had the weird sense that the mansion's unseen inhabitants were hiding from him; which he knew was silly. He told himself that Maryanne's rich lover had simply dismissed his servants for the night so they could be alone, but his gut instincts told him he was wrong.

Tony was faced now with two choices, either to climb the stairs that were near the living room or to walk down the hallway on his left looking for someone. He chose the hallway. He felt very nervous now and being on the ground floor meant he had a shorter distance to run if something was very wrong.

Because now, he'd begun worrying that maybe Maryanne wasn't okay—that he might have unwittingly stepped into a murder scene.

Still, knowing that he was intruding here, he proceeded with caution. He reached an empty dining room and was just about to turn around and go back to climb the stairs anyway, when he heard loud voices and footsteps approaching from further down the hallway. The voices sounded like the speakers were about emerging from a corridor ahead of him.

Confused, Tony ducked into the dining room, and when the voices kept approaching and he realized that he'd be noticed if he remained in the dining room, he dashed across to its opposite end and hid in the corridor it connected to, in a small nook beside the first door on the right. This door was shut but the smell of cooking seafood coming from behind it assured Tony that it was the mansion's kitchen; in addition to which he could hear joking male voices behind the door.

A few moments later, four people stepped into view in the hallway he'd just vacated. Two large brutish men shoved a third man ahead of them, this one naked and chained and trembling with fear.

The three men were followed by a busty naked woman who seemed to be painted red. But then Tony realized in horror that the woman was actually splattered with blood and that the purplish 'tassels' that decorated her bald head and her breasts and belly were shreds of skin and flesh.

Along with their male captive's whimpers, the smell of fresh blood reached him across the dining room.

Tony managed not to yelp in alarm, and then, as the quartet walked off beyond his range of view, he quickly turned and hurried off down the corridor, pausing only to open each door he reached and check where it led.

I'm getting the hell out of here, but I need to find another route out of this house.

Because, no way was Tony Cimini going back out the way he'd come in. Tony was now more frightened than he'd ever been before in his life.

He began praying that the blood and flesh plastered on the naked woman wasn't Maryanne's.

CHAPTER 17

Josie

The four exes watched Mrs. Pain and her two assistants stake their naked ex-husband down on top of the marble table. This was easy to do because the tip of each of the five points of the pentagram carved into the table contained a hole into which a steel peg had been sunk. Mrs. Pain dug a finger into each hole, hooked out the peg and then threaded one of John's chains through the hole in the peg's top, after which the chain was drawn tight and locked in place. Once all four of John's limbs were thus secured, a leather collar was locked around his neck and its own chain secured to the fifth peg.

Finally, John Miller lay there spread-eagled before his wives, completely humbled and mumbling and still looking perplexed at what was happening to him.

"Any last words, Johnny?" Candice had earlier mockingly asked him, while waving a long strip of duct tape at him.

"I'm sorry," John had pleaded. "I'm really—" But then the duct tape had shut off his voice, and next, as if to ensure he'd really be quiet, Candice had taped his mouth over three more times.

"Apology not accepted, Johnny," she'd then said with a wink.

***

John Miller was suffering from information overload. The revelation, after being held in seclusion for seven days, that his abduction was simply a plan by his ex-wives to get even with him had him in serious shock.

They found out! Oh no! Leroy warned me that this was gonna backfire!

118

John had still not recovered from that final video Mrs. Pain had shown him—herself chainsawing the 'pregnant traitor' into three and, oh God, what she'd done to the baby afterward.

John had belatedly realized who Mrs. Pain had murdered on video for his enter*pain*ment: There couldn't be two badly-tattooed brunettes on the planet with legs that hairy.

I had six exes . . . Sam is already dead . . . Candice, Josie, Lucy, Donna . . . they're here . . . Oh, my God, she sawed Maryanne to death! Maryanne always wanted to be pregnant, and now that she got her wish, Mrs. Pain went and murdered her!

Tears began streaming from John Miller's eyes.

***

Candice, mistaking the reason for John's tears, giggled at the other three exes. "Oh wow, look, girls, he's crying. He's really sorry that he hurt us."

"If he's really sorry, maybe we should just let him go," Josie suggested hopefully. She felt intense frustration, sitting here like this with John's left hand pointing at her chest and being unable to do anything to help him. (With Mrs. Pain now taking Maryanne's place at the table, one of John's secured limbs pointed at each of them like arrows, and his head pointed at Candice.)

"No, we are not going to let him go," Mrs. Pain replied Josie before anyone else could speak. "Not after all the trouble we went through to finalize preparations."

Josie nodded timidly. She didn't know whose blood and flesh that was splattered all over the bald woman, but she was willing to wager that it was Maryanne's; the red coating seemed to have a faint aroma of shrimp and cheese. She looked over at Lucy and Donna. Donna was lighting up a joint she'd taken from her large handbag, while Lucy was glaring at John with unmistakable hatred in her eyes.

Josie, who always used makeup sparingly, thought Lucy looked like an abstract painting, something cartoonish like her younger daughter Erica used to paint in kindergarten, with a giant red mouth and giant blue eyes, long garish fake eyelashes, and all her facial features distorted and overemphasized for maximum effect. Women like Lucy scared Josie; even when they were in relationships and clearly faithful to their partners, she couldn't stop thinking of them as home wreckers.

Josie nervously stuck a thumbnail in her mouth and proceeded to chew its silver coating off while focusing her attention on Candice again.

"Yes, we've spent too much time on our preparations," Candice agreed, with a nod in Mrs. Pain's direction. "Preparations like collecting his semen for a whole week."

"You never told us that bit," Donna said after taking a drag of her joint. "I thought we were just gonna sacrifice this motherfucker. What the fuck you need his come for?"

Josie scowled. "Yes, why? You aren't going to ask us to drink it, are you? If so, you can count me out already. I hate swallowing during oral."

Lucy said nothing, she just kept staring daggers at John, whom, once he'd heard the word 'sacrifice' had begun twisting and turning where he lay. Spread-eagled as he was on the marble table, however, the effect of his squirming was merely comical.

Candice laughed at the women's comments and pointed beyond Mrs. Pain, at the giant stone oval that stood in the far corner. "No, we aren't going to drink John's stale come, we need it to anoint the portal before it opens."

"Okay, so now that everything is properly set up, how *do* we kill this bastard?" Lucy asked, while digging her pink fingernails into John's right shin so that he winced in pain. "Let's get started, shall we? I'll die of impatience if I have to wait any longer to kill John Miller."

"Yeah, that's right," Donna quickly agreed, her milk-chocolate face creasing into a frown. "Let's get this over with. How're we gonna kill him anyway?"

"By erotic asphyxiation," Candice said.

"Huh?" The other three exes gaped at her, while with a wave Mrs. Pain dismissed her two hulking assistants. "Go wait for me downstairs in the living room," she instructed them.

"Yes, you heard me right," Candice told the women once the two muscular men had departed. "Our ex-husband will die of erotic asphyxiation."

CHAPTER 18

Death and the Woman

Just like Donna and Lucy, Josie was surprised to hear exactly how they were supposed to kill John.

"We're going to strangle him during sex?" she asked.

Donna giggled. "Wow, that's just deliciously kinky."

John was still alternately tugging at his bonds and mumbling entreaties to the women, but they spoke across his bound body like he wasn't even in the room.

"Well, technically, yes," Candice agreed. "But not the way you imagine it being done."

"How then?" Donna asked after exhaling a stream of marijuana smoke. "Choking someone while fucking 'em is the only kind of erotic asphyxiation I know."

Josie wondered too. At the moment she felt completely frustrated.

I came here to rescue John and just look what's happened. And it was all Maryanne's fault! If only she'd not been there in the basement.

But then Josie glanced down the table and her eyes locked with Mrs. Pain's. The blood-splattered woman winked back knowingly at her as if they shared a secret, and a sudden tremor of fear ran down Josie's back.

She knows, Josie realized. *She knows that I'm the traitor and not Maryanne. And yet, she doesn't care . . . she really doesn't care at all! Mrs. Pain just wants someone to hurt; anyone will do, and on any excuse at all.*

This knowledge both reassured and terrified Josie. The implication was simple enough: her rescue mission had failed. John Miller was going to be sacrificed here and now and there was absolutely nothing that she could do to alter that fact.

And there was also an unspoken warning in Mrs. Pain's cold smile and Antarctic gaze as she plucked a piece of bloody skin off of her left nipple and flicked it away; and that warning was as clear as a message painted on the sky in blood: *Don't you dare screw up again, bitch, or next time this will be you plastered all over me like this.*

Oh, Josie had no intention of screwing up again. Hell no, she didn't. *I've four kids to live for and they all need me!* She peered down at her vainly struggling ex. *Sorry, Johnny, I really do still love you, honey, but when all is said and done, you brought this on yourself.*

Tears came to Josie's eyes then, but she quickly blinked them away. *Oh no, I mustn't give the others any indication of my true feelings.*

Then Josie realized that Candice was looking at her with a smile on her face. *Oops, did I just miss something she was saying?*

"I vote that Josie does it," Candice said.

"Hey, why her?" Lucy immediately protested. "I want to do him! He's the reason I'm HIV-positive now. He's ruined my life and I want to . . . !" She was so enraged that she ran out of words and just stabbed her nails into John's foot instead.

"Hey, stop doing that," Mrs. Pain cautioned Lucy. "We need him unmarked. You know that."

Lucy looked from the bald woman to Candice, who nodded, so she pulled her hand away and just glared angrily at John.

"No, not you, Lucy," Candice said. "And not Donna either."

"Why not me?" Donna asked, exhaling smoke again.

"Because just like Lucy, you'll enjoy it too much, but for a different reason. Lucy will torture John and might waste too much before killing him, while you may forget while we're here and simply ride him to multiple orgasms."

"Yeah, that I might; it'll be good payback for all the blowjobs I gave him while we were hitched," Donna agreed with a laugh, then she gestured at Josie with her joint. "But why her then? Why not you?"

Candice shrugged. "Oh, I'd love to, but I'm too old and fat and my joints ache. For me, even getting up on the table would be too much trouble." She pointed to Josie. "But she's perfect; she's skinny and fit and . . ."

Josie still had no idea what she was supposed to do. Stab John with the ceremonial knife that lay by Candice's fingers? But no, they were talking about erotic asphyxiation so it couldn't be that.

" . . . And besides, she's seemed a little reluctant about everything so far, so we'll give her a chance to really dirty her hands now, so she won't think of running off to the police afterwards."

Josie's heart sank on hearing this. *Oh, does she know too?* But a quick glance at Mrs. Pain reassured her. When their eyes met this time, Mrs. Pain shook her head slightly. Josie nodded back and pretended nonchalance.

"Yeah, sure, I'll do it," she told Candice. "What am I supposed to do to him?"

Candice tapped the tabletop. "Climb up on here, then sit on John's face and smother him with your vagina."

Now Josie's eyes really widened in surprise. "What?"

Donna smoked and giggled and Lucy looked jealous. As much as the collar fastened around his neck would permit, their intended male victim gaped at them in turn, his dread evident in his eyes.

Candice nodded back at Josie. "It's simple enough. His lips are taped shut, so he can't breathe through his mouth. All you have to do is seal his nose shut with your vagina. You clamp it down on him and hold it there until he stops breathing."

"He lived by his dick and he'll die by your pussy," Donna quipped through a cloud of smoke. "That's just so fitting."

CHAPTER 19

John

On hearing the fate intended for him, John strained up his head and quickly stared in horror from one woman to the next. He couldn't orally plead with them, but maybe one of them might root for him to be set free if she noticed the imploring look in his eyes.

Candice was seated directly behind him. Then, as if sensing his desire to see her clearly, she leaned forward over him.

Candice, now middle-aged, nicely fattened up and matronly, her long cornsilk hair now mingled with stark gray strands. Her blue eyes were cold and utterly pitiless as she gazed down at him and stroked his face, with her lips curled in a satisfied smile. John had always known she was ruthless; it was one reason he'd been glad to divorce her once their marital problems had started.

Finally, she leaned back into her chair again and John turned his head towards Josie.

Josie was seated on Candice's immediate left. High-strung and borderline-neurotic Josie, the most clingy and possessive woman he'd ever had a relationship with. A wonderfully loving and caring mother, but a crappy partner to live with. He'd known all her successive marriages would fail—she just grated on a guy's nerves after a while.

At the moment Josie seemed even more on edge than ever. She was tugging on the ends of her blonde hair with her left hand while clawing his forearm with her right hand, but gently, not digging her silver fingernails into his skin the way Lucy had done.

Oh, I won't get any help from her, he thought. *She blames me for her own failures.*

The next chair, the one that faced his left foot, was occupied by Mrs. Pain. He now understood that his exes were seated around the table in the order of their marriage to him, and that Mrs. Pain was in

Maryanne's chair. Tears filled his eyes again and he blinked them away. *Oh, my beautiful, harmless redneck princess Maryanne with her love of stinky food and her sexy furred legs—how could Mrs. Pain be so cruel to her? And she had great breasts too.*

Okay, so he admitted that Mrs. Pain also had fantastic breasts.

John had always loved breasts. No two women had the same kind of breasts and yet all their breasts seemed wonderful and perfect to him. Big, small or almost none at all . . . like Lucy. He'd once even dated a comedienne who'd had a double mastectomy to preempt a hereditary tendency to breast cancer and so had had both of her breasts replaced by implants. She had had no nipples, and yet, still, her breasts had been just as alluring to him, had seemed to sing songs of her still-uncorrupted femininity into his ears when he rested his head on them, and had smelt and tasted delicious when he licked and sucked their sweaty surfaces.

The gore-covered Mrs. Pain was looking at him with the sort of interest a cat showed in a mouse; as if she wanted to play with him before killing him, or kill him before playing with him.

John quickly looked away from her. But although he'd intended to look at the next chair, at Lucy, his attention was instead diverted backwards, between Mrs. Pain and Josie, towards an unusual object in the far corner of the room. A huge oval rock stood over there—it had to be almost seven feet high, it almost touched the ceiling. What caught John's attention the most about the giant rock though, was the pentagram carved into its front surface. Remembering in horror that his exes had just said they intended to sacrifice him and that he was currently laid out on top of a similarly carved pentagram on this table he was bound to, he looked away from the giant stone, his frightened gaze quickly sweeping past Mrs. Pain's gory figure to the next chair.

Lucy was clearly mad at him.

Lucy—black hair, blue eyes and as desirable as ever even after all these years of only seeing her on Facebook and Instagram. Lovely Lucy, who was addicted to makeup. Lucy, who could spend two hours putting on her face, and then, if she noticed the slightest imperfection in what she'd so painstakingly done, was prepared to wipe it all off and start over afresh. And she was just as painstaking about her hair and nails and waxing her body. And about her complexion.

When they'd bought a tanning bed, she used to sleep in it at night; she used it so much that John was scared she'd develop melanoma.

Lucy had only stopped her compulsive tanning after the tanning bed caught fire while she was inside it. After that scare she'd sworn off tanning beds for life.

While married to Lucy, John had quickly understood that she was one of those women who wore heavy makeup to cover perceived imperfections in their souls, not in their bodies.

Despite his dire straits, John couldn't not roll his eyes at one detail about his gorgeous ex: *She's wearing fake eyelashes, for chrissakes—she's here at my goddamn funeral and she's as heavily made up as a drag queen and is wearing goddamn fake eyelashes!*

But then, in an instant, his irritation turned to intense sympathy for her. *Oh my God, what was that about her getting HIV? Oh shit, not that dickhead Hutch!*

On hearing about Samantha's suicide note on the news, John had thought Hutch's positive HIV status was a recent development. But no, so the sonofabitch had HIV all along?

John locked eyes with Lucy and all he saw there was death for himself.

I can't really blame her, he thought, looking guiltily away. *Dammit, Leroy Brown was right—I really should have stuck to one woman. But I had the whole divorce thing and my money to consider. That money is mine. These women never had a right to it in the first place!*

But then a chill settled over him, along with the realization that except a miracle occurred, he might very well be dead in a few minutes. *Please, please, please, God, make these crazy bitches take this damn duct tape off of my mouth so I can reason with them. I'll happily give them the prenup money now! I will, I will!*

But maybe God thought he was guilty too, because none of the women came to his rescue. Desperate again, and realizing now that time was fast running out for him, John shifted his gaze to his final surviving ex, his last hope.

Donna. His sultry mulatto. Her naturally kinked hair now permed flat, her milk chocolate complexion flawless as always. Once a prostitute and forever a prostitute. Even now she projected 'booty for sale' into the room. Ah, those big pouty lips painted with maroon lipstick, and her brown eyes like pools of lust. Okay, so yes, it had been a huge mistake marrying her, but she'd borne him a child and, oh yes . . . she did give incredible blowjobs.

But Donna wasn't even looking at him. She was smoking away; expelling marijuana clouds into the room and fanning the smoke away from her face with her other hand so she could see the others.

For a moment, John's gaze flashed back to Lucy and he considered the similarities and differences between these two women whom he'd married one after the other. It occurred to him now that part of Donna's attraction for him was how similar she'd seemed to Lucy at the time.

For one thing, they were both makeup addicts. But there was a discernable, very clear difference between Lucy's and Donna's use of cosmetics. Lucy looked perfect, like a painted doll, too delicate to play with in case one slipped and broke it; even during their marriage, she'd appeared too flawlessly put together to make love to, a man wouldn't want to dishevel those razor-straight bangs across her forehead, or ruin her red lipstick by smearing it on his erection.

Donna, on the other hand, always applied her lipstick, blusher and eyeshadow with a casual hand; in a way that was intentionally sloppy. She 'smeared' it on, as if to say, "Come help me smear it further." Even the hairstyles she chose spoke more of improvisation than planning.

Lucy's makeup was an inhibition, Donna's an invitation.

Donna still wasn't looking at him.

"Hey, Josie, hurry up, wilya?" she said, staring over John at the other woman.

Yes, that girl I met downstairs was right, John thought weakly, realizing there and then that none of his exes cared that he lived. *I'm totally fucked.*

CHAPTER 20

The Death of John Miller

Understanding that she simply had no choice in the matter, Josie nodded weakly and got up on the marble table.

First of all, while standing with her feet on either side of John's face, she peeled off her black silk robe. She wasn't wearing any panties under it—none of them were. Once she had handed the robe to Donna, it was simple enough to kneel over John's head. And for a moment—when his skin brushed against hers—she almost forgot what she was here for due to the pleasure of touching him again after so long.

But Candice's cold voice quickly brought her back to her present reality: "Okay, great. Now shift forward a little so that you're completely covering his nose . . . yes, like that . . ."

With his nose deep inside her vagina, Josie could already feel that John couldn't breathe. She adjusted her position slightly so that the edges of the lines cut into the tabletop didn't hurt her knees.

". . . Hold on to his hair, so he can't twist his head away from you . . ."

His head restrained like this, he was sniffing for breath inside of her, the continual sucking making Josie feel like her vaginal walls were collapsing. And she could feel her secretions dripping into his nostrils, clogging them. He sneezed inside her and she almost let go of his head in disgust; but then, suddenly, maybe because of this act, her love for him turned into intense hatred.

In an instant, Josie's mind filled up with all that she had suffered because of John Miller's callousness to her. The pain from her bandaged arm goaded her on: John was the reason why she'd injured herself too; all he ever seemed to do was hurt her.

Now he wasn't worth dog shit to her and she wanted him to die. Shutting her eyes, she gripped his hair even more tightly and pulled his head up into her crotch, and also pressed herself forcefully down on him, while at the same time spreading her thighs wider to accommodate him even deeper inside her body.

What was it that Donna had said: *Yeah, Johnny, you lived by your dick and now you'll die by my pussy!*

John was trembling beneath her now, his arms and legs flailing and kicking desperately . . . but weakly. Josie kept her sex sealed against his nose until he stopped moving, and even after that she remained the way she was positioned, with his face pressed against her crotch, until she felt Candice tapping her arm.

"Okay, you can get off him now," Candice said. "I've just checked his pulse. He's dead."

Josie opened her eyes. She was surprised to see both Donna and Lucy leaning on the table near her. Both were staring intently at her.

"Wow, that was some ride," Lucy said breathlessly. "Oh, I'm green with envy of you. I really wanted to be the one to do that to Johnny. Did you come? Did you come?"

Josie shook her head. "I didn't try to; I didn't want to. I just wanted to feel him die. And I felt it—it was . . . it was great."

"Wow, this is just so empowering," Donna said with a slightly stoned smile; she seemed to have finished her joint. "Us girls should do this to bad guys more often. Some niggas and players I know deserve this shit happenin' to their black asses."

"Get off him, Josie," Candice repeated. She was standing by John's left hand and nodding down at the still seated Mrs. Pain.

"Yeah, sure," Josie said, realizing that she still had John's head pressed to her crotch. She let go of his hair and his nose came unstuck from her vagina with a sucking sound. His head fell back onto the table and she looked down at it. John Miller's eyes were open and bulging, as if he'd tried to breathe through them while suffocating.

"Ugh, that's just gross," Lucy said, pointing at the stream of mucus flowing from the dead man's nostrils. "Is that yours or his?"

"I think it's mine," Josie said with some embarrassment. "He keep snorting it out of me."

"Get down off the table, girl, and put your ceremonial robe back on," Candice ordered stiffly. "Time is running away from us. We need to continue with the ritual before the window of magical opportunity closes for us."

"He didn't get an erection when he croaked," Mrs. Pain said from her chair in clear disappointment as Josie got down off the table. I was really hoping that he would."

"Okay now, girls, everyone back to your seats," Candice said once Josie was back on the floor and dressed again.

The ex-wives once more took their assigned chairs, only this time it was around a corpse. John Miller lay there before them like a man-shaped birthday cake.

"No, no, Donna, no more joints for now," Candice instructed when Donna, fresh spliff in hand, began searching through her handbag again for her lighter. "We need to concentrate on this. We'll be done here in an hour tops, and by then you'll have something to celebrate, I can assure you."

"Somethin' to celebrate?" Donna asked. "What'cha talkin' 'bout?"

"No time to explain now," Candice replied, waving her ceremonial knife at Donna. "Just wait and see."

And then she slit the dead man's throat, pulling the razor-sharp blade smoothly across his neck from left ear to right ear. John's neck gaped open.

Josie winced at the brutality of Candice's action, but to her surprise and relief, blood didn't spurt from John's throat and splatter anyone. Rather, the blood just gently welled out of him, exiting his body into the grooves carved into the top of the marble table. Once out of John Miller's corpse, the red liquid streamed along the grooves as if it was a living, possessed thing.

Josie felt chilled as she watched the blood fill up the lines of the pentagram, turning them a brilliant crimson. She still felt quite elated at how she'd killed her ex, but her fear of being arrested by the police was once more returning to bother her.

"Shouldn't his blood be squirting like mad?" Lucy asked.

"No, his heart has stopped beating and now it is draining out of him supernaturally," Mrs. Pain replied her question. "The table is pulling it out of him."

Then the bald woman got to her feet and bent over the table, dug her fingers beneath John's buttocks and lifted up his hips. "I'll just help it drain out faster."

"You do that," Candice agreed with a nod. "In the meantime I'll go fetch our cooks from the kitchen."

She left the chamber.

Josie looked at the other exes. Lucy was staring at the emptying corpse in morbid fascination. Donna just looked stoned.

CHAPTER 21

The Pig

Candice was back eight minutes later, followed by Ron and Lucy's brother Dave, who were both wearing white chef uniforms with mushroom-like toque hats and who were also pushing a long metal serving cart ahead of them.

By now John's body seemed to have been completely exsanguinated; no more blood tricked from the gaping wound in his neck and Mrs. Pain had since lowered his hips back down onto the table. The carved pentagram however sparkled with the blood that filled it and which seemed to course through it like a red river, or as if it was a living extension of the dead man's arteries and veins.

"Wow, that's a giant hog," Dave exclaimed on seeing the waiting corpse. "It's been ages since we've had to dress a pig this big."

"Hell yeah," Ron instantly agreed with him.

Assisted by Mrs. Pain, the two cooks got down to freeing John's arms and legs from their restraints.

Josie stared sharply at both men, who were acting as unconcerned as a pair of undertakers as they shifted John's corpse off the stone table and onto their serving cart, arranging him so that his head dangled down over one end of it and his feet hung down over the other. Finally they folded his arms neatly across his chest.

They're behaving like they see human corpses everyday. They're . . .

She looked over at Candice, who was supervising things. Candice's eyes met hers and she nodded back and silently mouthed "Magic" at her.

Josie nodded. Opposite her, Donna, her eyes closed, was humming a hip-hop tune to herself—sounded like that talentless kid 'Chill Bill' that her kids adored. She looked at Lucy instead.

Lucy nodded back at her and then, after gesturing to Josie to lean closer, she switched over from her own chair to Mrs. Pain's vacated one (which was next to Josie's), bent forward and whispered in Josie's ear: "Hey, remember what Candice said—that my brother and his friend wouldn't remember anything that happens here tonight? I didn't believe it myself, but apparently this magic stuff really works. You heard them referring to him as a pig, right?"

"Yeah," Josie whispered back. "Crazy, isn't it? But hey, do you really imagine that we're going to successfully summon a demon here tonight like Candice says?"

Lucy grimaced and shook her head. "No, of course not. What Candice did to Ron and my brother is just hypnosis like you sometimes see magicians do on TV shows. That's the sort of magic I was referring to. You know, illusions and suggestive mind control stuff, where you wind up thinking you're seeing stuff that isn't there. Hey, I can understand and accept that; but not supernatural stuff—sister, there's no such things as demons or angels. But you know what, Josie? I honestly don't care about that anyway. Me? I'm just here for the murder."

"Listen, that's what's bothering me. The damn murder we just committed . . . okay, that *I* just committed. Yes, he's frigging dead now and he deserved it, but how the hell does Candice intend to get rid of his remains? Because if there's an investigation, we'll all be going to jail. Yes, yes, I know I'm the one who killed him, but you're an accomplice too."

Lucy shrugged. "Oh, don't worry. I imagine she's got an incinerator in the basement. Lots of mansions have those to deal with their trash."

Josie looked up to ensure that neither Candice nor Mrs. Pain could overhear them, then figured she needn't worry about that. Both women were now standing over by the door of the chamber, along with Dave and Ron and the men's gruesomely laden cart.

Josie felt a sudden surge of intense revulsion. No, that body lying on the metal cart just couldn't be the man she'd once loved—the man she'd spent three years of her life with, the virile stud who'd made her feel like a real woman in bed and impregnated her with two kids. At the moment, John Miller looked like a turkey on its way to the oven. All that remained was to gut and stuff him.

"Okay, Mrs. P., we'll be off downstairs now," Dave was saying. "Are you sure you just want this porker garnished? You don't wanna roast it for some additional flavor?"

"It'll taste a whole lot better roasted," Ron added, with a pleased glance down at the dead man. "Trust us, ma'am, Dave and me, we're professionals at this. We've been in this cooking bizness for years. We've cooked hogs in every way possible. What I'd suggest is that we stick a spit right through this one's ass, slide it up to its neck and let it cook in that giant oven you've got downstairs." Ron then made the classic gesture of kissing his fingers and sweeping them back through the air. "Oh, yummy!"

"No, no, just do it like I said," Candice said with a cold smile, with Mrs. Pain nodding her agreement. "Just garnish it. And please hurry up, we've very little time before my VIP guest arrives."

"Okay, you're the boss, Mrs. P.," Dave agreed, and then he and Ron rolled their cooking cart out of the summoning room.

Candice and Mrs. Pain stood in the doorway watching them go, which gave Josie the time to quickly turn back to Lucy and whisper desperately: "See? I don't think she intends to burn his body up. She's crazy! Oh shit, this is gonna turn out badly. We're all gonna go to jail for this!"

"Calm down," Lucy said in a soothing voice, her rage seeming to have deserted her on their ex's death. "Listen, we'll let Candice have her fun tonight, and in the morning we'll discuss seriously about disposing of John's corpse. Worst comes to the worst, we'll get her husband Richard to help us convince her of the dangers of not destroying the body."

"Her husband? Lucy are you stoned like Donna? Listen: first of all, at the moment Candice's husband is in Panama, right? And secondly, the guy's a famous lawyer—there's no way he's gonna dirty his hands with this murder his wife planned."

Lucy smirked then and Josie had no idea why she'd done so until she explained herself: "Oh, don't be naïve, Josie. Look around us, at this damn magic chamber—it's up on the second floor of the mansion and not hidden in any way. Girl, the way I see the situation here, good old Richard Penderson the Third has to be as much involved in all this devil-worship stuff as his wife is. Have you looked in the guy's study? Fully half of the books in there are about summoning demons. He and Candice are clearly in it together."

"Yes, yes, I've noticed that. But maybe he's just going along with Candice 'cos he loves her a lot and—"

"Shush, they're coming back, we'll discuss it later," Lucy said and then she quickly pulled away from Josie and hurried back to her own chair again.

Josie spun around, leaned back in her seat and faked a smile as Candice and Mrs. Pain rejoined them at the table.

"So, that's settled," Candice said after sitting down. "Now that the boys are preparing the corpse, we had better get on with the final part of the ritual before John's blood dries up on us. Okay, girls, each of you dip your hands into the curve of the pentagram nearest to you. Make sure your fingers are covered with John's blood and then . . . Hey, hey, Donna, pay attention."

Donna's eyes fluttered open. "Yeah, yeah, sure, momma. What were you sayin'?"

Candice sighed. "Just dip your hands into John's blood and repeat this spell after me: Suot nek rae h'lleh fose tag eyho . . . "

"Suot nek rae h'lleh fose tag eyho . . ."

"Ecap semo ceben ot stelsu otpu nepo . . ."

"Ecap semo ceben ot stelsu otpu nepo . . ."

CHAPTER 22

Meet The Ex: Lucy

Except for the four years she had spent studying Marketing at Penn State University, Lucy Lowry had lived in Raynham all of her life.

Though ideally she should have relocated to Boston after graduation, which was where New England Face Inc. (or NEFI), the cosmetics company she worked for was located, she spent too much time flying cross-country to want to live in a high-population-density environment when she had time to herself.

Her hometown Raynham, with its population of less that 15,000 people, suited her perfectly.

Lucy had never understood why marriage was viewed as such a complicated deal. All you and your guy needed to do was love one another and things were certain to work out right. And so, when she had been married to John Miller that was what she had set out to do, to love and cherish him for the rest of her life.

And when things had nosedived between them, she hadn't understood why things had turned so bad.

Lucy was extremely intelligent, but she was also a woman who did not believe being smart meant you had to dress badly. She had never accepted the idea that being fashionable was the exclusive preserve of those without any brains in their head.

Throughout her life Lucy had taken care to look her best at all times, to make the best physical impression she could on her social environment.

Of course, many people misinterpreted her seeming obsession with makeup as narcissism, but they were wrong. Lucy was as socially minded as the next person in line, she just looked better than the rest of them, that's all.

Finding out that she was HIV-positive had hit Lucy with severe depression. Despite the fact that the ARV drugs kept her healthy, she could never escape the feeling that she was actually one of the 'walking dead.' Each time she watched a zombie movie, she kept thinking, *Yeah, they're just like me, exactly like me.*

Yes, she knew her feelings were irrational, and knew that her life could still be just as fulfilling as before, but even after all these years of therapy, she still found accepting her new state a major challenge.

Lucy had responded to her emotional crisis the best way she knew how—by applying more makeup.

CHAPTER 23

Megan

The knife, when Megan found it, seemed almost to have been waiting for her.

The knife, a ceremonial dagger with the kind of spookily curved blade that put you in mind of those horror movies in which bearded old Satanists sacrificed nubile young virgins, was also concealed in the most unusual of locations: tucked away under the mattress at the foot of the bed.

Megan had no idea how long it had been there for, but someone, most likely one of the goons or Mrs. Pain herself, had clearly stuck it there for some nasty purpose and then forgotten to retrieve it afterwards. Or maybe it had been left there so it would be handy when needed.

Megan felt a chill on seeing the dagger. Even though its blade was unstained, a faded dark patch on the rug beneath its location, cleaned but not properly, hinted at its possible prior violent use. Also, the knife's position of concealment at the foot of the bed seemed perfect for Mrs. Pain to pull it out during lovemaking and slash her lover's face, stab him in the guts, or worst still, slice his manhood off. Ghastly thoughts for sure, but the awful videos currently playing on the cell's television clearly demonstrated that Mrs. Pain's sadism and evil depravity knew no limits.

John Miller though, had clearly not realized that he had a deadly weapon so close at hand.

With her eyes Megan measured the distance from where she stood to the hoop on the wall that John Miller's chains had been attached to, and then she tried to recall exactly how long those restraints had been.

Or had the ceremonial dagger been left here under the mattress because, chained up like he was, John had no way to reach it anyway?

She decided that that had to be the case: no one had bothered to remove it from the cell because John Miller's chains prevented him from reaching it.

"But I'm not John Miller, and you guys have just caged a tigress," she said heatedly. "I may be seriously outnumbered here, but no way am I going down without a fight."

Then, suddenly noticing that the CCTV cameras in her cell moved when she did and as such were clearly tracking her actions, Megan quickly slipped the dagger into one of her jacket's inner pockets.

Hopefully, no one had seen what she'd just done. In fact, she was certain they hadn't. The goon who'd entered the room in the corridor to see Mrs. Pain had told the other one that Mrs. Pain's instructions were to call her on their way upstairs once they'd collected John from his cell.

And I don't think there's anyone else in the house other than Dave and Ron, the exes, and Mrs. Pain and her goons—that's everyone I've seen so far. So no one's watching me at the moment.

Satisfied that she was finally in a strong position to defend herself, Megan returned to the bed to endure more of MRS. PAIN'S GREATEST HITS.

CHAPTER 24

Tony

After walking the corridor that exited the dining room to its ending at a locked and bolted door, Tony Cimini turned back the way he'd come and retraced his steps.

This time he didn't bother with the doors again. He already knew that several were locked, one led to a bathroom, and one led down another corridor that he'd wasted time investigating only to finally discover that it led to a dead end crisscrossed by a maze of pipes and electrical wiring.

And then, right before he'd reached the locked back door, he'd opened a door that seemingly led to a basement. There were lights on down there but Tony hadn't bothered investigating the place. He was trying to exit this mansion, not venture deeper inside it.

There's gotta be a way outa here, a way that I can leave this damn house without needin' to use the front door, he thought.

Tony wasn't desperate yet, but he was very aware that he would be in a world of trouble if the blood-covered woman and her hulking cronies caught him in the mansion.

Dammit, this place has gotta be a gangster's house. Might even be one of Marko's.

Marko Velli was Boston's number one crime lord and Tony hoped he never had to tangle with the guy.

But no . . . no that's wrong. When I checked out the house address, this snazzy place belongs to some guy named Penderson . . . Richie Penderson.

Tony reached into his pocket for his cellphone to double-check the screenshot he'd saved and then scowled. *Damn, I left my phone in the car. Now, how'd I manage that? Yeah, my suspicions about Maryanne made me act sloppy. Well, ya know what? Screw Maryanne. If she wants this rich dude, she can have him. I just want outa here.*

The discovery that he didn't have his phone with him made Tony even more anxious to leave the mansion. If he got in trouble now, he had no way of calling the outside world for help.

Oh no, not now!

He'd arrived at the bend in the corridor that led towards the dining hall. Only now, unlike when he had hidden beside it earlier, the kitchen door was wide open and was spilling light out into the corridor.

But with no way out through the back door, Tony had no choice but to go forward. So that's exactly what he did, stepping silently and taking care not to make any noise. He could hear voices coming from the kitchen, the same ones he'd heard earlier.

I'll just dash past 'em and . . .

Then he peeked into the kitchen and almost wet himself from shock. He stood there trembling with his bladder threatening to lose control and drench him in urine.

Through another entrance opposite him, two men in cook uniforms were wheeling a corpse on a metal cart into the kitchen. The guy was dead, dead, dead.

Tony quickly recognized the dead man: *Oh no! It's that chained guy I saw them pushing past me a short while ago! They murdered him. Man, I gotta get out of this place!*

The chains were still attached to the corpse and they rattled as the two cooks positioned the cart next to a marble-topped island.

The dead man's head hung down over the front of the cart (his neck was a gaping hole) and his eyes seemed to be staring right at Tony and warning him: "Dude, you'd better run for your life while you've still got a life to run for."

Tony took the hint. Once the two cooks looked away for a moment, he stepped gingerly past the kitchen door and practically ran across the dining room. Next stop, the front entrance.

But once out in the hallway, he instantly skidded to a halt.

Oh, sweet Jesus and Mary Chain! You gotta be shittin' me!

Directly ahead in the living room, and barely five yards from the front door that Tony was headed for, sat the two men who'd earlier herded the dead man in the kitchen past the dining room. They were drinking beer and laughing about something.

Tony quickly stepped back into the dining room. There was clearly no way out there. Nor did he want to chance opening or breaking one of the windows opposite him.

Anything goes wrong with that plan and those two guys will be on me like maple syrup on pancakes . . . Damn, what I do now?

Hearing strange sounds from the kitchen, he crossed back to it again and peeked in and then grimaced.

Ugh!

The two cooks were kissing each other, their bodies tightly pressed together.

Tony took the opportunity of their distracted state to quickly step past the kitchen door again and then he turned to once more view the strange sight.

Okay, so these two dudes are homos.

Watching the two men kiss, Tony felt the normal unease that witnessing gay activity caused in straight guys.

But really, his unease went much deeper than that. What really bothered him about this scenario was the way the two kissing men seemed not to even notice the stiff right next to them. The dead man could have been plucked poultry or a shank of beef for all the notice they took of him.

The men broke apart. "Oh, honey, my ass feel so empty now," the shorter and slimmer of the cooks now told the other. "Do you think we have time for a quickie?"

Before replying, his taller and more muscular boyfriend glanced up at the wall, where Tony assumed a clock was hanging. "I guess so, baby. But it'll have to be a literal quickie or Mrs. P. will be mad at us"—he gestured down at the dead man—"if we don't garnish her pig quickly enough."

Tony got out of there fast after that; he had no desire to watch them sodomizing each other. With the front door closed off to him, he headed back down the corridor again.

I need to find a phone to call the cops. A landline. There's gotta be lots of 'em in a house of this size.

And it was this intention which led him down into the basement.

Yes, Tony had initially dismissed the basement as not being relevant to his search. But now it occurred to him that it might lead to one of those underground parking lots. Sure, there were three or four cars in the garage outside the mansion, but who was to say that a family this wealthy wouldn't have one or two vintage models parked under their house as well?

The point was, that such an underground parking lot would certainly have access to the outside of the house.

However, once Tony reached the basement he quickly revised his opinion. There was clearly no subterranean car park down here, just two long parallel corridors that looked like they ran the entire length of the mansion.

But then he also realized that all these doors along the two corridors couldn't be storerooms—one or two of them might be offices or work spaces—and so he began opening them to see if he could find a phone to call the police with.

CHAPTER 25

Boku Java

". . . H'trof e moc a vaju kobh trof moc."
". . . H'trof e moc a vaju kobh trof moc."

The spell completed, there was silence in the summoning room for a while.

A cloud of expectancy hovered over the women. The blood in the pentagram carved into the table top now glowed brightly. It had also become hot while the women were chanting the spell, so hot that both Donna and Josie had pulled their fingers out of it. Lucy's fingers were still stuck in the groove, but she had a pained look on her face, as if her fingers were boiling in the hot blood. Neither Candice nor Mrs. Pain seemed bothered by the heat.

"Nothing's happening," Donna said after a while with a petulant pout of her lips.

"No, you're wrong," Candice replied her. "At the moment a whole lot is happening in the supernatural realms." Then she nodded to Mrs. Pain. "Use the semen now."

Mrs. Pain nodded back at her and then got to her feet and picked up the silver goblet full of semen from where it stood on the table. She walked briskly to the huge engraved stone in the deepest corner of the summoning room and without ceremony flung the contents of the goblet at it and then stepped away from it.

Josie, Lucy and Donna had turned to see what Mrs. Pain was about to do, and now they all gasped. John Miller's collected semen didn't splatter against the rock surface like they had expected, but instead—and all three women saw this happen—the milky liquid formed itself into the shape of a pentagram in midair, and after spinning twice in place, this liquid pentagram slotted itself perfectly into the one etched on the rock.

"Holy shit, that sure is somethi—" Donna began saying, but then she shut up because something even weirder was happening now on the giant rock.

To the accompaniment of a series of soft clicking sounds that created the impression of a safe's tumblers falling into place, the white pentagram of sperm on the face of the rock was turning, first clockwise and then anticlockwise. It did this three times, with differing degrees of rotation, and then finally stopped.

"Oh wow, how'd that just happen?" Lucy gasped, looking as if she'd cut and run.

"Silence, girls, and keep still," Candice cautioned. "Watch—the portal is opening."

Yes, the portal *was* opening. The pentagram and rock were both fading away into nothingness and in their place a doorway was forming in the corner of the room; a normal-sized and normal-shaped opening that might have been there all along and merely previously hidden by the rock, except that . . .

Lucy rubbed her eyes. "Am I seeing things, or is that really John's come all around that door? And is it actually moving about?"

"Oh, how gross," Josie agreed on seeing what Lucy meant. The black rectangular opening was indeed framed by the semen that Mrs. Pain had thrown at the rock, and the semen did appear to be flowing in both directions around the doorway.

"Wow, cool," Donna giggled. "Just don't ask me to walk inside there. My momma didn't raise no fool."

"Something's coming out of the doorway!" Josie gasped. While still pointing sideways at the dark rectangle, she turned and stared at Candice with eyes wedged open by her fright.

Candice smiled coldly back at her. "Don't worry, that's the gentleman we've been expecting." Then she quickly turned to Mrs. Pain. "Go check on the cooks," she instructed her. Then she sighed. "And next time we're hiring for something like this, I think we'll go for some guys in their sixties. Those two young men only have sex on their minds all the time."

Mrs. Pain left quickly. None of the other three exes noticed her leave, they were too concerned with staring at the strange creature that was now emerging from the rectangular portal.

The thing was man-sized and vaguely man-shaped, but was mostly an unformed mess, as if someone had tried to build a sculpture out of jelly, with the expected problems where structural integrity was concerned.

A weird but also weirdly subdued smell accompanied it from its home realm.

The thing in the portal hovered there at the entrance to the room, seemingly gripping the portal's edges for support. Then it took a step out into the summoning room, at which Josie and Lucy both leapt out of their seats and hurried around the stone table to duck behind Candice. Donna shortly joined them behind Candice's chair and they all kept as close to the matriarch as they could.

Because, now that the jellylike creature was out of the portal, they could see its face; a face sunken deep into the ooze of its body, but nonetheless evil through and through. It had teeth too, black-rimmed jaws that flashed at them like distorted reflections in a fairground mirror.

"Behold Boku Java," Candice said delightedly. She sounded happier than any of the other exes had heard her sound since they'd first met.

Lucy scowled. "Java? Alright, girls, now listen," she told Donna and Josie while gawking at the creature, "if either of you two bitches dares make any coffee jokes about that thing, I'll claw your eyes out."

"Hey, that thing ain't made out of Johnny's come too, is it?" Donna whispered to Josie. Like Josie and Lucy, she too couldn't stop gaping at the creature they'd summoned.

"I don't think so," Josie whispered back, tugging at her hair with both hands while she attempted to master her fear and confusion.

"No, no, no—there didn't seem to be *that much* semen in the goblet," Lucy agreed. "I think that's its normal body form."

The demon—Boku Java—had now reached the stone table. With its mushy jellylike body seeming like it would collapse at any moment, the creature addressed Candice. "You performed the ritual correctly and I came," it told her. "I am willing to keep my side of our pact if you will keep yours." Its voice was surprising normal, a fact that calmed the three women huddling behind Candice a little.

"Excellent, excellent," Candice said, grinning and clapping her hands. She pointed to Mrs. Pain's vacated chair. "Please seat yourself, Boku Java. Refreshments will be served shortly."

The demon seated itself, which looked as if someone had upended a bowl of jelly over the chair and the portion of table closest to it. "The human world is a lovely place," it said. "I should visit it more often."

***

"So, you've visited our world before?" Lucy asked Boku Java, unable to stop herself. She was speaking to normalize the situation to herself; to prevent herself from cracking up. Rather than accepting the demon Candice had summoned as a supernatural being, Lucy was rationalizing it as an alien. She watched lots of space opera films and as such this was the logical way the demon made sense to her.

The demon looked at her in amusement. "Yes I have, Lucy Lowry, Napoleon summoned me twice. There was great feeding on battlefields back then."

Lucy nodded. She figured there was no point in asking the creature how it knew her name; extraterrestrials would of course have the telepathic ability to hack into her mind.

Also, she belatedly realized that at some point since they'd fled over to Candice's side, the blood in the table pentagram had all dried up—the circled star's grooves were deep black lines again.

***

Now that Boku Java was talking to them, Josie too found the demon's presence easier to accept. It looked like one of those daytime cartoon characters her two younger kids loved, like something from SpongeBob SquarePants' universe; or maybe even something from her two teens' creepy Japanese manga comics.

Maybe it's a cartoon that's come to life. I can accept that for a short while.

At the moment things had taken such a radical turn, had gotten so far out in left field, that Josie had forgotten the pain in her arm where she'd slashed herself; now when her arm hurt, the pain felt like a signal broadcast from far away.

The creature's smell, however, was something that niggled on the edges of Josie's nerves; something that couldn't really be placed, but which she was certain that, had it been more pungent, might have the potential to drive one crazy. And not crazy in the way that Maryanne's shrimp-and-cheese salad had affected her, but like *crazy* crazy—crawling-up-the-walls-in-a-padded-cell insane.

But still, she managed to smile at the horrible-looking jelly-thing with the sunken face and eyes like raisins.

"You're very welcome," she nervously addressed it. "Very welcome indeed. What exactly do you do for a living?"

The demon shrugged its half-formed shoulders. "I torture people in Hell," it replied. "It's a good job, but one occasionally desires a change of scene." It pointed a clawed hand that seemed about to drip off its body and splatter on the tabletop at Candice. "So these summonings do me a wealth of good."

Josie nodded. "Yes, I can see how that would be the case. It must be really hot in Hell at the moment."

The demon smirked nastily. "Lady, you've no idea how damn hot that fucking place is. Pray you don't arrive there soon."

Josie realized that Candice was tapping her leg.

"Huh?" she asked.

"You three girls need to return to your seats, so we can finish up with this," Candice said. "Go, go, go and sit, sit, sit now. Mrs. Pain and the cooks will be back upstairs any moment now."

***

"Yeah, sure," Donna agreed when Candice shooed them back to their seats.

She'd spent the first half of the interim wondering what sort of hallucinogenics her dealer had put into the weed he'd sold her. LSD or what the hell?

Then she'd accepted that what she was looking at was real, and still half-stoned, she'd begun pondering why the hell this Boku Java creature was so fucked-up looking. *Is it genetic or what? 'Cos if it is, I sure as hell don't wanna meet the motherfucker's parents.*

But still, once she'd sat down, she smiled coolly at it and said, "Hey, dude, I'd've offered you a joint, but Candice says no smoking till we're done here."

The demon laughed. "No hurry, Donna, we can both get high together later."

Donna considered high-fiving it, but then she decided that doing so might splatter its goopy hand to bits. She also didn't want the bother of wiping herself clean afterward.

So she instead looked at the portal, which was still wide open, a dark rectangle that gave her an impression of infinite depth.

"Exactly how deep does that thing go?" she asked Boku Java. "Hey, does it reach all the way down to the eternal Lake of Fire? I'm just askin' 'cos it don't seem particularly hot in there."

But she never got an answer, because that was when Mrs. Pain and the two cooks returned, with the two men whistling happily and pushing their cart ahead of them.

Donna looked at the contents of the supersized serving tray on top of the cart and sighed. Then regardless of what Candice was going to say about it, she opened up her handbag, pulled out a fresh joint and lit up.

***

With a gesture at the serving cart, Mrs. Pain grinned at Boku Java and said, "We've prepared him exactly the way you like them."

Dave and Ron had completely garnished John Miller. They had split him open from neck to crotch and had stuffed him with more kinds of vegetables than his four exes knew existed. John's eyes had been plucked out and peeled onions stuffed in their sockets. And like one sometimes saw in classic illustrations of roasted pigs, a large apple had been stuffed into his mouth as well.

In addition the two cooks had slit open the skin of his upper arms and thighs, dug deep troughs inside of them and stuffed vegetables inside those too. His removed innards lay around him on the huge metal tray, amidst piles of turnips and carrots and broccoli and potatoes and beets.

And the corpse, which was no longer pinkish in color but painted a dark orange and bright yellow and milky cream and catsup red from the mingled sauces and velvety garlic-butter baste it had been coated with, now smelled of mint and rosemary and lemon balm and whatever other spices and kitchen condiments the two men had had to hand.

Watching with clear anticipation as the cooks wheeled their grotesque offering towards it, the demon was already licking its lips, its mouth seeming to be the one part of its body that wasn't jellylike.

Lucy gaped as her brother and his boyfriend wheeled their cart around the table. She and Donna were positioned on the opposite side of the table, but she could see clearly enough. As much as she tried to feel empathy for the dead man, she couldn't. He'd had this coming to him for a long time; she only wished this could have happened while he was still alive to really suffer it.

Across from her, however, Josie turned seen-ghost-white as the men rolled the cart past her and parked it beside the jellied demon. She slammed a hand to her mouth to keep from throwing up, but that didn't help, so she leapt up and ran out of the summoning room.

Candice, who had been smiling serenely at the sight of the garnished body, nodded to Mrs. Pain. "Follow her. Make sure she's okay and bring her back here. And do it quickly. You know why."

Mrs. Pain left the room again.

Donna blithely smoked her joint, once more relieved to be able to reassure herself that what she was looking at wasn't as bad as it looked. Despite her previous statement to Boku Java, she didn't offer the demon a toke of her marijuana.

Gasping from the effort required to lift it, Dave and Ron heaved the giant tray containing the dead man up onto the table. They took special care not to bang the tray against the outstretched arms of the large metal witch-sculpture near Boku Java.

"Oh, yummy!" the demon exclaimed once the tray was set before it, and began eating.

***

None of the three women present (not even Candice) had ever seen anyone eat like that before.

Snuffling like a pig, Boku dug both of its hands and its entire head into John's body, from which loud sucking and squelching noises now ensued, while the corpse began jerking up and down on its tray like it was still alive.

"Wow, dude, you must really be hungry," Dave quipped with a broad grin on his face and a spaced out look in his eyes—he and Ron both looked more stoned than Donna did.

"Yeah, for real, dude," Ron agreed, picking up a chunk of chopped kidney that had just dropped to the floor and placing it somewhere on the table where it couldn't be knocked down again.

Boku Java was still feeding with its head buried inside John's body, and now a gap parted in the corpse's flesh and the women could see exactly what was happening; how the demon's mouth worked, with its gleaming teeth chomping at speed while its hands shoveled meat and vegetables between them at a breathless pace; its claws stripping flesh from John's bones almost faster than their eyes could follow. Meanwhile the anticipated collapse of its jelly flesh from the weight of the food packed on it never happened. Also, as the demon ate, it flooded the food tray with a yellowish saliva that stank like eggs gone bad.

"I ain't gonna comment on how gross this is to watch," Donna said serenely.

"Ugh, do we really have to watch this?" Lucy asked Candice with a pleading look. "I'm seconds away from puking like Josie's currently doing."

"Try to control your stomachs and emotions," Candice replied calmly, even though she too looked completely nauseated by the demon's unorthodox method of feeding; as though Boku Java's style of eating the sacrifices offered to it wasn't covered in her spellbook.

Bones included, the entirety of John's torso had already vanished into Boku Java's body, and the darkness of the ingested meat at once seemed to make the demon more solid. All that remained on the tray were the corpse's four limbs and its head. The demon now turned its attention to those, pulling the body parts and remaining vegetables and innards towards it and again digging its head right into the middle of the pile it had made. The slurping and snuffling sounds resumed.

And yes, the demon's flesh now looked more solid. In fact, its body now looked almost human in texture.

"There's something I want you all to see and it should happen any moment now, so you can't leave yet," Candice told her two female companions. Then she turned towards the door of the summoning room. "Where the heck have Josie and Mrs. Pain gotten to? I expected them to have returned by now."

"As requested, ma'am, here is the pig's heart," Ron said, sliding a covered metal dish across the tabletop to Candice. Then, while Candice stopped the dish with the heel of her palm and opened it and nodded at its contents, he turned away from her to once more stare at the feeding demon.

"Hey, dude, look at him go," he called out to Dave. "Dude really is hungry, bro! Dave, Dave, you listening to me, man?"

Dave wasn't. He was talking to his sister, who had turned her chair sideways to avoid looking at Boku Java. Dave was trying to serve Lucy a plate of raw guts that looked like sausage links.

"No, I don't want any of your damn *pig,* little brother," Lucy growled acidly at him. "Keep that shit away from me.

She was saved by Josie and Mrs. Pain's return.

Josie looked much better on her return to the summoning room, but only for a short while. Her fast exit from the room meant she'd been saved from experiencing most of the demon's revolting feeding process and now only had to watch it ingest John's head, which, while it did upset her stomach, found nothing in there for her to throw up.

But still Josie stiffened and froze where she was. Lucy was still fending off the plate of human guts that her brother wanted to feed her, and Donna's glazed eyes revealed that she was traveling somewhere far, far away, possibly even through the black recess across the room from which Boku Java had emerged.

And so, aside from Candice, it was Josie who first noticed the change in the demon and asked: "Hey, why does Boku Java now look like Johnny?"

"Huh?" Lucy, who was facing the door and not the table, asked. "What are you talking about?"

Josie was now trembling with fright in the doorway and looked like she'd turn and run away if Mrs. Pain hadn't had a firm grip on her. "Turn your frigging chair around, biatch," she whispered to Lucy in a scared voice. "This creature that Candice conjured up now looks exactly like our ex-husband who we just killed."

On hearing this, Lucy's lips parted slightly in surprise and then she violently shoved her brother away and quickly turned her chair around.

"Holy shit," she gasped on seeing that Josie hadn't been lying.

John Miller was now completely gone from the serving tray, which was instead filled with the demon's pungent yellow saliva. But John Miller now sat in Boku Java's place. The demon had become a perfect replica of the man they had just killed. It was of course completely naked, and its body also still flickered a little, as though it hadn't yet settled down completely in its new form.

Lucy tore her eyes away from the demon and stared at Candice, while rapidly jabbing her thumb in the transformed creature's direction. "Wh-wh-what is g-g-going on?"

"That's a real good question, homegirl, a wonderful question indeed," Donna said, waving her joint at the others. Then she pointed the joint at the demon, which had just finished eating John's head and was licking its lips. "I mean, hon, there's fucked up and then there's fucked up. I'm gonna need to take LSD to normalize myself after tonight."

"This is the reason to celebrate that I earlier mentioned we'd have," Candice told them. Then she smiled at the demon across the table. "How do you feel, Boku Java?"

The demon shrugged. "I'm good, I think. It always takes a while to get used to a new body. I like this body a lot. The last one I had belonged to an old woman with arthritis. Ugh."

"Hey, you mean it . . . or he . . . even *talks* like Johnny now? . . . Oops!" Donna's surprise at that fact had made her drop her joint. She scrambled to recover it before it burnt the rug.

Josie had recovered now. Staring warily at the smiling demon, she walked over and sat beside Candice again.

"How are you able to do that?" she asked the demon. "I mean . . ."

"Yeah, how exactly?" Lucy seconded her. Behind her, Ron was helping Dave up from where he'd fallen when she'd shoved him. As the demon had transformed right after Ron had turned away from it to gaze in amusement at Dave (who at that time had been focused on trying to feed his plate of raw guts to Lucy), neither cook had yet noticed the change.

"It's a simple trick," the demon replied them in the dead man's voice, with a look on its face that was so much like the late John Miller's that Lucy felt angry enough to want to kill him again, while Josie felt a quick return of her love for John and intense regret that she'd smothered him with her vagina. "I now know everything that John Miller knew even better than he knew it and I can do everything he could do better than he could do it."

(Along with Candice, the women now found themselves thinking of Boku Java as a 'he' rather than the 'it' that had seemed such a perfect pronoun when it had been in its original jellied form.)

"Including the ability to flawlessly sign John's signature, and a complete knowledge of all his passwords and confidences," Candice explained, as the demon waved 'his' fingers at them.

"He's going to impersonate John?" Lucy asked. "Is that what this is all about?"

Josie waved her hand to get Candice's attention. "Hey, hey, hey, you said we were going to leave John's heart for the police to find, so what's this sudden change now?"

Candice tapped the metal dish that contained their ex's heart. "Sending his heart to the police was merely my backup plan if this one failed. I wasn't sure that Boku Java's transformation would be convincing enough." She shrugged and gestured at the demon. "But, girls, you can see for yourselves how much they look alike. Personally I don't see any difference."

"Yeah, you're right," Donna agreed, pinching out her joint and quitting smoking for the time being. Then she peeked under the table for a few seconds. "Wow, bitches, even his dick seems the same size."

"I'm John Henry Miller's exact double, down to his fingerprints," the naked demon enlightened them. Then he gestured across to Candice. "Can I have his heart now?"

"Here you are then," Candice said, picking John's heart out of the dish and flinging it across the table at the demon.

The illusion of humanity about Boku Java was shattered for a second then, when, with his head arching forward like a dog's and his jaws spreading unnaturally wide, the demon snapped the heart out of the air with his teeth and wolfed it down.

Then 'he' was once more a man, though one with a bloodstained mouth and saliva dripping from his chin.

"Okay, ladies, that was some weird shit!" Dave Lowry said, his words reminding everyone that he and Ron were still in the room.

"Hell yeah, the jelly mold guy now looks like our pig," Ron agreed in a dazed voice, then added, "Hey, ladies, if you don't need us anymore for the moment, we'll just collect the tray and head back down to the kitchen with our cart. We gotta go load up the dishwasher."

"That's an excellent idea," Mrs. Pain laughed. Since Boku Java was now seated in her previous chair, she was standing behind Candice with her hands on Candice's shoulders. "But no more fooling around with each other, boys. We don't want your come in our breakfast now, do we?"

Dave batted his eyelashes at her. "Oh, Mrs. P. As if we'd ever do something naughty like that."

"You know we wouldn't," Ron agreed even more flirtingly. "We wouldn't want you to fist us both to death now, would we?"

There was a pause while Ron collected the scraps of intestine that Dave had been trying to feed Lucy from the floor and placed them before Boku Java, who once more exhibited the bestial side of his nature by wolfing them down in an instant.

"Ugh," Josie said. "I'll never, ever get used to seeing that."

"Me neither," Lucy agreed, then she addressed the demon: "Listen, if you're going to successfully impersonate John, you're going to have to stop eating like that."

Boku Java grinned back at her.

Donna nodded. "Yeah, man, you eat like that in Burger King or Taco Bell and you're gonna wind up in a padded cell somewhere."

Taking care not to spill its stinky yellow contents, Dave and Ron loaded the giant saliva-filled tray back onto their cart.

"Be seeing you, boys," Donna waved to them as they left the room. "Try not to have too much fun with each other."

Then she immediately turned back to Candice, her cappuccino-toned face serious. "Alright, now I think you've some explaining to do?"

"Yes," Josie agreed, with Lucy nodding also. "What point is there in us 'raising John from the dead' again as it were, when his will won't get read except he is dead? I thought securing his money for our kids was the whole idea here."

Candice rolled her eyes and sighed. "I'd have thought that by now you three would have cottoned on to the obvious here."

Josie leaned forward over the table. "*What* obvious?"

Candice sighed as if surprised that they all could be so obtuse, and then she pointed to Boku Java: "Ladies, to the general public, that man seated over there will be John Miller. That general public includes both his lawyers and bankers. Meaning . . ."

"Oh, now I get it," Josie said, wagging a finger in the air.

Candice nodded back at her. "Yes, honey. Meaning, no one is going to question him when he finally decides to give us ex-wives the prenuptial settlement money he's owed us for all these years."

Josie, Lucy and Donna turned to stare at Boku Java. The demon nodded back at them and they turned to stare at Candice again.

"Bitch, you're a friggin' genius," Donna said.

Josie and Lucy nodded their full agreement with Donna's statement. Both women had begun smiling.

"Of course, we'll only take what we're owed," Candice said. "Five million each for us wives—including Maryanne, of course—leaves four million each for our children, when six months from now, John becomes suicidal and decides to end his life."

She settled back into her chair and let her companions digest this.

Donna finally turned and addressed the demon. "Dude, you're gonna kill yourself for us?"

"Dying in this body presents no problem for me," Boku Java replied. "Each incarnation only permits me a six month period on Earth." He gestured back at the dark rectangle in the corner with the shiny liquid edges. "Once that time is complete, I must return home for a while." He opened his mouth and picked at his teeth with a fingernail. "But until then, I will feed regularly on delicious human flesh."

"Ugh. So it's not a one-time thing?" Lucy asked, looking warily at the demon.

"No," Candice enlightened her. "To sustain this human shape, Boku Java will need to eat human flesh at least twice a month." She shrugged. "I see no problem there. The state is full of homeless folk, winos and runaways and junkies that no one will miss."

Josie pointed over at the portal. "So you're just going to leave that open like that for six months? Won't someone—your servants, for instance—get curious about where it leads to?"

On her question the demon lost his previously nonchalant expression. "She makes a good point, Candice," he said. "You know the rules of my summoning. If anyone enters the portal before my allotted timespan is complete, I'll be summoned back home again."

"Oh, don't worry about that," Candice replied airily with a careless wave of her hand. "I've already figured that one out. Once we're done here, Mrs. Pain and I will cover your portal with a fake plaster replica of the rock that was originally there."

"We already have it prepared down in the basement," Mrs. Pain confirmed from her standing position behind Candice. Since the demon's human transformation she had been staring at him with intense lust in her eyes; her nipples were swollen and stiff and she licked her lips whenever he glanced at her.

"Good, that is perfect," Boku Java said. "Now, however, I still feel a little hungry. Do you perhaps have anyone handy that I can eat? Preferably someone still alive. It's been ages since I've tasted fresh and hot flesh and blood on my tongue."

Candice considered the question for a while. In Josie's opinion, this interval was too long, and when she could no longer stand the uncertainty and anticipation, she leapt to her feet and hurried off behind Candice again.

"Definitely not me," she yelped as she fled, with her robe almost tripping her up.

"Nor me either," Donna said, raising her finger to make her point. She didn't flee from her chair like Josie, but she kept glancing at her handbag, on the verge of breaking her vow to not smoke another joint tonight.

The thought of all the money she'd soon have made Lucy act braver than the other two women. "And you can't eat me or my brother either," she said, wagging a stern finger at the demon. Then she sighed sadly. "And besides, I don't think HIV-infected meat tastes particularly nice."

"Girls, girls, for heaven's sake stop panicking," Candice finally said, before pointing out: "We've two perfectly suitable candidates in the basement."

"We do?" Lucy asked in surprise.

"But of course we do, Lucy darling," Mrs. Pain said. "One of them is an ex-boyfriend of mine. The other, of course, is that girl who followed you here. The brunette."

Lucy looked surprised. "Megan? I'd forgotten about her."

"But I hadn't," Candice said. "And yes, I think this is the perfect way to dispose of her. I'm certain you've noticed that Boku Java's feeding leaves no traces behind."

"But we can't . . ." Lucy protested helplessly. "We can't just kill her."

"Is she worth five million dollars to you, Lucy?" Josie asked. "Because she isn't to me."

"Me neither," Donna said. "But I vote for shooting her in the head first. Or at least slitting her throat. That'll be merciful and humane. Being eaten alive is just so old-school."

"I want her *alive*," the demon disagreed with an angry scowl on his face, while thumping both of his fists on the tabletop for emphasis. "I want to taste her blood on my tongue, I want to feel her flesh shredding between my teeth when I bite into it. I want to rip her skin off of her bones with my fingers and shatter her bones with my fists and feel her muscles shredding as I pull them into my mouth while she screams and weeps and trembles in agony."

Donna leaned away from Boku Java and waved her hands at him in a pacifying gesture. "Sure, sure, baby; whatever you like. I was just thinkin' that seein' as you're now human and all, maybe you won't want her splatterin' all over you and making a mess of your sexy body?" She pointed to Mrs. Pain, who was still covered in blood. (*What is it with those giant red circles she paints around her eyes anyway?*) "But maybe you both have similar fashion sense." She sighed and then muttered under her breath, "Or lack of it."

"Candice, please," Lucy pleaded. "Megan is innocent. She had no idea what she was getting into when she came here."

"She shouldn't have broken into my house," Candice replied with an evil smile on her face. "But okay, to make you happy, I'll give her a sporting chance. How about if we let Boku Java decide for himself which of them he prefers?"

Lucy nodded, realizing she was defeated. If the demon chose Megan for his second meal, Megan it would be then.

With that evil smile firmly in place on her face, Candice enquired of the demon: "Would you prefer a male or female meal, sir?"

"Female, please," Boku Java replied without a second's hesitation, making Lucy sigh in dismay.

"An excellent choice," Candice told Boku Java, giving the demon a knowing wink. "This girl is young and tender, just the way you demons like 'em. Sorry, she's not a virgin but I'm sure you understand that there's a huge shortage of those about nowadays."

The demon nodded sadly. "So sad, Candice, but so true."

Donna glanced up from inspecting her fingernails and quipped: "Whoever imagined that the decline of Christian values in our society would be lamented down in Hell too, huh?"

Candice rolled her eyes at the remark. After shoving Josie back towards her seat again, she turned to Mrs. Pain. "Please go with the boys and fetch our juicy and tender female captive from her cell."

Mrs. Pain smiled even more coldly than Candice. "Of course, at once. I too see it as the perfect way to solve our problem of what to do with her."

Then, before turning to leave, she burst out laughing. "Hey, girls, I really should get something from John Miller's bank account too, you know. Remember I was his girlfriend for a whole week."

Candice burst out laughing too. "Oh, Mrs. Pain, you're killing me!"

CHAPTER 26

Meet The Ex: Donna

Donna Goines had grown up in an old east-Brooklyn house with bad doors, which meant that from a very early age she'd gotten used to hearing the sound of her parents making love at night.

During her high school years she'd wake up at 2 a.m. to get a drink of water and hear them going hard at it, working the bed springs like they were testing their endurance for the manufacturers.

Donna had never figured out which of her parents was the nymphomaniac one, her black father or her white mother. But the pair of them had kept banging away throughout her years of adolescence, until the concept of the necessity of constant sex had become more ingrained in her young psyche than the need for education.

Once she'd finished high school, Donna had begun working the streets as a hooker, both to earn money and to get laid as consistently as her mother was getting it at home.

And then the young hip-hop producer Raven Rave had picked her up for a quick blowjob, and had discovered how fantastic she was with her lips.

This skill at fellatio was a talent that Donna herself hadn't realized she possessed. Yes, she had noticed that most repeat clients of hers preferred her to suck them off rather having regular sex or even anal with her and were prepared to pay extra for her blowjobs, but she'd just assumed that the black guys she met disliked her smaller ass because she was half white.

Raven Rave had enthusiastically introduced Donna to several hip hop musicians and by extension to the high-class escort lifestyle.

Since then Donna had never looked back. In New York she was considered the queen of blowjobs.

One thing she had made sure to do though, was to use some of her earnings to repair all the bad doors in her parents' house, both so that she could get some sleep whenever she visited them (after having sex all day herself, she had no desire to listen to them have sex all night), but even more importantly so that her baby sister Tasha didn't wind up being subconsciously conditioned into a prostitute like she had been.

Donna made lots of cash as a prostitute, but she also liked spending lots of money; 'blinging herself up' so she didn't look like an also-ran on the hip-hop scene.

Nowadays Donna only had sex for money. It was the simplest way to conserve both her time and her energy. But she felt she needed to give up the game before her son Toby grew old enough to really understand what she did for a living, including why she took all those long trips while leaving him at his grandparent's house.

5

Every Woman is both Angel and Demon,
Heaven and Hell in equal measure,
Man's greatest misery and his greatest
treasure.

*

Life's a female dog and then you die
- Slain Jane (Superglue for Broken Hearts)

*

A fool angers his wife,
A madman angers his mistress.
A suicide angers them both.

CHAPTER 27

Megan

Unaware that two floors above, she had just been sentenced to a horrible and messy death, Megan was trying not go mad in her cell.

MRS. PAIN'S GREATEST HITS was still playing on the cell's TV and now it was close to driving Megan nuts.

She had so far found no way to turn off the television—there was no remote control in the room and the unit itself didn't have any controls that she could manipulate. She had looked for a HDMI cable to unplug, but there wasn't any; the TV seemed to be fed by wireless transmission. Its power cord also didn't either begin or end in any plugs that she could yank out—like a snake it emerged from the rear of the TV and similarly vanished into a hole in the wall.

And so, due to this inability to switch the damned thing off, Poor Megan, whose movie watching had previously been entirely dedicated to chick flicks and lighthearted Disney-princess fare, had just gotten through watching PAIN AND MARY JANE in which Mrs. Pain had hammered almost a hundred knitting needles—of bamboo, plastic, and steel—through a screaming woman's body.

There was no escape from the visual and auditory assault. Running into the attached bathroom cubicle didn't help. Megan had vomited twice already, but even while throwing up, the noises reached her loud and clear. Even if she shut her eyes, the screams of Mrs. Pain's victims were in themselves a kind of temptation; they made her want to see— no, they made her *need* to see what was happening to cause the sufferers such intense anguish. She'd plugged her ears with rolled-up tissue paper from the bathroom, but it hadn't helped; the ghastly shrieks still made it through her makeshift earplugs.

And so Megan had finally given up. Now she was sitting on the bed watching Mrs. Pain's enter*pain*ment show.

Just beginning now was DR. PAIN'S PAINFUL PERIOD PREVENTION PROCEDURE:

As she had a few times previously, Megan unwisely let herself be lulled into a false sense of serenity by the scene's opening montage of a hospital exterior and smiling doctors and nurses, medical carts being wheeled along brightly lit corridors, apprehensive kids tightly clutching their mothers' hands . . .

And then all of a sudden, just like a magic trick, she was once more viewing the naked sadist's torture room, or maybe the woman had more than one of them—this one seemed slightly different from the others.

In keeping with the previous hospital montage, this setup was a simple one. A red-haired woman lay naked on a bed—actually she was tied down spread-eagled on her back—and Mrs. Pain, who was wearing a nurse's cap and also had a stethoscope dangling between her naked breasts, stood beside her.

Megan was relieved to see that there was no surgical cart with surgical tools in evidence. But her relief was short-lived, because the bound redhead was awake and was staring at Mrs. Pain in an absolute terror that immediately communicated itself across to Megan; her green eyes looked like they would pop out of her face.

"Oh, come now, Mrs. Dawson," Mrs. Pain chided in the voice of an aggrieved physician. "You have to be strong here—surely you understand that this is all for the best. Those nasty period pains of yours must be cured."

"No, no no, I'm okay!" Mrs. Dawson pleaded. "I'm fine! I'm fine! Please, just let me go home to my husband and my kids."

"Oh, come on now, Mrs. Dawson," Mrs. Pain tutted disapproving. "Don't get all dramatic on me. You know as well as I do that this is all for your own good."

While speaking, she was sliding her hands down the bound woman's pale body to her crotch, and now the camera focused there also.

Mrs. Dawson's pubis was shaven bare, but very roughly, leaving her with several nasty cuts. The shaving had clearly been done just so that the viewer could clearly see what had been done to her.

And now Megan had absolutely no idea what to think anymore; horror had chased rational thought from her mind, because the top of a hand grenade protruded from the redhead's vagina, with the safety pin in evidence; if Megan didn't know any better she would have mistaken its ring for labial jewelry.

There was a lot of blood between the woman's legs, clearly resulting from the stitches that had been used to partially sew her vagina shut so that the grenade wouldn't slip out of her. Just as with her shaving, the stitching had been done very roughly and her labia had ripped in several places.

Megan took a closer look and saw that the grenade stuck in the captive redhead had been modified in some way. Not being a big fan of weaponry, it took her several seconds to figure out what the difference was here.

But then she got it: the lever-like thing on the grenade's side—she wasn't certain what it was called, but she knew about it because two years ago she had bought her soldier ex-boyfriend Tommy a cigarette lighter designed like a hand grenade for his birthday and squeezing that lever-thing was how one ignited it.

The point here was that Megan understood that after one pulled out a grenade's safety pin, that lever-thing was what stopped the grenade from exploding in one's hand.

But well, that side-lever-thing was missing here on this grenade that was stuck in Mrs. Dawson's vagina.

But no, further observation showed Megan that it wasn't actually missing, but it had been drastically shortened, sawn off very near to the safety pin itself, and the reason for this was instantly obvious: With an unmodified grenade rammed into Mrs. Dawson's sex, her vagina would function just like a hand, holding the lever down after the pin's removal and preventing the grenade from exploding.

But modified like this, once the safety pin went, so would she . . .

The camera focused on Mrs. Pain again.

She patted Mrs. Dawson's thigh. "So, in my expert opinion, ma'am, an explosive excision of your womb is the perfect solution here. After all, you can't have period pains if you don't have a womb, can you? Now, let's do this girl!"

"NO, PLEASE NO!" The bound woman instantly shrieked, with tears spilling over the sides of her face to be mopped up by her red hair. "OH GOD, GOD, SOMEBODY HELP ME PLEASE!"

Mrs. Pain frowned down at her. "Honey, you've just got to believe in yourself! You really can get better!"

"NOOOOOOOOOOOOOOOOOOOO!" Mrs. Dawson wailed as Mrs. Pain pulled the safety pin from the grenade and then ran off out of sight.

Time froze for Megan. She counted lifetime-long seconds while Mrs. Dawson flailed on the bed and in a grotesque spectacle, began thrusting her crotch upward in a futile attempt to pop the hand grenade out.

Megan tried to shut her eyes; but her eyelids seemingly wouldn't obey her.

The explosion was impossible to describe. There was fire and smoke and Mrs. Dawson's crotch and torso blew apart in a crimson shower like 4th of July fireworks. The camera must have been filming from behind a bulletproof screen, but even that screen sustained a lengthwise crack.

When the smoke cleared, all that was left of Mrs. Dawson were her legs, her arms and her head, which had been blown over the top of the mattress, which was now on fire, with most of its middle portion destroyed.

Well, most of the dead woman was still in the room, but she was splattered all over the walls and—as the camera obligingly now lifted to show the viewer—the ceiling as well.

As Megan fought against the urine that was violently trying to escape her bladder and wet her jeans, Mrs. Pain strode back into view with a fire extinguisher in hand.

While putting out the blaze on the bed, she pouted for the camera. "Well, that's another pretty patient cured—she'll never have to worry about period pain again!"

And then she dropped the extinguisher on what remained of the mattress and grinned at the camera again.

"And hey, African girls, my cure works for victims of FGM too, you know that female circumcision thingy? Having no orgasm ain't a problem if you ain't got no pussy. To book an appointment, call me on my toll-free gynae hotline: 1-800-666-PAIN. Yeah, girls, that's 1-800-666 . . . P . . . A . . . I . . . N . . . and I'll schedule an appointment for you too!"

Megan kept gaping, hugging herself tightly with arms covered in panic gooseflesh.

"And now, let's look in on our other patient, shall we?"

Megan froze. *What? There's someone else in the room?*

Indeed there was, as the camera now proceeded to reveal to her, panning right and showing Megan a glass wall in the middle of the room; bulletproof glass of course, because although also splattered with chunks of the dead woman, it was otherwise undamaged. This screen was clearly what Mrs. Pain had earlier run off to hide behind.

The glass wall had a door in it, which Mrs. Pain now led the way through, with the cameraman following, or maybe there was more than one camera and they were all automatic, because suddenly, in a matter of a split-second, the perspective shifted and Megan was staring at the room from its opposite end and seeing Mrs. Pain from a front angle rather than a rear one.

But Megan's main focus was on the naked, blonde-haired man bound to the bed in the middle of this half of the room. Just like the dead woman in the other section had been, he was spread-eagled, but in his case on his belly, not his back.

"Please, don't," the man murmured weakly, turning his face towards the camera. His pale eyes were puffy from weeping and his mouth was twisted into an agonized shape that told of his having endured unimaginable pain. "Oh, my dear God, woman—how could you do that to Melanie?"

"Now, now, Mr. Dawson," Mr. Pain said with a kindly smile, while stroking his face, "as I'm certain you just heard, my period pain cure worked a treat for your wife. The great news for you is that it's certain to also take care of those troublesome hemorrhoids you've got."

"No no, please, please, no!"

The camera now shifted from the man's face, moved down over his back and came to rest in the space between his spread buttocks, with Mrs. Pain helping the view by pulling Mr. Dawson's buttocks farther apart.

Megan gasped. Another, similarly modified hand grenade was stuck up Mr. Dawson's anus. It looked horrible, like a giant hemorrhoid that had turned cancerous. Much too big to fit in his ass naturally, it been forced into place, with the anal sphincter having torn apart at several spots to accommodate it, which accounted for all the blood on his buttocks.

Just like in his wife's case, the safety pin's ring glinted bright silver, awaiting the murderess' finger.

Once Mrs. Pain pulled that pin, Mr. Dawson was dead meat too, as the parts of his wife still dripping from the ceiling in the other half of the room so bloodily testified.

Megan cringed on trying to imagine the sort of insane reasoning required to modify an already deadly weapon to make it even more devastating.

What the hell had Mrs. Pain been thinking? Something along the lines of: *Alright, now I want to blow a man or woman to pieces; what the nastiest and messiest way to do so?*

Mrs. Pain tapped the grenade gently and made a show of halfway pulling out its safety pin, which made her male captive shriek in insane panic, and caused Megan to once again feel like the world around her had stopped.

But then the bald madwoman onscreen stepped away from Mr. Dawson and addressed the camera instead.

"I'm sure everyone watching already knows how this story ends, don't you? Well, you're right—he'll soon be cured too." She laughed uproariously, while beside her the bound man trembled and sweated bullets and wept in silent relief.

Megan only realized that she'd been holding her breath when Mrs. Pain's grinning image froze and a yellow banner was superimposed over it. The banner's black lettering read:

'Definitely to be continued, fans, but will Mr. Jerry Dawson, who has a weak heart, sadly die of suspense before Dr. Pain succeeds in curing him? To find out, be sure to watch DR. PAIN'S HEMORRHOID HELPLINE HOMICIDE in her GREATEST HITS, PART 2.'

***

I'll just keep pretending to myself that this is a horror flick I'm watching, Megan told herself as the screen faded to red, giving her a few precious seconds to retrieve the tattered threads of her fast unravelling sanity from the psychic ether and weave them back together again.

What I don't get about Mrs. Pain is how she can be so calm, so blasé about the horrors and mutilations she's inflicting on these people. Yes, she's excited— she's breathing hard and her nipples are hard and sometimes she even wanks herself—but her behavior in these snuff films goes far beyond simple excitement; beyond even the suggestion that she feels she's performing some necessary function by murdering all of these people. From what I'm watching, this madwoman seems to need her sadism the way the rest of us need air to breathe. She'll keep on killing and killing for as long as she can, with no compunctions and no ethical constraints.

The screen was still red. Megan felt her emotions normalizing. *And Candice and her husband Richard—because he too has to be a part of this insanity—it's happening . . . all being filmed here in his basement, isn't it? What do the two of them get out of this? Do they share these videos with their friends? Are all these grisly murders simply fun and games—enterpainment—for a jaded world elite?*

There was no mirror in either the cell or the bathroom, but staring across at the TV, Megan could see herself reflected in its red screen: a hunched-over woman in black biker jacket, denim pants and boots, and with long dark hair and staring eyes—gaping-like-mad eyes— seated on a wide bed.

Peering closely at herself, Megan decided she hated the look in her eyes. *I seem both helpless and hopeless. I am not helpless and hopeless!*

While the TV seemed to be making up its mind on what evils to show her next, she concentrated on visibly altering her facial expression, blinking her eyes several times and breathing in deeply, and turning up the corners of her lips from a frown into a cold and determined smile.

She liked how she looked now; like a fighter.

Now and again her right hand strayed inside her jacket and gripped the hilt of the dagger she'd earlier found beneath the mattress. She clutched her knife as if her life depended on it, because she realized that yes, judging on what she was viewing at the moment, her survival really did depend on this knife she'd found.

Showing me these films means that Mrs. Pain isn't bothered about anyone finding out what she's been up to down here, which means they aren't going to let me leave here alive tonight.

The clock on the wall ticked away interminable seconds, but Megan had long ago stopped noticing it; compared to the television it was a lesser, insignificant deity. At the moment she seemed to exist in a realm where time was either flexible or nonexistent. Mrs. Pain's videos had made it so.

The CCTV cameras placed up in the room's four corners still tracked Megan each time she shifted on the bed, but she had gotten used to them now. She was certain no one was behind them—at the moment, with everyone in the mansion seemingly preoccupied with satisfactorily disposing of John Miller, the video cameras had to be working automatically, recording footage to be reviewed later.

Megan no longer cared about why John Miller's exes wanted him dead so badly.

The television screen came alive again. 'MRS. PAIN IN "FUN-FILLED FISTING FAMILY FATALITY." '

This was as bad as everything that had preceded it.

Mrs. Pain was back in the same room, or maybe another one just like it, this basement seemed immense enough to contain eight or ten such torture chambers.

And am I even alone down here? Are there other people in other cells, each of them watching this same insanity on their TV screens and waiting in terror for Mrs. Pain to visit them and 'star' them in one of her flicks?

In the onscreen torture chamber, three people were bound over low gym horses that had been placed beside each other with about four feet of space between them. A man, a woman and a teenage boy of maybe thirteen years of age. The three of them were naked and the words 'Father,' 'Mother' and 'Sonny' had been written on their backs with a black Sharpie. They had apparently been kidnapped during a family outing—the mother was wearing large earrings and had on badly smeared makeup. The unfortunate family also had black ball gags shoved in their mouths. The video camera was filming them from the left side, but was elevated so that it recorded a partly overhead and partly side view.

What happened next was fast, brutal and sickening. Mrs. Pain grabbed up an axe and began hacking off the father's left arm, slamming her blade hard against the side of the gymnastic horse until his forearm and elbow separated from his body and fell to the ground. He didn't bleed much—Megan could now see the red wires between the man's shoulder and bicep with which the arm had been tourniqued so tightly that the wires had dug deeply into the skin.

Mrs. Pain leaned her bloody axe against her jerking male victim (who seemed about to pass out), picked up his severed forearm and waved it at the camera.

"The family that fists together stays together," she informed whoever was watching her. "Fisting gives one a true grasp of relationships."

Then she strode around behind the three bound people. "Who shall daddy do first? His darling wife or his darling son?" She giggled. "Oh, let's have some perversion here, shall we? Sonny it is!"

The mother was in the middle; the son was last in line. Mrs. Pain strode past the struggling woman and paused behind the boy. She regarded his pale buttocks for a short while, brutally stuck two fingers up the kid's anus, and then after pulling her fingers out of him, seemed to momentarily relent and consider the size of the severed forearm that she was holding.

Then she looked up at the camera again.

"Hmm, we seem to have a bit of a problem here. Daddy is too big for Sonny's derriere." Then she snapped her fingers as if she had just thought of something. "Oh, but not to worry, a little anal episiotomy will easily fix that."

"What?" Megan gasped aloud. "What?"

But Mrs. Pain had already dropped the severed arm, and was now in its place holding a pair of hedge shears.

"No!" Megan screamed at the TV as Mrs. Pain shoved one of the hedge shears' long blades into the kid's anus, with the expected instant gush of blood. "Stop it! Are you crazy!"

But of course Mrs. Pain qualified as crazy; Megan already knew that.

While the teenage boy froze and squirted bright red blood from his anus all over her, Mrs. Pain snipped his backside wide open.

Finally, she dropped the shears, tested the size of the hole that she had made by sticking her own fist inside it, said, "Okay, Sonny, now let Daddy show you the true depths of his love for you," and then she shoved his father's severed arm as deep inside him as she could, which was way past the elbow.

The kid jerked twice on the gym horse and died.

Mrs. Pain smiled up at the camera. "Now he knows what the expression 'a father's love' really means."

She strode briskly back to the father's side. He seemed half unconscious, but she quickly slapped him back awake.

"Don't be a lazy lover, honey," she told him in a mock cross voice. "Now it's time for you to make love to your wife also. Or why do you think God gave men two arms—if not to fist their families all the better?"

She picked up the axe from beside his dripping stump, walked around him to his right side and then patted his terrified and weeping blonde wife nicely on both of her cheeks and said to her, "And which hole would *you* prefer to be fisted in, honey—pussy or ass?"

The gagged woman merely shook her head in terror, and so Mrs. Pain answered the question herself: "Oh, let's be adventurous, girl—anal's the in-thing nowadays with all the kids; and don't tell me you've not been dying to try it yourself." She laughed. " '*Dying* to try it?' Get the joke, honey?"

Megan leapt off the bed when Mrs. Pain began hacking the father's right arm off.

Suddenly realizing that she'd so far overlooked a guaranteed method of switching the damned TV off, she hurried over to it.

The massive electric shock that hit Megan when she sliced into the TV's power cord with her knife almost knocked her unconscious, but as she slumped to the floor, she was relieved that her electric tormentor had finally gone silent. The sputtering wire assured her that the TV was off for good.

She remembered how John Miller had looked when the two goons had come for him; completely defeated and already accepting the inevitability of his fate.

If I'd watched that thing for a minute longer, she thought while catching her breath and watching the end of the severed cable spark, *I'd be in a much worse state than he was. Now all I have to do is wait until Mrs. Pain comes for me. I just hope it isn't right now, 'cos when she does arrive here, there's gonna be one hell of a fight, and at the moment I really don't feel up to fighting.*

CHAPTER 28

Tony

The first two basement rooms that Tony examined were storerooms, big rooms cluttered with the sort of junk everyone had at home and didn't know what to do with; things you had no current use for but didn't want to discard because they might be needed in the future.

The next door he opened revealed a large pantry, with amongst other things, a giant walk-in freezer in which several whole pigs dangled from ceiling hooks.

Tony shut the pantry door and forged ahead. But both subsequent rooms he checked were full of boxes of unopened cleaning supplies.

Wow, this basement is almost as stocked as Walmart.

Which brought Tony to a turnoff that connected to the parallel corridor on the basement's other side. He now had a choice; he could either walk directly ahead and continue searching on this side, or he could examine the rooms along this side corridor.

He chose the first option, but soon felt that he'd made a mistake, as the next three doors he tried were all locked.

Tony shrugged off his disappointment. He had now reached a second turnoff. Just like the first, this one also crossed to the parallel corridor. He looked back at the first one but decided that since he'd already arrived here, he'd better check along this one first.

The first room Tony entered along this turnoff was some kind of cell. It had a double bed, a bathroom in an open cubicle built into the wall, and weirdest of all, a giant TV set beside the wall opposite the foot of the bed. A set of chains—just like the chains on the dead guy upstairs—hung from a ring on the wall.

There were also several red splotches on the otherwise cream-painted wall that Tony instantly recognized as bloodstains.

Tony got out of there fast. *What the heck is this place?*

He wished he had his cellphone with him so he could take some snaps for the police. He was now certain though that the owner of this house had criminal connections; so maybe it was great that he didn't have a phone to take any snaps with: in the underworld snitches got their throats cut.

The dead guy upstairs then came to mind—had the man snitched on the mob?

Tony considered going back upstairs and checking if the coast was now clear, but then he decided to first finish searching along this connecting passage. If he hadn't found a working landline by the time he reached its far end, he'd simply loop back along the other lengthwise corridor and climb out of the basement.

He shut the cell door behind him and walked to the next door.

This was another cell, but this one was occupied. In the middle of the room, a man sat tied to a chair, with his hands bound behind him.

The bound man had been tortured, and very badly at that. He'd been partially scalped and his left ear had been cut off. His removed scalp and ear lay rotting in a metal tray on the surgical instrument trolley beside him, while the top of his head, the front half of which was an infected open wound around a hand-sized patch of bare bone, crawled with maggots. The skin of his face ended abruptly above his eyebrows.

His chest and arms were also violently slashed, with raw flesh showing where patches of his skin had been sliced off. All he had on were his underpants but they were soiled with blood and the smell of old urine was thick in the air.

In addition to all the savagery done to his body, the man looked partially emaciated, as if he'd been fed sparingly while held captive down here.

Tony stared in dread at the man, and then at the surgical trolley. The instruments that lay on it were all bloodied. The only unbloodied one was the gleaming machete that lay below the surgical tools, on the cart's lower shelf.

Tony at first thought that the man was dead; his eyes were shut and he seemed too mutilated to still be alive. But he was breathing, the motion of his chest was unmistakable.

Tony was about to turn and flee when the man opened his eyes.

"Help me!" he pleaded weakly.

Tony stepped back in horror. Four or five of the man's teeth were missing and the cracked whitish spikes that remained in their place spoke of them having been extracted by violence, maybe using the bloody set of pliers on the surgical instrument trolley.

"Who the hell did this to you?" Tony asked the captive. "How the hell did you get down here?"

"This is my goddamn house," the man replied in a voice that wavered somewhere between a whimper and a growl. "And my . . . my damn wife did this to me."

Tony gaped at him. "*You're* Richie Penderson?"

The victim nodded, his voice continuing to waver as he replied Tony: "Yes, man, I'm Richard Penderson. My wife Candice . . . she . . . she's gone crazy . . . she accused me of trying to kill her . . . she's crazy . . . she's kept me down here for two weeks now . . . says she's telling everyone I'm busy down in Panama . . . traveling where I can't be contacted . . . she and that mad bitch Mrs. Pain . . . ouch!"

"Wait, is Mrs. Pain the hairless chick, with the two muscular sidekicks?"

"Yes, that's her." Then Richard Penderson peered more closely at Tony. "Hey, who are you? I don't think I've ever seen you before."

Tony sighed and shook his head. "Man, I just followed my girlfriend here. I thought she was cheating on me with you."

"Cheating? With Me?" Richard Penderson laughed weakly. "Are you nuts? Your girl is probably as insane as my wife—she told me she and some friends of hers were going to attempt to incarnate a demon tonight."

"Incarnate a demon? What the hell's that mean?" Tony asked.

"It means to bring a demon into human form in our world," Richard Penderson explained in a very world-weary voice. Then he gasped at Tony: "Please untie me. Use one of the knives on the cart to cut the tape binding my hands together."

Tony quickly nodded and picked up a suitable knife from among the several in the bloody tray. Then, avoiding looking at Richard Penderson's bared and festering skull, he stepped behind the man and crouched down and sliced through the silver tape that both bound Richard's hands behind him and also secured them to the rear of the chair.

When the duct tape snapped open a few maggots dropped from Richard's head onto Tony's shirt, making him wince and jerk back and beat the slimy things off.

Wincing, Richard pulled his arms forward in front of him and began stiffly moving his hands about. "Hey, hand me the knife; let me cut my feet free."

"Here, let me do it for you," Tony offered, walking back around the chair.

"No, it's okay, I can manage. I'll be up out of this chair in a minute, and then . . ." He stopped speaking and wheezed for a few seconds. "And then we'll both go phone the cops."

The way Richard was wincing in pain as he moved his arms, Tony doubted that the man would be able to stand up even if he did manage to cut himself free, but he handed him the knife anyway.

Tony was thus very surprised a moment later, when Richard lunged forward and dug the knife deep into his belly and ripped it upward. Tony tried to get away from him, but Richard grabbed hold of his belt and held him in place and stabbed him deeply again. Tony had gotten shot once—this felt just as bad as that. In fact it felt worse, because, unlike the bullet that had hit him, this pain was moving through his body as Richard swept the knife through his bowels.

Richard finally let go of him. With blood now streaming down the front of his ripped-up shirt, Tony staggered back and gaped at Richard.

"What, what . . . what'd you stab me for, man?" He gripped his belly. It felt as if his intestines were spilling out of him, but they weren't.

While Tony slumped down to the floor in a pool of blood, Richard Penderson cut his ankles free from the legs of the chair and got to his feet. With his legs wobbling, he strode forward towards Tony and knelt beside him.

"Why? Why, man?" Tony gasped. He knew he was dying, but why the hell had this man he'd just freed attacked him?

"I'm sorry, man, but we can't call the police," Richard said with a frown. His voice was still weak, but he had a cold and ruthless look in his eyes. He gestured around them with his knife, the motion making him grimace in pain due to the stiffness in his arms. "This mansion of mine has too many secrets that I need to keep hidden." Then he burst into loud laughter. "And besides, Candice was right—*I did* fucking try to kill her. I just never thought that that sadistic bitch Mrs. Pain would betray me and take my wife's side. Yeah, I was fucking the big-titted bitch too, but I guess she figured Candice would be more receptive to her mad idea of torturing everyone she could catch."

Tony was fighting to keep his eyes open. He felt cold like he'd gotten lost in a blizzard in deep winter. His hands and feet were all numb. He felt like he was about to go to sleep for a long, long time.

Yeah, I'm a damn fool, he told himself as the cold threaded itself through him and darkness ate up the light at the edge of his vision. *I should've trusted Maryanne and not come here. So she wasn't cheating on me? Damn!*

But Richard Penderson was now grinning down at him; and the mutilated man's eyes now seemed somewhat crazed to Tony, as if his incarceration in here had driven him mad.

"Oh, I'm going to teach Candice to keep me down here and try to make me sign over all my property to her and her daughter before she makes me disappear," he said. "By the time I'm done with her, she'll be looking like a sideshow freak."

Tony's eyes shut then, but he felt Richard slap his face so he opened them again.

"Thanks for freeing me," Richard told him, waving the bloody knife in his face. "But now there's one more thing I need from you."

"What's that?" Tony managed to gasp. Then he howled in pain when Richard stabbed him in the gut with his knife again. Then Richard bent over him and the intense agony of the man's knife slicing away at his guts completely revived him for a while. Tony lay there gasping and wondering what the madman was doing to him now.

Finally, Richard Penderson straightened up again. With blood streaming down his arms he held out a large chunk of severed meat to Tony. The surface of the meat had a smooth purple texture that Tony thought he recognized.

"It's part of your liver," Richard explained to him. "They haven't been feeding me too well down here and I need some food in me to give me strength before I go upstairs to confront my wife and her witchy friends."

And then while Tony gaped in disbelief both at what he was seeing and what he was hearing, the man he'd just rescued lifted the chunk of raw liver to his mouth and took a large bite of it. Then he began chewing it, with the blood from the meat squirting out of the gaps where his teeth had been pulled.

"Yes, very tasty," Richard said between bites, reaching up and brushing maggots off of his exposed skull. "I feel stronger already."

Tony died just as Richard finished eating that first lump of his liver and dug into him with the knife for another.

He was glad to escape the madness he'd discovered here in the mansion.

CHAPTER 29

Megan

The silence in the cell helped Megan harness her mental resources. She forced all the horrible images she'd watched on the now dead TV to the back of her mind, and those that persisted in harassing her she converted to fuel for her determination to survive her current nightmare.

The last image she'd seen as she'd dashed forward to sever the TV's power cord—of a blood-splattered Mrs. Pain laughing maniacally while slamming her axe against the captive father's remaining arm—seemed indelibly burnt into her mind, as if it would haunt her forever.

But it'll only be able to haunt me if I survive tonight! Megan coldly told herself.

Then she heard footsteps approaching. She instantly felt fear: *It'll be just me against the three of them. Can I do this? Can I really do this?*

The cell door opened and she had no more time for worry or contemplation.

Mrs. Pain walked in and stepped aside from the door. Her two goons waited outside, visible to Megan through the doorway.

"Alright, girl, get off the bed," Mrs. Pain said languidly, but with a flushed look on her face as if she was close to orgasm; her body was as red as if she had bathed in blood. "Time to go meet your maker."

Megan didn't move from her position on the bed, which was up by the headboard, with her legs pulled up to her chest. "Why don't you come and get me?" she shot back with a smirk on her face. "You're nothing but a naked bully, bitch." She felt intense fear, but this was no time to show it.

Mrs. Pain's expression hardened. "Oh, we'll see how tough you are once we get you upstairs." Then she rolled her eyes and gestured out to the two men in the corridor. "Get her, boys."

The two men entered the cell and made for Megan.

From Megan's perspective, this was a whole lot better. True, both men dwarfed her in size, which was very intimidating, but they also both seemed to be normal thugs, not insane sadists like their female boss. They also hadn't featured in any of Mrs. Pain's videos, but Megan didn't think they would be adverse to hurting her badly if Mrs. Pain ordered them to.

So the trick was to strike first.

Once the first of the goons reached the bed, Megan uncoiled like a spring. She jerked her knife out from her jacket and struck like a snake.

The men were completely taken by surprise.

Aiming as precisely as she could, Megan slashed her knife at the neck of the nearer man. The glittering blade entered his throat with seemingly no resistance, and then she instinctively jerked it sideways to do the most damage. The man's neck opened up like a zipper, squirting blood all over her, but Megan could care less about that.

By the time he fell forward, she was already leaping down off the bed and lunging at the second goon.

This man had seen the knife and he threw up his hands to shield his neck, but she had different intentions anyway. Holding the knife tightly in both hands, she dug it into the left side of the man's muscular belly and dragged it hard right.

The goon howled as the razor-sharp ceremonial knife (which had clearly been intended to slit the throats of innocents) 'unzipped' his belly too, revealing his wet and gleaming intestines.

The man screamed again in agony and grasped at his belly as his guts spilled out of him.

Behind her the first man was already dead and now this one was incapacitated too, but Megan knew her danger was far from over. She still had Mrs. Pain to contend with; and the bald woman frightened her much more than the goons did.

And yes, as quick as lightning, Mrs. Pain was already stepping around the wounded man's side.

But Megan somehow managed to move even faster than lightning. She shoved the wounded man at Mrs. Pain, flung a single glance sideways and saw that her plan had worked and that the two of them had fallen to the floor together, and then, leaping over Mrs. Pain's hands as they clutched at her, she ran out of the cell.

"Come back in here!" Mrs. Pain, her eyes mirrors of frustrated rage, yelled at her as she slammed the cell door shut and then locked it.

"Yeah, right," Megan replied under her breath. "If I did that I'd be as wrong in the head as you are."

And then she turned and ran off.

***

She quickly realized that she had no idea which way to go. And that was odd because it really shouldn't be rocket science to leave here. But apparently, in her haste while fleeing the cell she'd gotten her bearings mixed up and had headed the wrong way down the passageway, and while searching in a panic for the exit she'd gotten completely turned around.

She stood there, wiping her bloody hands clean on her jeans while trying to get her bearing right.

This is a basement, not a maze, for crying out loud! All I need to find are the stairs to the ground floor. Then I'll break a window and be out of this damned place.

She was very aware that time was of the essence to make her getaway. In the corridor beside her she thought she heard Mrs. Pain thumping on the door of her cell.

Yes, Megan had somehow arrived back near her point of departure. And from here, standing at the right end of the turnoff on which her former cell was housed, at its junction with one of the two corridors that ran the length of the basement, she could see just one stairwell, and this one was situated almost in the middle of the corridor; it definitely wasn't the one she'd earlier been brought down.

"Calm down, just calm down—the exit must be down the other corridor," she told herself, turning away from the stairwell and returning her attention to the turnoff. 'I'll just hurry back and—"

She froze and backpedalled out of sight in the longer corridor. "Who the hell is that?"

She would have doubted she'd seen anyone at all, would have written the person off as a merely a hallucination caused by her current terror, but she could clearly hear heavy breathing coming from the turnoff.

After taking a deep breath to calm herself, she pressed her body tight against the wall and dared to peek into the corridor again.

Oh no, she hadn't been hallucinating.

A naked and bloody man, who looked like he'd recently been one of Mrs. Pain's victims, was standing at the other end of the turnoff. Megan could clearly see the set of wet red footprints that trailed his progress along the corridor.

The man had been badly slashed up all over and his mouth and face were covered with blood. But worst of all, he appeared to have been scalped. From what she could see of him as he stood there, his head was a festering mess, the stink of which reached her and tickled her nostrils.

But the most bothersome thing about the man was the gleaming machete he was gripping in his right hand. His other hand seemed to be clutching a dripping piece of purple meat; at least that's what it looked like to Megan.

The man hovered there at the end of the turnoff for about fifteen seconds. (She now recalled seeing a man being scalped in one of the first enter*pain*ment videos she'd watched, but couldn't tell if it was this same man.) She couldn't make out his face clearly, but he seemed indecisive, as if he was trying to make up his mind about something.

Then she remembered the stairwell behind her, and understood why the man was standing there. She saw now that the man's bloody footprints in the turnoff began at a door almost opposite the cell she'd been held in. From the direction of those footprints, it looked as if the man had first walked from that door to the end of the corridor and then, like herself confused about his directions, had turned around again.

He hasn't noticed me, but he's thinking of climbing these stairs behind me. Dammit, I hope he doesn't decide to come over here!

If the mutilated man walked back into the turnoff, she would have no choice but to head down the corridor away from where she thought the basement's exit was, wait until he'd climbed the stairwell, and then when he was out of sight, return and cross to the other corridor to resume her flight. That would take longer, but this man was a complication she'd didn't need. She nixed the option of waiting and ambushing him—now that she was on her way to freedom, she saw no need to take unnecessary risks.

This scalped and badly mutilated man was an unknown factor to Megan and despite her recent display of bravery and her victory over Mrs. Pain and her goons, she figured it would be best to avoid him if she could.

But the man didn't head her way, instead he shook his head in apparent angry frustration and then turned and shambled off out of sight, leaving more red footprints in his wake.

Megan scowled. *Hey, you, I was planning to head over there to look for the basement exit!*

It was only after he had vanished from view that Megan realized that it would have been more to her advantage had he had crossed towards her to use the stairwell. Because now he was headed in the same direction that she wanted to go. And since he was ahead of her, he could easily ambush her.

Then, shaking her head, she corrected that last detail: *No, he can't possibly ambush me, not with the way he's leaving those telltale bloody footprints everywhere.*

Still, Megan did not think it wise to set off after him. She did look down at her knife and consider taking the mutilated man on. But, *No, he looks even more desperate than I do,* she finally decided.

Then after kicking the wall in disgust at this new twist of bad luck, she walked the short distance to the nearby stairwell and began climbing it.

I'll just see where this staircase leads to.

One flight up she found no exit, just a bare brick wall where she had expected the door from the landing to be.

Megan sighed. She didn't feel she should return to the basement, so she kept climbing.

She had better luck at the second floor landing. Here she found an arched exit with a gate, and the gate was wide open. And here the stairwell connected directly to a passageway.

Megan stepped into the passageway and began walking.

I wonder where this one leads, 'cos it seems really long, she thought after a while.

Indeed the corridor was a very long one. For a while it ran along the wall of the house—Megan could tell this from the horizontal slits in its upper half that let in air and diffused moonlight—but then the corridor made a sharp right turn and bent into the building.

And suddenly, Megan arrived at a dead end. The weak moonlight behind her revealed that she was facing a black wall.

What? she gasped. *What the . . . ?*

She was about to start weeping tears of frustration at having her escape thwarted again, when she realized that the 'dead end' ahead of her was actually just a thick black curtain and that she could hear voices on its other side.

Ooops, I'm back upstairs at the summoning room, she realized in shock.

She hurried forward to see what was going on.

CHAPTER 30

Bloodbath

Megan didn't feel safe at all in her current place of concealment.

She suspected that this particular stairwell and corridor she'd used were probably used to bring people up from the basement to be sacrificed. But it was also a long way back to the basement from here, much longer than it had taken to arrive there when she'd been led through the house as a captive, and so she figured this route would only be used if the homeowners wanted to keep their actions hidden from their guests or servants, for instance. And tonight that clearly wasn't the case.

But still, once she was discovered to be missing it was merely a question of time before someone thought of searching this secret corridor for her.

But she just as clearly couldn't return to the basement. So she had to exit through here.

And this time I'm armed. But me against five women? Not good odds, but Mrs. Pain is really the only one of them who scares me and until these ladies up here cotton on to the fact that she's trapped downstairs in the basement, I've a good chance of making it past them.

She carefully pulled aside the dark curtain for a look. The marble table was directly ahead of her and the women were joking and laughing. Maryanne wasn't with them though.

Megan ducked back into cover when Candice glanced her way, and then after a short wait she peeked out again.

"You're no lady, Donna, that's for certain," Josie was saying, looking just as stressed as on the previous times when Megan had seen her. Her blonde hair was as mussed up as if she'd been trying to pull it out by its roots.

"Oh, I'm a lady, Josie," Donna retorted. "You, you're just a woman."

"What's the difference?" Lucy asked, leaning towards Donna.

"A *lay-dee*," Donna explained sweetly, "is a woman who gets laid. Which I do regularly. And I get paid to get laid too."

All the women burst into laughter and it was now that Megan realized that there was an additional, male voice laughing along with them. She slid the cloth a little farther aside and saw the man's form, just the back of his head.

"Hey, what's keeping Mrs. Pain?" the man asked. "She should have been back with the girl by now."

Megan recognized the man's voice.

Hey, isn't that John Miller? I thought they were gonna kill him, and now they're all laughing like they're best friends. What exactly is going on in this crazy house? 'The girl' must mean me. What do they want me for?

But Megan never got an answer to that question. She was still peeking around the edge of the black curtain, and wondering how they had managed to shift that giant rock in the corner aside to open the doorway over there, and where they'd kept the rock afterwards, when a frenzied and bloody form burst in through the door of the summoning room.

Then breathing heavily, the bloody form settled down and glared at the assembled women.

It's the wounded guy from downstairs! Megan realized, seeing clearly now how horribly mutilated the man's body actually was. Mrs. Pain (who else could it possibly be?) had done a total number on him. In addition to losing a large portion of his scalp and his left ear, half of his teeth seemed to have been pulled out. She could hardly believe the fact that there were maggots tunneling through the flesh that remained on his head.

And then Megan made an even more shocking connection: *Hey, isn't this Candice's husband Richard—the man whose photo is hanging on the wall of the study down the hall?*

"Richard!" Candice yelped on seeing the frightening man. "What are you doing up here?"

"Is this is your husband, Candice?" Josie asked in horror.

"What happened to him?" Lucy added in equal horror. "Did he piss off everyone in Panama?"

"He looks like he raped Mrs. Pain and then she got even with him," Donna said.

"He has suffered a lot of pain," John Miller explained to the exes in a calm voice. "And now, understandably, he wants revenge on all four of you for that pain."

Lucy, Josie and Donna turned and gaped at John.

"But-but-but we had nothing to do with him looking like that!" Lucy gasped in a desperate voice, as, with a crazed look on his face and murder beaming from his eyes, Richard Penderson raised his machete high and headed for them.

"Now, Richard, don't you dare do anything foolish in here!" Candice shrieked at her husband, leaping to her feet and shoving away her chair.

But Richard Penderson was already swinging his machete at them. Candice was safely out of his reach for the moment, so instead he struck out at Josie before she too could escape from him. Josie had just risen from her seat when the machete sliced right through her head. Half of Josie's skull landed on the table and spun like a top, while she herself wobbled in place for a few seconds before slumping down dead.

"And now for you three bitches!" Richard yelled, brandishing his bloody machete at Candice, Lucy and Donna.

The three women shrieked like one woman with three voices.

***

Though frightened and perplexed by this sudden outburst of violent bloodshed, Megan meanwhile had troubles of her own. She was tempted to simply turn right around and flee back downstairs again; but she thought she heard voices behind her, out in the corridor.

Maybe I'm imagining them, or maybe I'm not, but I'd rather take my chances with this crazy guy up here, than go back down to the basement and chance running into Mrs. Pain in the state of mind she's certain to be in after my escape from her and her goons. And this time she's sure to be armed too. She might even have a shotgun.

Megan also considered how very long the corridor behind her was and the fact that there were no exits along it.

If I get trapped in the corridor, I'll be trapped, period.

Thinking about the corridor's length also helped her understand why, when she had earlier encountered him down in the basement, Richard hadn't crossed the corridor towards her to climb the stairwell that had brought her here.

Oh, I get it now! It's his house, so he knows about that gate on the second floor. I think he wasn't sure if it was locked or not; and if he'd found it locked, he would then have had to descend the stairs again and make the same journey through the house to get here. And even if the gate hadn't been locked, it's a much longer trip this way, and with the way he's all sliced up, the guy must have wanted to conserve his energy for this big showdown.

Seeing as retracing her steps to the basement was completely out of the question, Megan quickly scanned the summoning room, looking for an alternative way out of danger. And she quickly found one:

Hey, that door over there where the rock used to be. That has to lead to somewhere else in the house. All I have to do is sneak across to it while no one's watching and I'll be out of here, and hopefully this nightmare will be over.

But she would need to wait a little for a good opportunity, as Richard Penderson was now advancing on the three surviving exes.

And so Megan, gripping her knife so tightly that it felt like a part of her body, slipped fully into the summoning room and crouched out of sight behind John Miller's chair, awaiting her chance to dash to safety.

***

Candice had escaped from her husband with her ceremonial knife in hand, and now, with him blocking off the chamber's main exit, she had no choice but to confront him.

Once up on her feet, Lucy had run around the table to stand behind Candice, almost bowling Megan over in her haste. Lucy's abrupt flight had been so panicked that she had not even paused to see whom she'd hit on her way to safety.

Megan was doing her best to assess the situation calmly, she was constantly turning left and right behind John Miller's chair and straightening up a little for a few moments to peek around it and over the tabletop before ducking back down again.

She was trying to pick the right moment to run for the door in the corner that she intended to escape through. She would have loved to throw caution to the wind and run for it now, but to reach it she would first have to make a detour around a low stone table that projected well out from the wall, and on which stood the large metal sculpture of the witchy woman that she had noticed earlier when the goons had brought her in here. Making that detour would bring Megan within easy reach of Candice and Lucy; but most importantly Candice, who was holding a ceremonial knife very much like her own.

Megan thought that the reason why Candice and Lucy didn't simply turn and run away through that door themselves was because then they would have the madman at their backs and wouldn't be able to stop him hacking away at them.

But Donna, who had been sitting on Candice's immediate right, and who for that reason was still on the other side of the table from her co-exes, and who could possibly have made it safely to the summoning room's main entrance and escaped, had made no attempt to flee either. Donna was out of her chair, but was crouching by the table with her handbag in hand. She was also popping several colored pills into her mouth.

Alright no, Megan agreed after a quick peek, *Richard has to move further into the room before Donna has a surefire chance of getting away. And as far as I can see, he's not moving—he really wants to kill them all.* She gave him a quick once over. *With the way he's been cut up like that, I can't blame him for being completely pissed off at them all. But, ouch!—dude's gonna need one hell of a hair transplant—his skull is visible beneath that mess of rotting meat and grubs on his head.*

To Megan's mind, the weirdest thing of all about this situation, was how the naked man in the chair—John Miller—had so far shown no reaction to Josie's murder. In fact, as Megan watched Richard and Candice warily circle one another, she was certain she heard John Miller chuckle to himself. And then she heard him sucking and chewing on something.

What on earth is he eating at this time?

Megan had intended to make her break for the doorway then, but after a quick peek around John's chair revealed that he was eating Josie's brains out of the part of her head that had fallen on the table, she felt petrified. She sank down to her knees and began hyperventilating. Even after watching all those 'enter*pain*ment' videos that Mrs. Pain had played to her in her cell, seeing the seated man dig Josie's brains from her skull cap and slurp them into his mouth was

191

the most horrifying thing Megan had ever seen. She really needed time to recover from that.

Meanwhile, Richard and Candice had their deadly marital showdown. Each spouse was clearly wary of the other; and twice Richard leapt back as his wife swiped at him with her dagger, which she seemed rather expert at using.

But then, Candice, seeing she'd got Richard on the back foot, lunged at him, intending to stab him in the throat. But he had merely pretended to retreat from her to draw her in and make her lower her guard. By the time Candice understood this and began retreating herself, Richard's machete was already slicing into the side of her neck.

Candice's head separated from her body and flew sideways. Her body fell back against Lucy, who had been hiding behind her.

Lucy screamed in fright when Candice's blood squirted up all over her face, and then she fainted. She slumped against the projecting table, and by so doing once more prevented Megan from fleeing.

Megan cursed her bad luck. *What the hell is the matter tonight? I simply wanna leave this damned mansion! But each time I try to, something or someone gets in my way. Trying to leave this place is worse than trying to check out of the Hotel California!*

She glanced nervously over at the black curtain which hid the doorway through which she had arrived here. *Maybe I should just head back down—* She checked herself. *Oh no, screw that. I'm not handing myself over to Mrs. Pain on a silver platter. I don't—*

"Thank God I brought along my health insurance," Donna said behind her, interrupting her thoughts.

Health insurance? What health insurance? She spun around and saw that Donna had just pulled a small gun out of her handbag.

But Donna also looked confused. "What the hell's wrong with this freakin' thing?" she was asking herself. Then she looked up and seemed to notice Megan for the first time. "Hey, homegirl, I can't get this fucker to work," she whispered to her.

Megan noticed the distracted look in Donna's eyes and knew she was stoned. She was possibly high on pills, though the room also had a faint reek of pot.

"I think you need to cock it first," she quickly explained. "Try pulling back the slide like they do in the movies."

"Oh yeah, cock," Donna muttered. "Now there's something I truly understand."

Megan relaxed a little. *Oh goody, so Donna has a gun. In our current situation that's a great equalizer. I just hope she shoots the right person with it.*

***

The reason why Megan and Donna could hold their conversation amidst the ensuing bloodshed was because something really weird was happening now.

After having dispatched Candice to the great beyond, Richard Penderson had been walking towards the slumped Lucy to kill her too, when John Miller had suddenly gotten to his feet and walked towards him.

Richard had paused in his stride and raised his machete to hack at John, but then John had gestured to him and said in an calm voice, "Don't be an idiot, man. You know who I am. Let me pass. I just wanna feed on your wife's body. You can kill them all if you like and I'll dispose of all the evidence for you."

A brief flare of recognition flashed in Richard's eyes then and he smiled and stepped aside to let the other man pass. He turned and watched John Miller kneel down beside Candice's headless corpse and seemingly bury his entire head in her belly.

***

Donna and Megan saw this too. The sight made Donna drop her gun and she scrambled to pick it up again.

"Yeah, that sure is a great way to dispose of the evidence," Richard nodded to himself. "Alright, back to killing you evil torturing bitches."

On the floor by the table, Lucy was just waking up from her faint, blinking her eyes weakly and trying to remember who she was and where she was. With his machete raised to deal death, Richard stepped towards her again, but then Donna leapt up from her crouch.

"Hey, motherfucker, you ain't killing shit!" Donna yelled at him while pulling the trigger.

Megan prayed that Donna had remembered to cock the gun first.

It appeared she had: her first shot caught Richard Penderson in the thigh, making him stagger back and almost drop his machete. Donna fired at him again, but either she wasn't used to firing guns, or she was simply too stoned to shoot straight, because her second shot went

193

wildly to Richard's left and instead struck the metal sculpture on the table.

Megan gasped as the bullet ricocheted past her head, practically parting her hair; that was how close it had been.

Alright, I've hung around here long enough! Donna's gonna kill me if Candice's husband doesn't!

She leapt to her feet and ran. Richard was still examining his shot thigh and with Lucy still lying flat on the floor, all Megan had to do was leap over her and she was at the doorway, which she now noticed in passing had a glossy white frame, as if it was freshly painted.

***

Megan hurried through the doorway, but instead of finding herself in a corridor or in a second-floor room with a window she could leap down from, instead she seemed to be . . . nowhere.

She was inside a dark space with no walls that she could see. The darkness was walls around her and she also had the impression of intense heat beyond it.

She glanced back. The summoning room shimmered beyond the opening like a reflection in a mirror. Lucy was staggering to her feet and looked scared out of her wits, while Donna was firing at Richard again, but he'd now ducked down in a corner and she missed. Josie's legs were visible beneath the end of the table.

Megan was standing out of position to see John Miller eating Candice, which she was grateful for.

Then she turned around again to face the darkness that hemmed her in on three sides.

Oh shoot, what the hell is going on now? Where the hell am I?

And now 'Hell' seemed to be an appropriate word. All around her Megan could hear people screaming, multitudes yelling in anguish at the top of their lungs. And along with the screams of all these unseen people, she heard even louder laughter, from voices so loud and deep that they seemed to belong to giants. And once more, she had the impression of inferno-level heat beyond the blackness.

I've gotta get out of here! she thought in dismay. *This door leads straight to Hell!*

It was an impossible truth, but also an undeniable one. And while she was still thinking this, a force grabbed her—it felt like a giant hand picking her up—grabbed her around the midriff, lifted her well off her feet and then flung her out of the black space.

And as it flung her out, she heard someone laugh and cackle: "Get lost, woman, you've no business being in here."

***

Megan flew back out of the portal as if launched on a jet of wind. After traveling several yards in midair, she skidded across the top of the marble summoning table and then crashed down on its other side.

She lay there stunned by the shock of her impact with the floor. A glance back at the door from beneath the table revealed that it had now vanished. The rock with the pentagram carved on it was now back in place in its original corner.

What the . . . ? Megan wondered. *What . . .?*

However, this was no time to wonder. The deadly contest still raged in the room. Megan staggered back up to her feet.

Then she yelled at Donna, "Look out!"

Donna had been staring at Megan in surprise. And that distraction had just cost her. Seeing and seizing his opportunity, Richard leaned over the table and slashed down at Donna's gun arm. Donna howled as her hand came off at the wrist. She spun towards Megan and some of her spurting blood splashed Megan in the face. Richard swung at her again, but Donna backed away from him, clutching her gushing stump and moaning. She fell down and Megan leapt over her and ran for the room's main entrance.

But now she found her way blocked by John Miller. And the man was irate.

"Oh no, you're not leaving here alive, you little fool!" he growled at her. "You've gone and ruined everything for me!"

Megan had no idea what he meant by that, but she knew he meant business. His head was covered with blood and some of Candice's flesh was stuck to his face. Peeking behind him she could see that large portions of Candice's corpse were missing now—including her bones—gone like they'd vanished into thin air.

Looking back at John Miller, who was wiping blood from his mouth with the back of his hand, Megan now remembered that she had a knife and could defend herself. But then she realized she'd lost the knife. The loss had to have happened when she'd been flung out of . . . out of Hell?.

John advanced on her and she retreated from him and desperately scanned the floor for Donna's dropped gun. Of course the gun would still be attached to Donna's hand but that couldn't be helped. But Megan couldn't see either the severed hand or the gun it held. Donna herself was out of sight beneath the table, still moaning in pain, but her moans were weak, as if she was slowly bleeding to death.

On the other side of the table Richard was bent over and was hacking at Donna's exposed legs with his machete, but then Lucy sneaked up behind him and slammed a large vase down on his head. The vase shattered and both of them collapsed out of sight and then Megan heard Lucy shrieking "You asshole! You asshole!" in rage as she pummeled him with her fists.

But none of that helped Megan as John Miller was still advancing on her.

And then Megan made it past the end of the table and her back hit the wall.

Oops, I'm done for! she thought a moment later when John Miller grabbed her by the throat.

But even though his grip around her neck seemed one of steel, John Miller didn't seem to be himself any more. His form was altering, changing from that of a man into something she didn't understand.

John seemed to be turning into jelly. The flesh color was leeching out of his skin by the second and was being replaced by a sickly and sticky transparence.

"You've ruined everything, you bitch!" the jelly man moaned at her as his body transformed and then also began evaporating. "Humans aren't permitted into the demon realms while I'm incarnated out here!"

"Whatever, dude," Megan gasped weakly and prized his now weakened fingers off of her throat. "Just get the heck away from me!"

She kicked the evaporating thing that had been John Miller away from her. It hit the chair it had been sitting on and fragmented into pieces that slid to the floor and skidded across the tabletop.

Megan felt intense relief as she watched the chunks of jelly evaporate into nothing.

But then, just when she thought she was out of the woods, she both heard a gunshot and felt a stabbing pain in her belly.

Oh, not now! she gasped, looking down at herself and seeing the blood leaking through her tee shirt. The pain was so intense that she slid to the ground by the wall, but not before looking up to see who had shot her.

She had been shot by Lucy. Lucy was holding Donna's pistol and was glaring at her. Lucy seemed to be even more angry with her than 'John Miller' had been.

"You stupid, stupid fool, you've gone and ruined everything for us," Lucy said, stepping forward to stand over Megan and pointing the gun in her face. With blood splashed all over her head, Lucy was no longer the fashionable 'painting-perfect' beauty that Megan had known. Now she looked totally grotesque and her anger made her seem even more ugly.

"I wish you people would stop saying that," Megan told Lucy, gesturing around weakly at the bodies strewn across the room. "None of this bloodbath is my fault."

Lucy shook her head. "No, you stupid bitch, this is all your damn fault. If you'd just listened to me last night and gone away none of this mess would have happened, would it? But no, you had to be a smartass and insist on following me here and now see what you've caused? Your nosiness has just cost each of us five million dollars!"

Megan let Lucy rant. She didn't agree with her. The way Megan saw it, Richard was clearly to blame for all the deaths and any financial losses; he'd been the one who'd done all the killing before Lucy had knocked him out with the vase. But Megan was in too much pain to argue with Lucy. And besides, Lucy still had the gun pointed at her face.

"And what the hell did you do to Mrs. Pain?" Lucy raged on, while her motions billowed her silk robe about her body. Then she kicked Megan hard in the shin. "Answer me! I know you did something to her, because when you stepped over me a short while ago you had a bloody knife in your hand! That was Mrs. Pain's blood, wasn't it, you nasty little bitch?"

"No, it wasn't hers," Megan gasped weakly. "Listen, this is what happened—"

But Lucy was past listening to her. "Yes, Candice was right to want to kill you," she said, stepping back from Megan and taking careful aim at her face. "You're definitely not worth five million dollars to me."

Megan assumed she was going to die then. There seemed no way she could avoid losing her life.

But right before Lucy fired, Richard Penderson surged up from the floor and hacked her in the head with his machete.

He caught Lucy in the side of her face. Blood spurted from Lucy's face and the machete strike meant that as she pulled the trigger, she spun away from Megan, just enough that her shot went wide of Megan's head and zipped away through the curtain that covered the secret corridor entrance. Megan heard the slug zinging off stone walls behind her.

Richard jerked the blade of the machete out of Lucy's head. Lucy immediately slumped to the floor and began twitching.

Megan stared up at Richard. The man looked even worse after Lucy's dramatic assault on him. Lucy seemed to have broken his nose. Blood streamed from his nostrils as he stepped towards her.

Worse yet, from Megan's point of view, Richard Penderson had a completely crazed look in his eyes; a totally pissed off look that told her he clearly thought she was one of the women who had schemed against him and kept him captive in the basement and had him mutilated.

Can tonight possibly get any worse for me? Megan thought dryly as the madman came closer and smiled down at her. Sweat ran from her armpits and her breasts felt like they were glued to her tee shirt. And the bullet in her gut burnt like fire. *Aw heck, here I am saved from a bullet in the face just 'cos this guy wants to hack me to death instead.* She rolled her eyes heavenward. *You know, God, if you're so interested in collecting me tonight I'd have preferred to have been shot dead by Lucy!*

Richard lifted the machete up over his head to strike her and she tensed in anticipation, readying herself for its first cut, because for certain, this was going to hurt a whole lot.

And then, as if Megan was watching a replay of what had just transpired between Richard and Lucy, Donna rose up from beneath the table with one of the ceremonial daggers clutched in her remaining, left, hand; Megan thought the dagger was hers, she didn't recall Candice's knife being bloody.

Donna looked terrible; the skin and flesh of her legs hung in ribbons where Richard had hacked at them. Her black robe was a tatter of bloody rags fluttering around her body. But she had managed to tighten a cord—it looked like the strap of her handbag—around the stump of her severed right wrist to stop the bleeding.

"You crazy motherfucker!" she growled in a weak voice as she lunged at Richard. "Look what you've done to me! How am I supposed to earn a living without a hot body?"

Now alerted to her presence behind him, Richard forgot about killing Megan and spun around to attack Donna instead.

Immediately he was facing her, Donna stabbed him in the belly, and then she ran him into the side of the table, with the force of the impact making him drop his machete. Then she stabbed Richard deeply again in the side; and then they both collapsed to the floor together.

Neither of them got to their feet again. Richard lay there, bleeding out and looking perplexed, while Donna gave a long last gasp and died with a stoned smile on her face.

Megan just gaped. Then she whistled in relief.

I'm good now, right? All I need to do is get up and I can walk away from this mess before the cops arrive.

But she wasn't about going anywhere. Her wound hurt too much for her to move. She didn't think she was bleeding to death, but maybe it would have been better if she had been, because now, in the silence that filled the room along with the mass of corpses, she could hear footsteps approaching along the main corridor.

Oh shit, not Mrs. Pain! Not now!

She began desperately looking around for the gun that Lucy had shot her with.

Blood streaming from his mouth, Richard glared at her in anger. From where he lay on the floor, he grabbed up his machete again and weakly tried to slash her legs with it, but she kicked him hard in the head and he fell back limp and motionless. She had either killed him outright or just knocked him unconscious, she had no time to find out which.

Where the hell is that damn gun?

She couldn't find it. But then she leaned back against the wall and relaxed anyway.

It hadn't been Mrs. Pain on the way at all. Dave and Ron were staring into the summoning room in shock.

"Dude, what the hell happened in here?" Ron asked.

"Good thing we called the cops when the shooting began, but what the . . . everyone seems to be dead."

"Hey, Dave!" Megan called out weakly. "Dave, over here!"

The two cooks saw her and ran over to her side.

Dave crouched down beside her. "Meg, what are you doing here?" he asked in a confused voice.

"I followed Lucy here and . . . Ouch!" A burst of pain ripped through her belly and she shut up.

Dave nodded and then seemed to grow even more confused. "Yeah, okay. I remember promising you that I'd send your money over on Wednesday . . . But I don't know what happened. I remember coming here with Lucy on Tuesday night but nothing after that. Hey, Lucy ain't dead too, is she?"

Then Dave saw his older sister lying motionless on the other side of Donna. He left Megan's side and went over to Lucy. He knelt beside her and lifted her up to his chest and rocked her, her blood smearing all over him as she swung motionless in his grasp.

"Lucy, Lucy, oh shit!" Dave wept as he rocked her. Then between bouts of crying he gazed at Megan. "What exactly happened in here?"

Megan shook her head. "Guys, you really don't wanna know that."

"But we do, we really do," Ron replied her, crouching beside her and gesturing around the corpse-filled room. "Neither of us can remember anything that happened after Tuesday—it's like there's a blank space in our minds and . . ."

They all heard the sound of police sirens outside then and Ron gestured in the direction of the sounds. "And then we heard shooting upstairs and called the cops and . . ."

Megan relaxed. *Oh yes, I'm really safe now.*

". . . But what Dave and I can't understand," Ron went on, "is how three whole days seemed to have slipped past us without us remembering a thing about them."

Megan looked over at Dave.

He looked up from rocking Lucy and weeping and said, "Yeah, I was gonna wire your money to you on Wednesday like I'd promised, but on Tuesday night I came over here . . . and then 'Boom!' just like that it's now Friday night . . . no, it's now early Saturday morning, and I don't know what happened between then and now."

Megan figured that the spell Candice had cast on the two cooks had worn off immediately she died.

Peering beneath the table, she looked over at Candice's remains. Large portions of the matriarch's body seemed to have been dissolved away by acid and her severed head was nowhere in sight either. What was left of her looked so horrible that Megan turned away in disgust.

She stared instead at Josie, who was missing half of her head, and then closer to her, at both one-handed Donna and at Lucy who had a deep red trench cut into her face. And of course, Richard lay beneath Donna with his blood soaking into the red rug.

Yeah, what really happened in here? she asked herself. *What was all that crazy stuff with John Miller? What was that all about?*

Then she realized that Dave and Ron were still waiting for her reply.

"Trust me, guys, in your case ignorance truly *is* bliss," she told the two perplexed men as the sound of police sirens halted against the mansion's walls. "Just let the boys in blue figure everything out."

Then she fell silent and waited patiently for the paramedics.

CHAPTER 31

Meet the Ex: Famous Last Words

Except for Candice, whose inherent ruthlessness had unfortunately made her very receptive to her second husband's occult and sadistic interests, none of John Miller's wives were naturally evil women.

There also wasn't any of them who hadn't been head over heels in love with John when she'd married him. Even Donna, who found it impossible to keep her thighs shut once there were men nearby, had loved John in her own unfaithful way.

But there are situations in life that drive everyone over the edge. In some cases, little things; in others giant things.

And John Miller had unfortunately managed to trigger off that kind of adverse reaction in these five women, and push four of them far beyond the boundaries of what they normally considered right and wrong behavior.

See, sometimes you don't even need a butterfly to get the butterfly effect.

Who was to blame in the end for what happened? John or his exes? Folks, the jury will be out on that judgment for a long, long time to come.

CHAPTER 32

Megan, Anderson & Futana

The two Boston detectives who visited Megan in her hospital room in the Raynham Outlook Clinic three days later seemed to be a mismatched pair.

The senior of the two detectives, Tom Anderson, was a burly and grizzled middle-aged man who looked as cold as ice. His partner, Laurie Futana was a woman who seemed unsuitable for police work of any kind. Her figure and looks were such that she could have made a fantastic career either strutting a catwalk somewhere or performing onscreen in any number of Hollywood blockbusters.

Tom Anderson and Laurie Futana. These were the pair who came to ask Megan the questions she had been dreading answering. After the nurse showed them into her hospital room and adjusted her bed to a half-sitting position, they sat beside her and smiled at her.

Megan frowned back at them. She was well on her way to recovery now and her prescription of painkillers meant she wasn't in much discomfort, but she was wary of getting too deeply involved in the police investigation. She folded her arms over her bandaged midriff and attempted to look both tough and nonchalant.

But she discovered she needn't have worried. Though Tom Anderson had an unpleasant look to him, in reality he was easy enough to get along with, as was his beautiful partner.

And the detectives quickly made it plain to Megan that they weren't about accusing her of any wrongdoing. All they wanted to know was exactly what had transpired in the Penderson mansion on that bloody Friday night.

They also wanted to know what had happened to the kidnaped John Miller. Along with lots of CCTV footage of John in his basement cell, they had also found John's clothes and ID in another of the basement rooms; and random splashes of his blood had been found on top of the summoning room's marble table. But where was he?

"Okay now, Miss Kemp, before coming to see you, we've of course already interviewed the two guys who called us out to the mansion," Detective Anderson explained. "The problem is, neither of them can remember a thing that happened after Tuesday night."

"And they aren't lying either," Detective Futana added in her pleasant voice. "We've run series of lie detector tests on the pair; and the results confirm that they're both telling the truth. Lucy Lowry drove her brother over to the Penderson mansion on Tuesday night and Ronald James joined them shortly afterward and they both met with the late Mrs. Penderson, but after that they both remember nothing."

"And so, Miss Kemp," Anderson went on, "At the moment, you're the only one who can possibly tell us what really went on that night. All we've got at the moment are lots of stiffs and a crazy connection to a missing man."

"Five of John Miller's ex-wives died in that building," Futana said. "No, I mean four of them. Lucy Lowry is still alive."

"She is?" Megan asked in surprise. "I thought she'd died."

Anderson shook his head. "It was touch and go for a while, but she'll pull through. Ms. Lowry lost her right eye though and the depth of the cut into her head means that she's also lost control of her left arm for good—that arm is completely paralyzed now. But she'll survive." Then he peered inquisitively at Megan. "She's the one who shot you, right?"

Megan nodded. She'd already told the police that much, along with how she'd escaped from the basement. "But the gun was Donna's," she pointed out. "Richard Penderson was trying to kill all the exes and . . ."

"That bastard," Futana spat, giving Megan a hint of the steel that lay beneath her beautiful burnished blonde exterior. "He's still alive too—in intensive care. And from there he'll be going straight to prison; one of those 'two hundred and ninety-nine years without parole' sentences."

Megan nodded. When the paramedics had arrived that night, they had found it impossible to pry the bloody machete out of Richard Penderson's grip and had had to carry him off like that. Talk of undeniable proof of his being the murderer.

"And considering the extensive incarceration setup down in the Penderson's basement, his wife was clearly in on things too," Futana added. "What an evil couple."

"Did you arrest Mrs. Pain?" Megan asked the detectives. "You know who she is, don't you?—the bald woman in the basement? I told the police all about her."

On her question, Anderson and Futana exchanged pregnant looks that immediately told Megan something weird was amiss.

"What's the matter?" she asked. "You arrested her, didn't you?"

Instead of the 'yes' or 'no' answer she expected, Futana waved the question aside.

"Forget that for a moment," she said. "Before we go any further with this, I think I need to explain a little about why we—meaning Tom and I—are the ones interviewing you now."

Megan looked oddly at them both. "What's there to explain? You're the Massachusetts police, aren't you?"

"Well yes, Miss Kemp, but in actuality it's much more complicated than that," Futana replied her, leaning forward in her chair and then gesturing sideways at her male partner. "See, Tom and I here are like the BPD's version of Mulder and Scully." She paused and smiled at the 'Huh?' expression that now came over Megan's face, and then went on: "You know—the X-Files?"

Megan slowly nodded.

"Well, we're the Boston Police Department's version of that TV show."

"Meaning we get all the stuff that either doesn't add up or that scares the willies off of everyone else," Anderson added. "You know, miss, the sort of stuff the department has to sweep under the carpet and yet still needs someone investigating, but off the records. Those cases that no one else wants to touch even using the proverbial long spoon required to dine with the Devil."

Megan nodded again, though she was still uncertain where all this was headed.

Futana nodded too. "What we're trying to tell you, Miss Kemp, is that at the moment we're dealing with such a case. Now as far as the press and general public are concerned, this is a cut-and-dried case of a lunatic going on a rampage out of jealousy."

"Jealousy?" Megan asked.

"Yes, jealousy," Futana replied with a grim smile. "That's how we're feeding it to CNN, Fox News and the other news hounds. We're telling them that Robert Penderson discovered his wife and John Miller's other four exes holding a meeting about how much they missed being married to him and then he snapped and butchered them all."

"But that's ridiculous!" Megan protested. "Those five women all hated the guy!"

"Maybe, but the public are lapping it up. We've got four dead women, we've got a motive, and we've got a killer found with the smoking gun—"

"Laurie, you mean 'bloody machete,' not 'smoking gun,' " Anderson interrupted with a good-natured smile on his face.

"Whatever, man," she retorted with a smile of her own and then resumed addressing Megan: "The point I'm making, Miss Kemp, is that presented that way, it's a simple cut-and-dried case. As far as the public are concerned what happened in the Penderson mansion was a simple crime of passion taken to extremes." She frowned and then sighed. "But we, of course—meaning the cops—know there's a whole lot more to it than that. And as usual, it's up to Tom and I to unravel everything . . . off the record of course."

"Hey, you're leaving out Lucy," Megan reminded them. "Won't she be prosecuted for shooting me?"

Futana shook her head. "No, the state won't be prosecuting Lucy Lowry."

"But why not?" Megan asked heatedly.

"Well, to avoid complications," Futana explained. "We haven't interviewed her yet. We tried, but at the moment she's too doped up to say anything coherent and—"

"What damned complications?" Megan interrupted. "I don't see anything complicated about this! The bitch was about to blow my head off when Richard got her from behind."

Anderson sighed. "Girl, we both believe you, but in a court of law, the jury are certain to buy any plea of innocence Lucy makes. After all, it happened in the heat of the moment, with a maniac in the room trying to kill you all."

Megan scowled at him and let it go. At least Lucy hadn't gotten off scot-free, she'd been maimed and partially-blinded, and wouldn't be gorgeous anymore.

"Oh, there's a lot more to it than that," Anderson went on. "The thing is, like Laurie was just saying, Lucy is heavily medicated at the moment, and when we tried talking to her, she began blabbing about stuff that could complicate things for the law—magic and stuff like that. We've managed to convince everyone that she was hallucinating at the time, and have asked her lawyer to tell her to S.T.F.U., because with the mess on our hands we really can't have the damn woman raving about demons and paranormal transpositions in court . . ."

Megan decided then that she really liked Detective Futana. Anderson, not so much.

Anderson now pulled a small camcorder out of his jacket and switched it on, then he placed it on the cabinet next to Megan's bed and angled it to face her. "Now, miss, whatever you say to us from this point onwards is completely confidential and entirely off the record. We may file an edited version of it, but our report won't have anything in it that will ever get you in trouble with the law. Do you understand that?"

Megan nodded, though she still felt suspicious of him and was wary of being filmed. She pulled her bedcovers up around her chest and asked, "Alright, what do you want to know?"

Anderson didn't directly answer her question. "Okay, now Laurie's just told you what we're selling to the public. But even though most of that's true, there's still a whole lot of unanswered questions. Now, we know that Richard Penderson killed three of John Miller's exes, and that the fourth dead ex, the pregnant one we found sawn in pieces in the basement, was killed by he and his wife's female associate. Hey, Laurie"—with a look of intense displeasure on his face, Anderson turned to his partner—"what's that poor woman's name again?"

"Maryanne," Megan told him before Detective Futana could reply. "Oh, my God, so she was sawn in bits?" The dead woman's grisly fate horrified her. *She was killed by Richard and his wife's female associate?* "Hey, that was Mrs. Pain's doing, wasn't it?" She stared from one detective's face to the other. "But you didn't arrest her, did you? But why not? Are you going to let Mrs. Pain get off scot-free like you're letting Lucy off? But you mustn't. You simply can't let her out on the streets again. Mrs. Pain is a *total* psycho. Just watch her *Greatest Hits* recordings and you'll see what I mean. Hey, listen, I locked the insane bitch in that cell and . . ."

Megan suddenly realized that her voice was getting quite loud and so she lowered it to prevent a nurse from entering and ejecting the detectives.

But still, she must have been too loud anyway, because the door shortly opened and a nurse, a blonde woman with large glasses and a bright red smile, poked her head into the room. This nurse wasn't the one who had earlier shown Anderson and Futana to Megan's room and must have only just begun her shift. Megan didn't think she'd seen her before.

"Is everything alright in here?" the woman asked. "I thought I heard some shouting."

Megan quickly wagged her head back at her. "Oh, I'm fine. I was just surprised at some of the details the detectives were telling me."

The blonde nurse nodded and then checked her watch. "Okay then, detectives, I'll leave you with her. But you'll need to be quick. She's still very weak and it's almost time for her to take her medicine and get some rest."

"We'll be done here in a jiffy," Futana replied brightly.

The nurse exited and shut the door behind her.

"Mrs. Pain wasn't in the cell, Miss Kemp," Futana calmly informed Megan once the nurse had gone. "Yes, yes, the cell door was locked, but there were just two dead men in there."

Megan looked perplexed. "Mrs. Pain wasn't in there?"

"No, she wasn't there," Futana repeated. "One of the walls in the bathroom in John Miller's cell is actually a hidden door, one that unlocks by inputting a code into the same keypad that controls the hoop for the chains. Once the secret panel is unlocked and slid aside, behind it there's a tunnel that leads to an underground car park, which we suspect is how they smuggled all their victims into the basement in the first place without the mansion staff noticing. And once you'd escaped, Mrs. Pain must've figured the jig was up and fled in a hurry. She clearly escaped that way."

Anderson nodded and added: "To give that devil Richard Penderson his due, it was a well-planned torture and murder setup they had going down there, one we'd never discovered in a hundred years if you'd not gone over there that night. You may not have noticed it while you were down there, but the mansion basement is actually split in two halves."

"Two?" Megan asked. "It all seemed one large space to me."

Futana nodded. "Yes it is, but there's a control room down there where pressing a button activates a pair of retractable walls that once slid into place, divide the basement into two perfectly segregated halves. All the cells are located in one half of it, and once sealed off, that side of the basement is completely soundproof, while the second section contains the pantry, house supplies and occasional offices."

While adjusting his tie, Anderson added: "Those of the Penderson's house staff that we've so far questioned claim they had no idea the mansion's basement was that large, and we've no reason to disbelieve them."

"So why open it up that night then?" Megan asked.

"Candice apparently wanted to show off to the other exes," Futana replied.

But, shaking his head and wagging a finger at his partner, Anderson disagreed: "No, that's not it, Laurie. It simply took less time to arrive at the summoning room from the basement if one walked through the house than if one climbed up to that side passageway Miss Kemp found and used. Coming and going by that secret route must surely get to be a pain in the ass after a point. And with the servants all dismissed for the weekend, why stress themselves with going the longer way?" Anderson shrugged at Megan and jerked a thumb at Laurie Futana. "That's my take on their reasoning anyway, though Laurie insists that opening the basement's secret half had entirely to do with Candice's vanity."

Megan nodded, uncertain which version to accept, then she said, "But you really need to find Mrs. Pain." She regarded the two detectives with agitation etched on her face. "You have got to find and arrest that woman—she's utterly nuts. She and the Pendersons were running a frigging slaughterhouse down in their basement. She showed me videos of herself . . . her *Greatest Hits* . . . oh shoot!"

The horrible memories almost started Megan weeping.

Detective Futana patted Megan's leg gently. "Try to calm down. We've already watched all of Mrs. Pain's recordings, and the evidence against her is damning too."

"Thirty-four people were murdered in those videos," Anderson said softly. "All of them tortured in ways I had never thought possible. I'll never get the images of what happened to the Dawsons out of my head for as long as I live. And the murderess now seems to have vanished into thin air."

With a lump in her throat, Megan remembered who the Dawsons were—the poor couple who'd had hand grenades forced into their bodies. Judging from the totally aggrieved look on Detective Anderson's face now, Mr. Dawson clearly hadn't survived his 'performance' in MRS. PAIN'S GREATEST HITS, PART 2 either.

"And in addition," Futana added in an angry voice, "Finding Mrs. Pain might prove difficult, as she seems to not have any fingerprints."

Megan gasped. "No fingerprints?"

Anderson laughed coldly. "Well, she touched just about everything in her video rooms but her fingers leave no ridges that can give us any clue as to her real identity."

"I don't understand," Megan protested in some alarm. "How is that even possible? Was she a demon, or what's going on here?"

"Oh, there's nothing remotely supernatural about it," Laurie Futana explained. "It's just a question of a skin graft in which the skin at the end of the fingers is replaced with smooth skin from elsewhere on the body. Either that or an acid treatment that dissolves the friction ridges away. Or, psycho that she is, she could have burnt her fingerprints off. Just criminal science, really."

Megan looked at Anderson who nodded his agreement and then said, "Anyway, that's just part of the oddity of this case. We'll work on it and see what we come up with."

Futana said, "But for now, we'd like you to tell us exactly what happened to you in the Penderson's mansion. Everything you saw, everything you did; everything . . . from the moment you entered till the moment when the police and paramedics arrived. Try not to leave anything out, please." She smiled. "And don't worry, Miss Kemp, Tom and I have already watched the CCTV footage of your escape from your basement cell and that's as clear cut a case of self-defense as I've ever seen in my life. Those two dead bastards deserved what they got."

This information came as a huge relief to Megan, who had been scared she could be prosecuted for killing the two goons.

Still, extremely conscious of the video camera beside her that would be recording everything she said, she flung Anderson a guarded look. "For real?"

Anderson nodded back. "Yeah, miss, for real. The world's a better place with those two scumbags dispatched to Hell. You're in the clear there. Now, please tell us exactly what happened . . . and *please* try to remember everything that you can about John Miller in particular."

"Pardon me for mentioning this," Futana interjected, "but part of the problem here is that the missing man was dating Tom's girlfriend's younger sister. So in a way this is a very personal case for him."

John Miller was dating his girlfriend's younger sister? Megan looked at Detective Anderson curiously.

The big man nodded back at her again. "Yeah, it's true. Barbara's been going nuts ever since Johnny went missing."

Megan nodded. "Yeah sure, I'll tell you everything I know, but you're not gonna believe most of it."

She had been expecting the normal kind of patronizing reply one got to similar statements, but instead of giving her that reaction, Anderson and Futana both laughed softly.

"Oh, there's very little that *we* don't believe can happen, miss," Anderson finally told her. "Trust me, in our time spent investigating Massachusetts' paranormal activity, we've seen it all."

"Yeah, we've seen things *you* wouldn't believe," Futana agreed with a calm smile on her beautiful face. "Things that would both curl your hair and then straighten it out again. So tell us your tale, however unbelievable it may seem. You're in good hands here."

So Megan told them. Speaking slowly so as not to drain her strength, she explained how she'd gone to collect the money Dave owed her and instead met Lucy, and everything that had followed.

The detectives stopped her a few times and asked her to clarify some details, but mostly they just sat back and listened, occasionally nodded to one another, and let their camcorder capture her testimony.

Once she was done speaking, Anderson had an additional question for her:

"So what you're saying is, that John Miller acted differently each time you saw him? Can you please go over that once more?"

"Exactly," Megan agreed with a quick nod. "I saw him downstairs when they locked me in his cell and were taking him off to kill him, and at that time he was this scared old guy who had no idea what he was doing down there. . . . And the next time our paths cross, he's become this cannibal guy who eats brains, and the next thing I know, he's turning into jelly and evaporating, which was great for me since he was strangling me at the time."

She groaned. "C'mon, man, gimme a break here. I already told you that you wouldn't believe most of what I said. Thinking back now that it's over, I find it hard to believe myself. Once you detectives leave, I'm gonna try and forget it all, or I'll wind up needing psychiatric care."

"Oh, but we do believe you," Anderson quickly reassured her. "We're just trying to tie our loose ends together." He looked at his partner. "What do you think, Laurie?"

She frowned. "I think it's safe to conclude that John Miller is gone for good. Remember how Lucy was babbling about the demon eating his corpse?"

Anderson sighed. "Laurie, I need to think up a real good explanation for Grace and Barbara."

She shrugged. "We can always claim Penderson dissolved Johnny in an acid bath. That way there's no need to show anyone his remains."

Anderson nodded grimly. "Yeah, that'll work." Then he turned back to Megan, who had now begun feeling tired and who was stifling a yawn with her palm.

"Okay, thanks, miss," Anderson said. "You've been a great help to us and we'll leave you now to get some rest."

"That's all?" Megan asked through another yawn. "I'm done with the police investigation?"

"More or less," Futana replied. "But of course, at some point in the near future—by which I mean as soon as Richard Penderson is well enough to stand trial—you and Lucy Lowry will both have to give evidence against him in court. Just routine stuff: you'll tell the judge and jury what happened after he burst into the room; as much as you both recall of him killing the ladies. The DA's office will contact you about that."

Anderson nodded. "Yeah, by then we'll have sent them our edited version of this video interview so they'll know what questions to ask you . . . and Lucy too once we've properly interviewed her. And maybe by then the two cooks will have recovered their memories and can also fill in some gaps in your testimony for us."

"Don't count on it, man," Megan said. "Candice was specific that they wouldn't ever remember a thing that happened in her house."

"Okay, I won't count on it then," Anderson replied with an ugly smile.

The two detectives got to their feet, with Anderson picking up the video recorder from Megan's bedside cabinet, switching it off and putting it away in his jacket.

"Alright, we'll leave you to get some rest," he repeated with a nod and then he and Futana stepped towards the door of the hospital room.

"Hey, how do I get back my motorbike and my cellphone?" Megan asked.

They turned towards her again. "Oh, your Harley's at the Raynham police station," Futana replied. "You can collect it from there once you're feeling better. But your cellphone . . ." She turned to Anderson for a moment. "Tom, do you remember if they found her cellphone in the mansion?"

Anderson shook his head. "I ain't sure."

"Mrs. Pain's men took it away from me when they captured me," Megan explained. "It should have been on one of their bodies."

"We'll enquire about it for you," Futana said. "If the forensics guys have it, we'll have it sent over to you."

"Thanks," Megan said.

CHAPTER 33

Megan

Megan felt really good once the two detectives had left. The late afternoon sun shining outside her hospital room seemed to mirror her own bright future.

I escaped from that horrible place. Now all I need to do is find a new job, find a new guy, and get on with my life. She grinned. *Yeah, but first of all, I need to get my money back from Dave!*

The bespectacled nurse hadn't yet returned with her medicine so she pressed the call button to summon her. The interview with the police had weakened her considerably and now she wanted her bed lowered again so she could take a nap. Before getting shot, Megan would never have believed that talking could be so tiring.

The nurse didn't come on Megan's first call so she buzzed her again.

A short while later the door opened and the blonde nurse walked in, carrying a tray with Megan's pills and a hypodermic syringe.

There were also a couple of other objects on the steel tray, one of which Megan immediately recognized.

"Hey, that's my cellphone," she said, pointing to it.

"Yes," the nurse agreed and handed it over. "The female detective gave it to me and asked me to pass it on to you. She'd apparently forgotten it in their squad car."

"But they just said . . ." True, the explanation made no sense to Megan but she realized she had other worries. Her cellphone felt wet. And the wetness wasn't water, but some reddish substance that smeared over her hands and dripped down onto her hospital gown and onto the bed.

Is this blood? She stared in surprise at her reddened fingers, then looked up at the nurse again. "Hey, what's going on?"

But the nurse was already pulling off her blonde wig. She was bald beneath it, and once she'd also removed her spectacles, Megan immediately recognized her as the missing Mrs. Pain.

Why didn't I . . . or the detectives recognize her earlier? Oh my God—she's wearing green contacts . . . but even her voice sounds different now!

This was confirmed to Megan when Mrs. Pain reverted to her normal voice: "Did you really think you'd escaped from me, you fool? No one, absolutely no one, ever escapes from Mrs. Pain!"

Realizing that her life was in danger and she had no time to waste here, Megan lunged for the nurse call button. But Mrs. Pain knocked the call button off the bed before she could reach it. And then before Megan could yell instead, she slapped a wide strip of duct tape over her mouth and looped it around the back of her head.

Tired out by her long conversation with the two detectives, Megan was unable to match Mrs. Pain's speed. She was still trying to remove the duct tape gag, when she saw the crazy woman grab up a knife from the medicine tray. The knife was a ceremonial dagger with a glittering long and wavy blade.

Oh no!

Megan tried to roll off the bed, but once again Mrs. Pain moved too fast for her to escape. She leapt up onto the bed, pinned both of Megan's arms down by her sides with her legs, and then plunged the dagger deep into Megan's belly.

"Goodbye, bitch," Mrs. Pain said as Megan's eyes gaped open from the sudden hot burst of agony in her belly, which felt like she had just been shot all over again. "Consider this payback for ruining my cushy setup at the Penderson mansion!"

With a sadistic smile on her face, Mrs. Pain stabbed Megan again. Blood squirted up from Megan's body and stained them both. Megan flailed about on the bed, praying that someone would come to her rescue, but no one did; no one seemed aware of the desperate struggle occurring here in her room.

Mrs. Pain jerked the bloody knife out of Megan's belly and placed it against her throat instead.

Megan realized she had absolutely no hope of surviving this assault. Though she bravely refused to give up fighting for her life, she knew her resistance was useless.

And then, with a cold smile of triumph on her lips and a total lack of mercy in her cold green eyes, Mrs. Pain dug her knife deep into Megan's neck and slit her throat wide open from ear to ear.

Megan gaped at Mrs. Pain in stunned and agonized disbelief, snorted a torrent of blood from her nose, and then died.

The End.

ABOUT THE AUTHOR

Wol-vriey is Nigerian, and quite tall.

He believes there actually are things that go bump in the night.

He writes horror fiction—for adults only, please. And also some surrealist stuff.

Wol-vriey blogs at: *http://oddityfarm.wordpress.com*

.

WOL-VRIEY
BIZARRO AND TRANSGRESSIVE FICTION

BOSTON POSH (BUD MALONE #1)

In 2028 AD, the USA is a nation ravaged by hungry dragons and dinosaurs. In Boston, Massachusetts, private eye Bud Malone is hired to rescue a kidnapped heiress. But nothing is as it seems.

Malone works to unravel a tangled web involving Boston Chinatown, a 200-year-old woman with a 9-year-old body, white robots, a human-liver-eating psychopath, a golem, a porcelain dragon, and a snake goddess with a crush on him. There's also a woman obsessed with chicken sex. Then Malone meets Posh Lane, a gorgeous call girl who's desperate to quit her pimp.

Romantic sparks ignite between Posh and Malone, but Posh's past suddenly catches up with her in a BIG way. To save Posh, Malone agrees to run a quest for Earth's new rulers, the Forks. But, Malone has no idea that agreeing to the Fork's odd request will send him on the weirdest trip he's ever been on in his life.

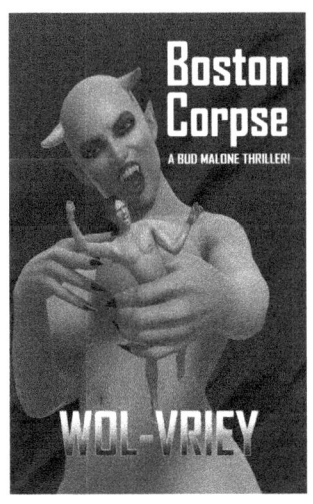

BOSTON CORPSE (BUD MALONE #2)

MAGIC CAN BE MURDER! - Drag queen Lucy Tang is back in Boston, and is hell-bent on settling her vindetta against casino owner Sookie Ling. And suddenly, Bud Malone, PI, has the case of his life to resolve.

When Boston's robot police force are baffled by a mind transfer case, they come to Malone for help. The one person who can likely help Malone out here is the witch Soledad Bathory. But Soledad seems to know a lot more than she's telling him. It's a case not made easier when Malone meets Soledad's beautiful cousin, Josephine 'Slave' Bailey. Slave has her own plans for Malone, most of which involve teaching him BDSM and making him her new Master.

Oh, and Rick Rogers owes Sookie Ling a whole lot of money, a gambling debt that's going to be literally Hell to pay!

BOSTON CORPSE - Not your average detective novel!

Burning Bulb

WOL-VRIEY

BIZARRO AND TRANSGRESSIVE FICTION

BOSTON LUST (BUD MALONE #3)

"Bless it, Father, for she has sinned."

Seven murdered gay women, all their bodies completely drained of blood. All also with large parts of their bodies dissolved away like acid has been pumped into their veins.

Bud Malone has to find the female vampire preying on Boston's lesbian population.

Then Malone meets the beautiful Trudi Carmen and the case gets even more tangled. Trudi needs Malone's help in recovering a ring that's gone missing. But how in the world is one little black ring related to either the dead women or their killer?

Resolving this case will lead Malone deep into Lucy Tang's legacy—The Abstracta. And then to the city of Genesis.

Boston Lust—Just when you thought Bean Town was safe to visit again.

HELL DANCER

Six people find themselves trapped in Detention, a nightmare realm where the demonic Schoolmaster is hell-bent on reforming them . . . until they die.

Porn superstar Venus Deluxe came to Springfield, MA to party, and next found her life hanging by a thread. One wrong answer will mean her death.

Suspended BPD detective Tanya Rockford was trying to stop one kind of violence, but found a terrifying another. With her and her companion's lives hanging in the balance, it's going to take all of her courage and resourcefulness to escape this hell she's stumbled into.

Porn stud Chad Cannon has made a career from his ten-inch penis. Here in Detention, however, it's his brains that matter. He'll soon be hoping all the pot he's smoked over the years hasn't completely messed up his memory.

The three students, Sherri, Jordan, and Mike? They were all just in the wrong place at the right time. Will anyone survive Detention? The evil Schoolmaster doesn't plan on letting that happen . . .

Burning Bulb
PUBLISHING

WOL-VRIEY
BIZARRO AND TRANSGRESSIVE FICTION

VAGINA MUNDI

Rachel Risk is a professional thief with super-strong hair that can stretch like tentacles to manipulate objects. Ashley Status has both a digitally augmented brain, and 'muscle-purses' in her arms and legs in which she stores inflatable objects—cars, guns, rocket launchers, etc.

When Raye is framed as the fall girl in a jewel robbery, the pair flee Chicago's vengeful robot gangsters and take refuge in the Hotel Bizarre, where the gorgeous 'vagina singer,' Femina, is performing for a week.

But the Hotel Bizarre is even stranger than its name suggests, and very soon Raye and Ash are involved in an deadly adventure, a struggle for survival the likes of which they'd never imagined possible—with loads of deviant sex, drugs, music, and violence at every turn. And just what is the old woman in the skin desert really doing with all those cats glued to her walls?

VAGINA MUNDI—a Bizarro Hymn in praise of WOMAN!

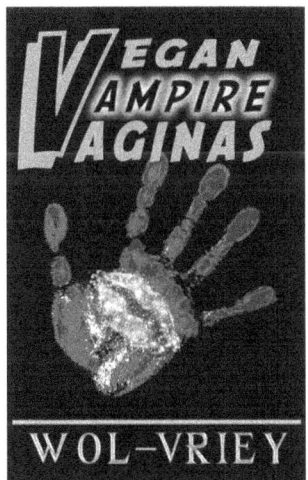

VEGAN VAMPIRE VAGINAS

The biggest bank heist in US history. And Tom Palmer can't remember pulling it off. And no, this isn't your standard case of amnesia. After a one-night-stand gone horribly wrong, Boston salesman Tom Palmer wakes up with a vagina implanted in his left hand. Then his day gets worse.

Tom is transported across space-time to a nightmare version of Boston, one where the Bizarro virus has transformed half the population into cannibals. Worst of all, Tom discovers that in this new Boston, he's the infamous gangster Pussypalm, wanted for robbing the Federal Reserve Bank of Boston a year ago. He also learns that the vagina in his hand is prophetic, i.e. it talks . . . after sex.

With 130 people left dead during his bank heist and six billion dollars missing, Tom knows he's living on borrowed time. It is in his best interests not to remember anything. Because once he does . . .

Burning Bulb

WOL-VRIEY
BIZARRO AND TRANSGRESSIVE FICTION

VEGAN ZOMBIE APOCALYPSE

In the post-apocalypse worlderness, zombies rule the earth. They're allergic to meat, and brains literally make them explode. Zombies now eat blood potatoes, parasitic tubers grown in the flesh of humancows corralled in maximum security farms. Two fugitives meet in the ancient ruins of Texas. The first is Soil 15-f, a womancow who's escaped her farm a week before she's due to be killed and her blood potato crop harvested. The second fugitive is Able Kane, former head necros food technician, now sentenced to death for heresy. But Soil is no ordinary humancow.

Unknown to herself, she's the vegan zombie agricultural revolution, and the zombies desperately want her back. And the necros equally desperately want Able Kane dead. He's fled with a forbidden discovery which will reshape the world for the worse if used. And Able is just hardheaded/misguided enough to use it.

MELANIE NEMESIS CATCHPOLE

In Springfield, Massachusetts, Melanie Catchpole is hired to fetch back a magic teddy bear worth millions of dollars from a warehouse across town. Problem is, the warehouse is down in Springfield's O-Zone—that totally weird sector of the city where Bizarro fell to Earth. The 'O' is a fairytale land, a place where dreams and nightmares literally live and breathe..

Worse still, the gingers—mutant cannibals—prowl the O. The gingers have already eaten everyone else Melanie's employers sent to get back the magic teddy bear.

Accompanied by the handsome but ruthless Doug Fisher (who she finds sexy but doesn't dare entrust her heart to), Melanie enters the O-Zone. Melanie and Doug are instantly caught up in an adventure they'd never have believed credible even if written as fiction . . . and Melanie's used to experiencing the very weird as the norm.

And now, additionally, there's a mystery to unravel: What does the dark, freezing-cold being called The Fixer want with Mary, the barkeep's daughter?

Burning Bulb
PUBLISHING

WOL-VRIEY
BIZARRO AND TRANSGRESSIVE FICTION

BIG TROUBLE IN LITTLE ASS

From Bizarro master storyteller Wol-vriey comes a truly weird western tale that will leave you awe-struck and on the edge of your seat...

In the town named Little Ass, tight-assed prostitute Rosa overhears a gunslinger's plans to assassinate rancher Edison Bennett. Once the badass Bennett learns of the plot, he ensures there'll be hell to pay for any attempt on his life!

Yes, it's going to take all of gunslinger Jude's shooting prowess, his eclectic collection of strange firearms, a trusty horse that requires an owners' manual, and the help of the lovely and invigorating Nell (who's EXTREMELY odd when the going gets weird), to survive the Bizarro hell that Edison Bennett unleashes in order to hold onto the land that he'd stolen from Madam Zizi.

BIZARRO 101 (A BASIC PRIMER)

Welcome to the strange place:

A collection of 37 flash fiction stories designed to introduce one to the Bizarro/New Weird Genre.

Weird, dreamy, nightmarish, absurd, sad, surreal, humorous . . . this collection of tales is all this and more.

***

"This primer is the very essence of any and all styles and types of Bizarro writing. Wol-vriey collects, distills, and bottles up these 37 tiny stories for your sensory enjoyment. This is an absolute must read for anyone new to the genre, because it demonstrates the scope of what Bizarro is, and what it can be."
                    –Teresa Pollack, Bizarro commentator and blogger

Burning Bulb

WOL-VRIEY

BIZARRO AND TRANSGRESSIVE FICTION

Dr. Orgasm

Courtney Taylor is young, intelligent, beautiful, and successful. She also has a boyfriend who loves her deeply. The problem is, no matter what Courtney does, she can't climax during sex.

When Florence Rigid's communist forces destroy the city of Metaphor, Courtney and her friends Teresa, Highball, Miki, and Heather are cast into the midst of a quest to find the only person able to save the land of Innuendo—Dr. Carol Orgasm, wanted by the communists for developing the O-Pill, a wonder drug that grants women sexual ecstasy on demand.

The communists will do anything to get their hands on the O-Pill and prevent its reaching the millions of Innuendo's women. But Courtney desperately wants that pill too. And so it's now a race between Courtney and the communists to find Dr. Orgasm first.

And Courtney has no choice but to win this race. She must win it: For her own orgasm . . . and for the freedom of female sexuality everywhere.

PUSSY TRANSMISSION

Pussy Transmission were the most decadent Pop Art ensemble of the 90's. Led by the beautiful painter Isis Lynch, the trio revolutionized the art world. Then suddenly, without explanation, Pussy Transmission vanished into historical obscurity. Now, twenty years later, three women come to Lynch Place. Lily and Nina are journalists desperate to interview Isis Lynch. Raven, on the other hand, wants to find her boyfriend, who's gone missing inside Isis's house. Raven's worried—she's heard that Pussy Transmission broke up because Isis began dabbling in black magic . . . with devastating results. All three women will shortly wish they'd never left home. Particularly once the rats in Lynch Place start warning them that they're going to die . . . and Raven meets Betty Butcher, the bouncy supernatural psycho who's intent on chopping her into bits. Pussy Transmission, Baby! Just because . . .

Burning Bulb
PUBLISHING

WOL-VRIEY
BIZARRO AND TRANSGRESSIVE FICTION

GIRLS ARE NOT SMILING

Welcome To The Road Trip From Hell

Pagan is demon-possessed.

Lori is suicidal.

Britt is just terminally pissed off.

Meet three young Boston women on the run from the law, each with problems that will fuse into more than the sum of their individual parts, becoming a holocaust of sex and violence and terror, a literal rain of blood and horror and gore and evil.

And if that wasn't already bad enough, Pagan's pet demon is slowly transforming her into something both unspeakable and unholy. Truly, these girls aren't smiling.

BLUE NIGHTMARES

Consummate EVIL is coming. It is relentless and unavoidable. It is Blue.

Jessica Schreiber is seeing things. Very horrible things. Since arriving in Raynham for what should have been a relaxing vacation, she's been seeing *The Big Blue*.

Jessica is smelling things too—dead and rotting things that she can't see. She is sure those dead and rotting things are dead people. Lots of dead people.

Jessica's worst nightmares will soon become her reality. Her reality will soon become a terrifying nightmare.

The tentacled residents of the House of Death have a lot that they wish to show Jessica Schreiber. They have a lot that they wish to tell her. But will she survive long enough to learn their lessons?

Burning Bulb

WOL-VRIEY
BIZARRO AND TRANSGRESSIVE FICTION

BRAINCHEW

It was supposed to be a simple jewel heist, but it went badly wrong. Chuck got shot and died.

Lance hid his friend's corpse in the Pleasant Street Cemetery. But that was a big mistake—there was something undead, something extremely hungry . . . something eXXXtremely horrible, buried in the Pleasant Street Cemetery.

And Lance had just woken it up.

They called the monster Brainchew because it ate brains. Human brains. And it preferred those brains fresh from the heads . . . of the living.

And now it was awake again, Brainchew planned on feeding big-time tonight. Oh hell yes, it did.

BRAINCHEW 2: OUT OF THEIR HEADS

After Tiff Hooper recognizes Josh Penham, the man who abducted her and kept her in his basement and abused her, she brings her three friends to Raynham for a night of well-deserved revenge on him.

Only things don't go according to plan.

It is never a good idea to leave a corpse in Raynham's Pleasant Street Cemetery. You run the very real risk of awakening what lies underground there. And that thing—Brainchew—is more horrible and more evil than anything the average mind conceives of even in its worst nightmares.

Brainchew is back! And this time the monster is extra-hungry. But there are plenty of delicious human brains about tonight, and Brainchew intends to eat them all before dawn.

Burning Bulb

WOL-VRIEY
BIZARRO AND TRANSGRESSIVE FICTION

DARIA: AN EROTIC NIGHTMARE

Even the best laid women can go wrong.

Daria Simpson is HUNGRY. She's HUNGRY for sex and bloodshed and death.

Shelly Parker just wanted to have a threesome with her boyfriend Craig and her best friend Erica. Everything was shaping up nicely for their weekend of sexual fun and games, until they stopped at the creepy Crossway Diner and met Daria.

From the moment they met Daria, EVERYTHING went wrong for them; and it went wrong in the most horrific and terrifying of ways!

Daria: Paranormal service has been resumed.

WET BONES

Greg is about learning the hard way that you don't mess with Aunt Grace.

Nine completely fleshless skeletons recovered in the Massachusetts woods. Two detectives on the trail of a horrible, hungry monster.

Broken-hearted Allie Jackson has a date with a creature from Hell.

Things are about to get well out of hand for everyone, and in horrifying, terrifying ways they don't expect.

Burning Bulb

WOL-VRIEY
BIZARRO AND TRANSGRESSIVE FICTION

MR. UGLY

When a rotting corpse appears and starts butchering Raynham's youths, there's really only one question that needs answering:

Is this faceless and rotting monster Peter Howard, or isn't it?

Problem is, Peter Howard died 15 years ago. So how can he possibly be back from the dead and murdering people with such relentless and incredible brutality?

Peter's mother Malicia, who's just been released from the lunatic asylum may have the answers to the crazy puzzle, but the two detectives investigating the deaths don't even know the right questions to ask her yet.

BRUTAL

Jane Winters is 28 years old.

She works as a checkout cashier in a department store. She's an attractive woman with a winning personality. She has both a photographic memory and an I.Q. of 189.

She's met the man of her dreams.

But she's also a cannibal with a unique and very scary mode of operation.

The group known as TULIP (The Urban Legend Investigation People) are out to either prove or disprove the legend of Insane Jane.

But have TULIP bitten off more than they can chew?

Burning Bulb
PUBLISHING

WOL-VRIEY
BIZARRO AND TRANSGRESSIVE FICTION

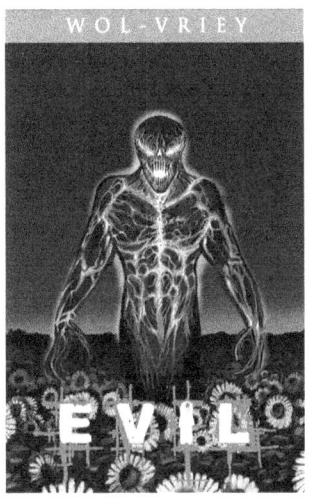

EVIL

The Evil began the week before Sylvia Stewart's 30th birthday.

Cathy Higgins died.

The Bargainer resurrected Cathy . . . for a price.

The price? Cathy's father Ronan had to plant some seeds for him.

But these were no ordinary seeds the Bargainer gave to Ronan Higgins. These were seeds from Hell: seeds which required human flesh as both soil and fertilizer.

And meanwhile, the unsuspecting Sylvia Stewart went ahead with the plans for her birthday party, which was to be held on Ronan Higgins' sunflower farm . . .

666

Ohio's State Route 666 stretches 14.7 miles between Zanesville and Dresden.

Most days, it's just a normal road with a funny name.

But for six minutes on the 6th of June each year, Route 666 becomes a gateway to somewhere else . . . a gateway to Hell.

Each year 13 unfortunates get trapped in the 666 underworld, with no way to get back home.

This year though, things are going to be very different. For one thing, there are currently a whole lot of turbulent human emotions at play in the underworld. And also . . . the psycho Al Gore is just about completing his collection of human heads.

And . . . what the hell is a church doing in Hell, of all places?

Burning Bulb

WOL-VRIEY
BIZARRO AND TRANSGRESSIVE FICTION

THE CLEAVERMAN

It began as a joke, a gag to pass the time that turned deadly. One rainy August night in Raynham, MA, nine friends jokingly invoke the evil phantom butcher called the Cleaverman.

These nine friends get a whole lot more than they ever bargained for. Because there's only one way to return the deadly Cleaverman back to the darkness he came from, and that is to solve his riddle, which starts: "Tell me the name of John Cleaverman's wife . . ."

And human beings being what we are, even with the Cleaverman out to butcher them all, our nine friends still manage to stir A WHOLE LOT of human misbehavior into the deadly mix.

At the rate they're going, it'll be a wonder if anyone survives THE CLEAVERMAN at all.

PERVERSE

When 21-year-old Heather Forrest accompanies three of her friends on a weekend trip up to Vermont, she has no idea what she's getting into.

Because, during a brief stop in the western Massachusetts woods, the girls get kidnapped and things go rapidly downhill from there. Soon Heather and her friends are fighting for their lives, fighting to survive the most perverted and impossible situation imaginable. And meanwhile, Hank Rollins is also in the woods, hunting the unholy monster that killed his wife and son . . . and he's hunting it with live human bait.

Oh yes, there will be blood. And there will be terror and buckets of gore also. And truly horrible atrocities will happen. Most definitely so.

Burning Bulb
PUBLISHING

WOL-VRIEY
BIZARRO AND TRANSGRESSIVE FICTION

THE VIRGIN

10 million dollars in prize money. 1000+ video cameras, lots of deadly weapons, 10 Suitors, 5 Virgins & 3 Hours . . . to keep your hymen intact.

Hailey Osborne wants to sell her virginity for a hundred thousand dollars. But then she's made an offer she really can't refuse: how about competing to win ten million dollars in a no-holds-barred underground game show, where all she has to do is remain a virgin?

There's just two problems:
1. Four other women also want that prize money.
2. There's ten suitors all contesting to take Hailey and the other virgins' precious hymens . . . by any means necessary . . .

But hey, it's just for 3 hours, right? How hard can it possibly be ? Hailey Osborne is about to find out.

THE BOOK OF ATROCITIES

Bestselling author Drake Melville has been missing for three years now. Drake vanished after publishing The Bleeding Oysters, an epic novel that set new standards for depictions of sleaze and depravity and human monstrosity in popular fiction. On vanishing, however, Drake Melville left a message for everyone, saying he'd 'left town' to go work on his follow-up novel The Book of Atrocities. The problem was, no one could find Drake. It seemed like he'd vanished off the face of the Earth. And now, three years later, Drake has just sent messages to his ex-wife Liz, his current (and abandoned) wife Melody; and his younger sister Chloe . . . asking them to meet him in Raynham, MA. Drake says he's now completed The Book of Atrocities and is ready to present it to the world. But there's a whole lot that Liz, Melody, and Chloe Melville don't know about Drake's Book of Atrocities. And unfortunately they're on their way to find out those excruciatingly painful truths. Because, see, Drake Melville is a VERY EVIL man with a VERY EVIL plan . . .

Burning Bulb

WOL-VRIEY
BIZARRO AND TRANSGRESSIVE FICTION

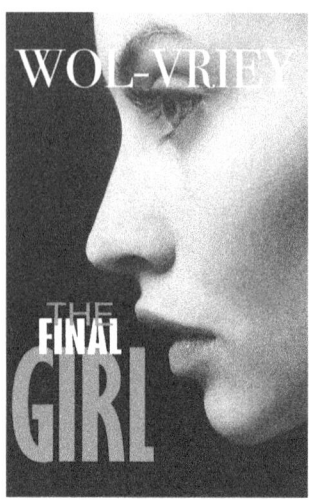

THE FINAL GIRL

Here there be monsters . . . because we made them.

At a secret location, 8 young women assemble to compete on the ultimate reality/game show—The Final Girl. The 8 contestants are: A young wife and her grown-up stepdaughter, a police detective, a prostitute, a nurse, a school teacher, and unemployed twin sisters.

The Final Girl is a no-holds-barred show beamed to an audience on the Dark Web, a show where murder is permitted and mutilation is encouraged.

The Rules:
1. Avoid being killed and eaten by the show's monsters and bogeymen.
2. Find the prize money—24 million dollars in cash.
3. Hold on to the money.

But only 1 woman can win. And to win The Final Girl reality show, that woman will need to be even more bloodthirsty and ruthless than the show's monsters.

Have a seat, everyone. The most dangerous game is about to begin!

WOMEN

John Miller must die . . . TONIGHT!

Megan Kemp initially went to the Penderson Mansion to collect a debt. But from the moment she stepped in there, getting back outside proved extremely difficult. And then what had merely been difficult for Megan suddenly turned deadly. Because something was going on in the Penderson Mansion that night. Five VERY ANGRY women had a score to settle, and no obstacle on earth would stop them. . . . And no one would get in their way and live to tell the tale either.

"John Miller must die," the women had decreed, and it looked like the forces of Hell would help them accomplish their deadly aim tonight.

But as the night progressed, Megan, who was now trapped in a deadly game of cat and mouse in the Penderson Mansion, found that despite her own troubles, her biggest question was: "What the hell did John Miller do to anger these five women this much?"

Beware, folks . . . sometimes things really do go too far!

Burning Bulb
PUBLISHING

www.ingramcontent.com/pod-product-compliance
Lightning Source LLC
Chambersburg PA
CBHW071311250626
47159CB00004B/1387